4/98

The Midden

By the same author

The Midden
TOM SHARPE

THE OVERLOOK PRESS
WOODSTOCK • NEW YORK

First published in the United States in 1997 by
The Overlook Press, Peter Mayer Publishers, Inc.
Lewis Hollow Road
Woodstock, New York 12498

Library of Congress Cataloging-in-Publication Data

Sharpe, Tom.
    The midden / Tom Sharpe.
    p.   cm.
    I. Title.
PR6069.H345M54   1997   823'.914—dc21   97-9909

Originally published in Great Britain by André Deutsch/Secker & Warburg

Manufactured in the United States of America

ISBN 0-87951-801-4
FIRST AMERICAN EDITION
9 8 7 6 5 4 3 2 1

*In fond memory of Montsé Turró
and with thanks to Jaume, Maria Carmen, Pep and
Kim and everyone at the Hotel Levant, Llafranc*

Chapter 1

It was Timothy Bright's ambition to make a fortune. He had been brought up in the belief that every Bright had made a fortune and it seemed only natural to suppose he was going to make one too. All his life the evidence of the family's success had been around him, in the houses all Brights he knew lived in, in the furnishings of those houses, in their acres and ornamental gardens, in the portraits of Bright ancestors on the walls of Bright mansions, and above all in the stories the Brights told of their forebears whose exploits over the centuries had amassed the wealth that allowed contemporary Brights to live so very comfortably. Timothy never tired of hearing those stories. Not that he fully understood their import. And he certainly didn't understand that twentieth-century Brights, and in particular his father's generation, had done practically nothing to increase or even maintain that wealth. In fact, thanks to their public school education and the smug conceit this engendered in them, they had done a great deal to waste the family finances and influence. They had also done the country no great service by wasting themselves. While the older and politically influential Brights had used their peculiar talents to ensure that wars were almost certain to take place, the younger members of the family had died with courageous idiocy on the battlefields. Whether this had helped the family finances no one could be entirely sure, but what wars and their own preference for playing games and killing birds instead of thinking and working hadn't done, death duties and indolent stupidity had.

All this had been hidden from Timothy Bright. One or two elderly aunts grumbled that things weren't what they had been in their day, when apparently every house had had a proper butler plus a great many indoor servants, but Timothy hadn't been

1

interested. In any case the few domestic servants he had occasionally seen sunning themselves in the desultory sunlight against the wall of Uncle Fergus's fine old kitchen garden at Drumstruthie hadn't impressed him. This was hardly surprising. The rest of the family disapproved of Uncle Fergus. He was an exceptional Bright and a very rich one. Thanks to a life of unstinted service in various unhealthy and inexpensive parts of the world (he had been Vice-Consul in East Timor and had even been considered for the Falklands) Fergus Bright had been prevented from sharing in the financial fiascos of his brothers and cousins. His last appointment, as the Governor of the Royal Asylum near Kettering, had been most rewarding and, thanks to the discretion he showed in the matter of his extremely well-connected patients, he had been handsomely rewarded. In spite of this, and perhaps because of his strange parsimony, Uncle Fergus had been held up to Timothy as an example of boring rectitude and of the social dangers of a good education.

'Uncle Fergus got a First at Oxford,' Aunt Annie was fond of saying to annoy her brothers and was always rewarded by a shout of 'And look where that got him – East Timor' from the other Brights, only a few of whom had been to university. So, in spite of the wealth that allowed him to keep up Drumstruthie, the example of Fergus was a negative one and Timothy had been encouraged to find his heroes in Uncles Harry and Wedgewood and Lambkin, all of whom played polo and shot and hunted and belonged to very smart clubs in London and who spoke of having had jolly good wars somewhere or other and who seemed to live very comfortable lives without having to think about money.

'I just don't understand it, Daddy,' Timothy had told his father one day when they had gone down Dilly Dell to watch Old Og, the handyman, training his new ferret by setting it down an artificial warren after a pet rabbit because, as Old Og said, 'They ain't no real coneys about what with this MickeyMousitosis like, so I has to make do with a shop-bought one, see,' which Timothy Bright did understand.

'But I still don't understand money, Daddy,' he persisted as the ferret shot down the hole. 'What is money for?'

Bletchley Bright had taken his protuberant eyes off the unnatural world of the warren for a moment and had studied his son briefly before going back to more important things like dying rabbits. He wasn't entirely sure that Timothy's question was a proper one. 'What is money for?' he repeated uncertainly, only to have Old Og answer for him.

''Tis for spending, Master Timothy,' he said and gave a nasty cackle which, like his archaic rustic language, took him a lot of practice. 'Spent by thems that has it and stole by thems what ain't.'

'Well I suppose that is one way of looking at it,' said Bletchley uncertainly. His only act of public service was to be a Magistrate in Voleney Hatch. The discussion was interrupted by the emergence of the young ferret with a bloodstained muzzle.

'He be a little beauty, bain't he?' said Old Og affectionately and was promptly bitten on the thumb for this lapse. Stifling the impulse to say anything more appropriate than 'Lawsamercy' he stuffed the ferret into his jacket pocket and hurried off to get some Elastoplast from the Mini-Market in the village, leaving father and son to wander home for kitchen tea.

'You see, my boy,' said Bletchley when they had gone two hundred yards and he had had time to marshal his thoughts. 'Money is . . .' He paused and sought for inspiration in a muddy puddle. 'Money is . . . yes, well I don't quite know how to put this but money is . . . Good gracious me, I do believe I saw a barn owl over there by the wood. It would be wonderful to see a barn owl, wouldn't it, Timothy?'

'But I want to know where money comes from,' said Timothy, not to be so easily distracted by nothing more than a pigeon.

'Ah, yes, where it comes from,' said Bletchley. 'I know where it comes from. It comes from other people paying it, of course.'

'What other people, Daddy? People like Old Og?'

Bletchley shook his head. 'I don't think Old Og has very much,' he said. 'You don't if you do odd jobs and things like that. Of

3

course, he's very happy. You don't have to have money to be happy. Surely they've taught you that at school?'

'Mr Habbak earns ninety-one pounds a week,' said Timothy. 'Scobey saw his payslip on his desk and he says it isn't much.'

'It's not a great deal,' said his father. 'But then schoolmasters get their board and lodging and that means a lot, you know.'

'But how am I going to get money? I don't want to be like Mr Habbak,' Timothy persisted. Bletchley Bright looked dourly round the faded winter landscape and finally revealed what was evidently the family secret.

'You will make money by becoming a Name,' he said finally. 'That will happen when you are twenty-one. Until that time I would appreciate it if you would never mention the topic of money again. It is not a subject at all suitable for a Bright your age.'

From that moment Timothy had been sure he was going to make a fortune because he was Timothy Bright and his name entitled him to one. And since this was so certain, he didn't have to think too much about how he was going to do it. That would come later in some natural way when he was twenty-one and had become a Name. In the meantime he had some of the problems of adolescence to cope with or enjoy. Having developed a taste for blood sports with Old Og he underwent a temporary religious crisis during what the school chaplain, the Reverend Benedict de Cheyne, called 'his sixteenth year to Heaven' in an explanatory letter to Timothy's parents.

'We frequently find that sensitive boys do tend to have fantasies of this nature,' he wrote after Timothy had decided to reveal all during a confessional hour with him. 'However I can assure you that the impulse towards undue holiness tends to pass quite rapidly once the initial sense of sin wears off. I shall of course do all I can, as Timothy's spiritual adviser and consort, to hasten this change. We shall be taking our holiday in a cottage on Exmoor at Easter. I have often found that this period of isolation is helpful. Your obedient servant in God, Benedict de Cheyne.'

'I must say I find his emphasis on sin disturbing,' Bletchley told his wife when he had read the letter several times.

'What do you think they are going to do on Exmoor?' Ernestine asked. 'It gets so terribly cold there at Easter.'

'I prefer not to think,' said Bletchley, and left the room before she required him to discuss the nature of Timothy's fantasies. He shut himself away in the downstairs lavatory and tried to exorcise the memory of his own adolescent lusts by studying photographs of a collection of mole traps in *The Field*. He'd have liked to use one on the Reverend Benedict de Cheyne.

But Mrs Bright raised the topic again at dinner that night. 'Of course I blame Old Og,' she said as they sat down to scrambled eggs.

Bletchley's fork paused. 'Old Og? What on earth has Old Og got to do with it?'

'Timothy has been exposed to ... well, Old Og's baleful influence,' said Ernestine.

'Baleful influence? Nonsense,' said Bletchley. 'Old Og's all right. Outdoor sports and so on.'

'You may call them that,' she went on. 'In my opinion they are something else. To allow a sensitive and delicate boy like Timothy to be exposed to ... well, Old Og.' She stopped and looked down at her plate.

'Exposed? You keep using that expression. If you're telling me Old Og exposed himself to ...' Bletchley shouted. 'By God, I'll thrash the blighter ... I'll –'

'Oh, do shut up,' Ernestine said. 'You're making an absolute fool of yourself. You're not capable of thrashing him. No, that dreadful creature exposed Timothy to two terrible temptations.' She paused again. Bletchley was about to rise from his chair. 'One was that awful animal with blood on its snout killing a pet rabbit –'

'He had to,' Bletchley interrupted. 'There weren't any wild rabbits about and he had to train it on something. And anyway it was not an awful animal. It was Old Og's young ferret, Posy.'

'All ferrets are awful,' said Mrs Bright. 'And as if that were not enough to turn the child's mind, Og had to take him to some frightful girl in the village and expose him to . . .'

'Expose him?' Bletchley said. 'He didn't do anything of the sort with me. He exposed her. Ripe as . . . Now, what's wrong?'

'You are a vile, disgusting, and hopelessly impotent man. I can't think why I bothered to marry you.' And Ernestine Bright left the table and went up to her room.

'I can,' Bletchley told the portrait of his grandfather, Benjamin. 'For money.'

But in due course the Chaplain's forecast proved correct. Timothy Bright came off Exmoor with all dreams of a religious life quite gone. He had a different attitude to the Reverend Benedict, too. Instead he followed the usual course for boys of his sort and failed his A-Levels.

'Bang goes your chance of Cambridge, my boy,' his Uncle Fergus told him when the results arrived – Timothy was up at Drumstruthie for the summer – 'There's nothing for it now. You'll have to go into banking. I've known an awful lot of fools who've done remarkably well in banking. It apparently doesn't require any real thought. I remember your Great-Uncle Harold was put into banking and you couldn't wish for a bigger fool. Dear fellow, as I remember him, but definitely short of the necessary neurons for anything else. Not to put too fine a point on it, I'd say in the modern jargon that he was so mentally challenged it took him twenty minutes to do up his tie. But a fine fellow for all that, and naturally the family rallied round to train him for his new profession. I seem to think it was your grandmother's Uncle Charlie who found the way. He owed a bookie at Newmarket rather a large sum and in the normal way would have avoided the fellow for a bit. Instead he got the family to put up the necessary cash and Charlie did a deal with the bookmaker. He agreed to pay up in full immediately provided the bookie took Great-Uncle Harold on and showed him the ropes. Bookie thought Harold was an idiot and accepted, and when he'd graduated Harold went on as a banker in the City. Did damned well too. Ended up as Chairman of the Royal Western, with a gong. They said he had a knack of knowing what a chap was thinking just by looking at his hands. Extraordinary gift for a fellow with no brains to speak of. I daresay you'll do very well in banking and the family could do with some financial help just now.'

Inspired by the example of his great-uncle, Timothy Bright had tried to persuade his father to put up the money to apprentice him to a Newmarket bookie, only to meet with an adamant refusal to waste money.

'You've been listening to Uncle Fergus's tommyrot,' Bletchley told him. 'Uncle Harold wasn't such an idiot as all that, and what Fergus forgets is that he was a mathematical genius. That's what accounted for his success. Nothing to do with watching clients' hands. From what Fergus says anyone would think he was some sort of tic-tac man.'

'But Uncle Fergus says he always looked at —'

'He was so short-sighted he couldn't see clearly that far. What he could do was work out square roots and some things called prime numbers at the drop of a hat. Nearest thing to a human calculator in existence.'

In spite of this Timothy Bright followed his uncle's example to the extent of attending a great many race meetings at which he gave bookies a considerable amount of money and learnt nothing at all. All the same, he did go into banking, and on his twenty-first birthday became a Name at Lloyd's.

Bletchley tried to tell him what a Name was. 'The thing is,' he said awkwardly, 'the thing is you don't have to put any money up. All your capital stays in investments or property or whatever you like. I suppose some people leave it in Building Societies. And every year Lloyd's pay you premiums. It's as simple as that.'

'Premiums?' said Timothy. 'You mean like insurance premiums?'

'Precisely,' said Bletchley, delighted that the boy had caught on so quickly. 'Just like insurance on the car. Instead of the company getting the premiums, Lloyd's distributes them among the Names.

It's a wonderfully fair system. Don't know what we'd have done without it. In fact Brights have been Names since Names were invented as far as I know. Hundreds of years probably. Been an absolute Godsend to us.'

On this somewhat lopsidedly optimistic note the interview ended. Timothy Bright was a Name.

A few years later Timothy had made something of a name for himself. Coming to the City at the beginning of the eighties his opinion that the world was his oyster fitted in exactly with the views of those then in power. From his position in the investment branch of the Bimburg Bank he was soon able to play a surprisingly important role in restructuring the stock market. Long before insider trading became such a well-publicized practice, a few of the shadier and, in the opinion of some, shrewder stockbrokers had used Timothy as an intermediary in the certain knowledge that they could talk through him without his having the faintest understanding of the issues involved. It was this enviable reputation for involuntary discretion which, more than anything else, led to his consistent rise up the investment banking ladder. When Timothy Bright was urged to push shares he pushed them, and when told to talk them down he did that too. And of course the Bright family benefited from his popularity, in particular Uncle Fergus, who regularly caught the night train from Aberdeen simply to take his nephew out to lunch and quiz him about the week's business. From these unnoticed interrogations Fergus Bright returned to Drumstruthie a richer and more knowledgeable old man. Of course it required all his skills as an interpreter or even a code-breaker to sift the genuine information from the useless bits with which Timothy had been programmed, but the effort was clearly worth the trouble. Uncle Fergus was able to buy cheaply shares that would shortly rise to quite astonishing heights while selling those that would presently fall.

It was largely thanks to Uncle Fergus's interventions in the market that Timothy was eventually promoted from Bimburg's investment branch to the Names Recruitment Bureau at Lloyd's. This wasn't its official title and its existence was strenuously denied, but its work consisted almost entirely of spreading the word to the millions of newly 'enriched' Thatcherite home owners that becoming a Name at Lloyd's had the advantage of being socially most acceptable and, at the same time, inevitably rewarding. As house prices shot up and the Prime Minister spoke of Britain's new economic success, Timothy Bright did what he was told and recruited new Names to help pay for the anticipated losses on asbestosis, pollution claims, and a host of other disasters. Life was joyful. He moved in a world of self-congratulation and socially accredited greed. In his clubs and at weekend house parties, at political conferences and intimate dinner parties, Timothy Bright could be relied upon to say that prosperity had finally come to post-war Britain and that the Prime Minister had saved the nation from itself. In return for this idolatry he was favoured with fresh confidences about privatization plans and those companies that could expect government contracts. The flow of supposedly confidential information grew so steadily that Fergus was persuaded to take a room permanently in an hotel rather than spend so much time travelling backwards and forwards from Scotland. He was especially delighted to have news in advance of the coal miners' strike, and made provision for the outcome by investing in Nottingham Trucks Ltd and their spare parts subsidiaries.

'A fine man and a Scotsman, MacGregor,' he said when Timothy told him who was to be appointed to the Coal Board to inflame Scargill.

Even Bletchley Bright, normally an exceedingly cautious man where any of his son's financial advice was concerned, was tempted to invest – though not in anything connected with coal or along the tortuous lines laid out so carefully by Fergus. He took his son's advice literally, and lost nearly everything in Canadian gold.

'That's the last time I listen to that blithering idiot son of yours,' he told Ernestine. 'The little moron definitely said gold was going to make a terrific come-back. Said he had it from some blighter in the Bank of England. And now look where it is. No wonder the country's in a stew.'

'Now, now, dear,' said Mrs Bright, 'Timothy is doing brilliantly and everyone thinks so. There's no need to spoil things for him. After all, we're only young once.'

'Thank God,' said Bletchley and went off to commune with Old Og, who thought the world was in a dreadful mess too.

'Bain't seem to be no sense in it,' Og told him. 'Had a fellow from the Ministry round said us had to gas all badgers. I told him we got no badgers but he don't hear like. "Got to gas 'em cos they got TB," he says. I tells him straight. "I don't know about that," I says, "and we still haven't got no badgers. You'm come to the wrong place for badgers unless you want to gas Master's shaving brush, that being the only bit of badger round here." '

Bletchley found comfort in the old man's words. They took him back to a world that had never existed in which summers were perpetually sunny and it snowed every Christmas.

In many respects Timothy Bright's world was as unreal as his father's memories. He too went through the eighties believing what the PR men told him and, while politicians and businessmen lived in the hope that their optimistic words would produce the prosperity they proclaimed was already there, Timothy Bright really believed it was. With the sublime ignorance that finds no excuse in law, he thrived in the praise of criminals and timeservers like Maxwell and his acolytes and took the view that a prison sentence was no bar to social advancement. In Timothy's world no one resigned or was punished for negligence or worse. The Great Hen squawked self-congratulations over the City, and Maxwell silenced his mildest critics with the harshest of libel writs and made Her Majesty's Judges accessories to his terrible crimes. And Timothy thrived. He was a merry idiot and everyone loved him.

And just as suddenly he was a bloody swine and no fool after all.

10

Chapter 2

As with everything else in his life it took Timothy some time to realize that anything was wrong. He went about what he called his work in the same way as before and frequented the same clubs and wine bars to discuss the same topics and tell clients what shares to buy or sell, but slowly it did begin to dawn on him that something was different. People seemed to drop out of his society without any warning and a number of friends he had advised to become Names began to remind him of his advice.

'But I hadn't the foggiest that things were going to turn nasty then,' he explained only to be called a damned liar.

'You knew as far back as '82 that the American courts were going to award asbestosis victims huge sums –'

'All right, I knew,' Timothy admitted. 'But I didn't know what asbestosis was then. I mean it could have been the measles or something mild like that.'

'But you knew about the huge awards that were coming. And what about pollution? You were there at the meeting when the whole dirty scheme for recruiting new Names to help pay was first mooted. And don't bloody well say you weren't. We know you were. You went there with Coletrimmer.'

'Well, yes I did,' said Timothy unwisely. 'I remember the meeting but I had no idea the sums were going to be so large. Anyway, I didn't fix for you to go into that Syndicate.'

'Didn't you? Then how come you managed to stay out of it so well?'

'I was only doing what Coletrimmer advised,' said Timothy.

'Oh, sure. That's a likely story. Coletrimmer's up the spout himself and you're sitting pretty. Why don't you follow his example and sod off to South America some place?'

In this new and harsh world Timothy found himself increasingly isolated. His clubs had become the focal points of an unpopularity he could not face and, while he still saw a few old girlfriends from the heady days of affluence, his own financial position deteriorated so drastically that he was unable to entertain them in the same style and they drifted away. 'Timothy Bright's such an awful tick,' he heard a girl he had been fond of say as he stood in a crowded train. 'He was naff enough before. But now. Ugh.'

To make matters worse still, Uncle Fergus gave up coming to London and let it be known he didn't want 'that moron Timothy' anywhere near Drumstruthie. Timothy took this particularly hard. For once he had offered his uncle some good advice and had warned him there was likely to be war in Kuwait. It had been entirely due to Fergus's habit of finding the kernel of truth behind the arrant nonsense that Timothy usually talked that he had decided no war was likely and had invested heavily in Iraqi Oils. Fergus's losses had been very considerable and the old man had never forgiven his nephew. As a result Timothy had nobody at all sensible to turn to when his own financial problems developed. And they developed with alarming rapidity. The house he had bought in Holland Park at the top of the property boom had required an enormous mortgage. As the recession developed and his work tailed off, he found himself unable to keep up his mortgage payments. And, as if that were not enough, he found himself involved in the Lloyd's scandal and owing hundreds of thousands of pounds. In a few months Timothy Bright's world collapsed about him.

It was at this point that he recalled his ambition to make a fortune and the method his Great-Uncle Harold had used. Timothy turned to horse-racing and gambling. Having lost nearly everything on the horses he borrowed heavily and, using an infallible system he had read about, bet everything on the roulette wheel at the Markinkus Club. The roulette wheel ignored the system and when Timothy finally pushed back his chair and stood up there was little he could do except accompany two very thickset men to the office for what they termed 'a quiet word with the Boss'. It was rather more than a quiet word. By the time Timothy Bright left the casino twenty minutes later he was in no doubt what his future would be if he did not pay his debts within the month.

'And that's generous, laddie,' said Mr Markinkus, who was clearly in an expansive mood. 'See you don't miss the deadline. Yeah, the deadline. Get it?'

Timothy had got it, and in the dawn light filtering slowly over London he tried to think where to turn for help. It was at this dark moment that he found the inspiration that was to change his life so radically. He remembered his Great-Aunt Ermyne who had gone to her demented death repeating the never-to-be-forgotten words 'You must always look on the Bright side' over and over again. Timothy had only been eleven at the time but the words, repeated like a mantra as Auntie Ermyne was wheeled down the corridor at Loosemore for the last time, had made a deep impression on him. He had asked Uncle Vernon, Ermyne's husband, who seemed to be in a talkatively good mood, what they meant. After the old man had muttered something about a few years of freedom and happiness, he had taken Timothy by the hand and had shown him the family portraits in the Long Gallery.

'These are the Bright side of the family,' he had explained in tones that suggested ancestor worship. 'Now when things look darkest, as they generally do, I'm told, just before the dawn, it is to the Bright side that we always look. Here, for instance, is Croker Bright shortly before he was captured by the French. His forte was piracy on the high seas and after that the usual silk and brandy smuggling. He was particularly feared by the Spanish. Died in 1678. We owe a great deal to him and to his son, Stanhope, here. Stanhope Bright was a fine fellow. You can see that. He was a slave trader and became the founding father of the Bristol Brights. Very rich man indeed. His cousin over here is Blakeney Bright, also known as Mangle Bright, not, as people would have us believe, for any good agricultural reasons but for the invention of a particularly devastating form of high-speed beam engine. I forget what it was supposed to do but I do know it was only used in coal mines where very high casualty rates were perfectly acceptable.'

Old Uncle Vernon had moved on down the Gallery extolling the virtues of Bright ancestors while Timothy had learnt how one Bright after another had made a fortune against quite amazing odds of character and circumstance. Even after the abolition of slavery, for instance, the Rev. Otto Bright, of the Bright Missionary Station on Zanzibar, had done a remarkable fund-raising job for the Church by supplying well-favoured young men from Central Africa to discriminating sheikhs on the Arabian peninsula while his sister, Ursula, had pursued her own feminine tendencies by persuading a number of young women from Houndsditch to join what she called 'secular nunneries' in the less amenable ports of South America. Even as late as the 1920s several American Brights who were the direct descendants of Croker Bright had collaborated with the bootlegger and gangster Joseph Kennedy in rum-running during Prohibition. Uncle Vernon remembered some of them.

'Fine fellows who followed the family traditions,' he said and quoted another old family maxim. ' "Where there is a demand, supply it: where there isn't, create one." That is an old saying that dates back to Enoch Bright, a contemporary of Adam Smith and the truer Tory. The saying is at the very heart of modern economic practice and Croker is a good example.'

Now, standing in the grey dawn off the Edgware Road, Timothy recalled his uncle's words and looked on the Bright side. It wasn't at all easy but he did it. He still had his job of a sort at Bimburg's Bank; he had a flat in a friend's name in Notting Hill Gate and a new motorbike, a Suzuki 1100, in place of his old Porsche, which he kept in a lock-up garage; but above all he had the Bright family connections. These were his most important assets and he meant to make use of them. With their present help and the example of past Brights to inspire him he would find a way out of his temporary difficulties and Mr Markinkus's threats and make his fortune. With renewed optimism he hurried back to his flat and spent much of the day asleep.

Over the weekend he racked his brains for a way forward. Perhaps, if he went home and asked Daddy to lend him some money . . . No, he'd done that too often and the last time Daddy had threatened to have him certified as a financial lunatic if he ever mentioned the word 'borrow' again in his presence. And Mummy didn't have any money to lend. Perhaps if he wrote to Uncle Fergus and told him . . . But no, Uncle Fergus had a 'thing' about gambling and had once preached an awful sermon at his strange Presbyterian Church about 'Gambling Hells' which he seemed to think of quite literally. There was absolutely no member of the family he could ask for help in his predicament. 'You'd think someone would be willing to supply the money considering the demand I have for it,' he thought bitterly. And then on the Tuesday just when he was almost past thinking and was at his lowest ebb, he received a telephone call at work. It was from a Mr Brian Smith who suggested that Timothy drop by for a drink at El Baco Wine Bar in Pologne Street on his way home that night. 'Say 6.30,' said Mr Smith, and rang off.

Timothy Bright considered the invitation and decided he had nothing to lose by accepting it. Besides, there had been something about Mr Smith's tone of voice that had suggested he would be well advised not to reject it. At 6.25 he entered the wine bar and had hardly ordered a Red Biddy when the barman told him that Mr Smith was through the back and waiting for him. Without wondering how the barman had known who he was, Timothy took his drink through the door.

'Ah, Mr Bright, my name is Smith but you can call me Brian,' said a man who didn't look or sound like any Mr Smith, or Brian for that matter. Timothy had never set eyes on him before. 'Good of you to come.'

'How do you do?' said Timothy, trying to be formal.

'Pretty damn well,' said Mr Smith, indicating a chair on the other side of the desk. 'I hear you don't do so good, no?'

'Nobody's doing very well in this depression . . .' Timothy began, before deciding Mr Smith wasn't talking in general terms. He also appeared to be cleaning his nails with a cut-throat razor. Mr Smith smiled – or something. To Timothy it was definitely not a proper smile.

'Good, so we understand one another,' said Mr Smith, and apparently cut an errant fly in half in mid-air. 'You want some money and I got some you can have. How does that sound to you?'

'Well . . .' said Timothy, still overwhelmed by the fate of the fly, 'I . . . er . . . I suppose . . . that's very good of you.'

'Not good. Business,' said Mr Smith, now glancing in a hand mirror to assist him in using the razor to defoliate a nostril. 'Want to hear more?'

'Well . . .' Timothy said hesitantly, wishing he wouldn't flourish the razor quite so casually.

'Good, then I tell you,' continued Mr Smith. 'You gotta motorbike, big Suzuki eleven hundred, yes?'

'Yes,' Timothy said.

'You gotta uncle?'

'Actually, I've got quite a few.'

'Sure, you gotta lots. You gotta one who's Judge. Judge Sir Benderby bloody Bright?' interrupted Mr Smith. 'Right?'

'Oh yes, Uncle Benderby,' said Timothy, and swallowed drily. Uncle Benderby terrified him.

'Your Uncle Benderby done some friends of mine some big favours. Like fifteen years,' Mr Smith went on. 'You know that? Fuck.'

Timothy didn't know it but he could see that Mr Smith had just nicked his nose. The situation was most unpleasant. 'I'm sorry about that,' he muttered. 'He's not very popular in the family either.'

Mr Smith dabbed the end of his nose with a blue silk handkerchief and hurled the razor expertly at the desk where it bisected a cigar. He got up and went into the toilet for some paper.

16

'Got a yacht called the *Lex Britannicus*?' he said while dabbing his nose with the paper.

'Yes,' said Timothy, mesmerized by the performance.

'And your Uncle Benderby sails it out to a place near Barcelona for the winter and brings it back to Fowey for the summer. Then out again in September. Right?'

'Quite right. Absolutely,' said Timothy. 'It's an awfully rough time to sail. With the equinoctial gales, you know. But Uncle Benderby says it's the only time to be a real sailor.'

'He'd know, wouldn't he?' said Mr Smith with a nasty smile. The red-stained paper on his nose didn't improve his appearance. 'Well, you and Uncle Benderby ought to get together. Soon. Like you ride your flash bike down there with a present for him.'

'A present for Uncle Ben –?'

'That's right. A present. What you do is this . . .'

For the next ten minutes Timothy Bright listened to his instructions. They were very clear and to Timothy's way of thinking didn't add up to anything in the least attractive. 'You want me to catch the ferry from Plymouth to Santander with my bike and drive to Llafranc and meet someone who will have a package for me and I'm to put it in the sail locker on Uncle Benderby's yacht without him knowing? Is that right?' he asked.

'Sort of. Except you'll be taking something with you maybe so you earn your money both ways. That way we know you've done the job proper.'

'But this sounds very dubious to me, I must say,' Timothy protested, only to be cut short.

Mr Smith reached into a drawer in his desk and brought out an envelope. 'Take a look at piggy-chops,' he said and pulled out a colour photograph and slid it across the desk.

Timothy Bright looked down and saw something that might once have been a pig.

Mr Smith let him savour the sight. 'Right, you want to end up like piggy-chops there all you have to do is not do what I say. Right?'

17

'I suppose so,' said Timothy, who definitely didn't want to end up looking like that indescribable pig. 'I mean, yes, of course. Right.'

Mr Smith put the photo back in the envelope and picked up the razor again. 'You will get the ferry from Plymouth on the twentieth. That'll give you time to arrange leave from the bank. You're owed some. Like three weeks, and you're taking it.'

'I suppose so. Yes, all right,' said Timothy with a lopsided smile. The dreadful man seemed to know everything about him. It was terribly disturbing and frightening.

'So you do what all good yuppie stockbrokers do. Sell in May and go away. Here's your ticket and some spending money. Anything else?'

'I don't think so.'

Mr Smith picked up the razor again and smiled. 'Oh yes, there is,' he said and leant forward with the razor. 'And don't you forget it. There's this.' His left hand produced a brown paper parcel carefully tied with string. He laid it on the desk top and allowed Timothy to study it. 'Don't try and be a bigger smart-ass than you are. You'll end up piggy-chops and no mistake. And this is your present for the Pedro other end. Lose it and . . . You better keep this picture for a reminder like.' His hand went back to the drawer and the photo of the pig but Timothy shook his head.

'I don't need any reminder,' he said. 'I've got it all straight.'

'So where do you meet the Pedro?'

'Up the hill past Kim's Camping,' said Timothy.

'When?'

'I go past at eleven-thirty every night for three nights from the twenty-fourth through the twenty-sixth and he'll be there on one of the nights. But how will I know he's the right person?'

'You don't have to. He'll know you all right. He's got a nice picture of you, hasn't he? One of the nice "before" ones. He'll pick you up.' Mr Smith took the piece of bloodstained paper off his nose. 'Then he'll give you the article to put in the sail locker. How you get on board is your business but you'd better have a good excuse if you're spotted.' Mr Smith's tone had changed. He was no longer a foreigner and he didn't even sound very London. 'Unless of course you want to just visit Uncle Benderby, pay him a nice social visit. Nothing wrong with that. You do what you want.'

'But won't the … er … package I put in the sail locker be noticed?' Timothy asked. It was a question that had been slowly gaining shape in his mind.

Mr Smith shook his head. 'It will be noticed, and then again it won't. He'll have had it before. Like it's one of his fenders, see. Just like all the others. Nice and worn too. Identical to the one that went missing a few days ago. And in due course, like June, dear old uncle is going to sail into Fowey and you'll have been home and comfy in bed long before he gets here.'

'I see,' said Timothy, with the feeling that he was unlikely ever to be comfy in bed again. Even his father had admitted he was scared of Benderby Bright and said he found the Judge's sentencing on the harsh side. Judge Bright had several times given it as his opinion that drug smugglers and pushers should get a true life sentence without the possibility of parole. And it was well known that he had been the toast of the evening at the last two annual dinners of the Customs and Excise Officers Association. The prospect of stowing a fender containing goodness only knew how many kilos of an illegal substance in the sail locker of the *Lex Britannicus* filled Timothy with almost as much terror as the dreadful process called 'piggy-chops'. Not quite. Judge Benderby Bright was not a dab hand at skinning pigs with razors. Yet. It was hard to tell what his feelings would be if it ever came out that his nephew had been party to planting a fender full of drugs on him. On the other hand it was almost inconceivable that the yacht would ever be searched by the Customs officials in Fowey.

'You got nothing to worry about that side,' said Mr Smith, reading Timothy's mind. 'About as likely as the Pope handing out condoms in St Peter's Square.'

He paused and toyed with the razor again. 'One more thing,' he said. 'One more thing you got to remember. You go anywhere near the police, even go past a cop shop or think of picking up the phone, like your mobile, you won't just get piggy-chops. You won't have a fucking cock to fuck with again first. No balls, no prick. And that's for starters. You'll have piggy-chops days later. Slowly. Very slowly. Get that in your dumb fucking head. Now.' Once again the cut-throat razor quivered into the desk top and stayed there.

Timothy Bright left the wine bar at 8.15 clutching the brown paper parcel and with an envelope in his pocket containing five thousand pounds. If he did what he was told, Mr Smith had said, he would get another twenty-five grand when he returned. It was exactly the sum he needed to pay Mr Markinkus at the casino. That night he got drunk before going to bed.

In the morning he was late in getting to Bimburg's Bank. There was a letter waiting for him. It informed him that as of 18 May he had no need to apply for three weeks' leave. Timothy Bright had been made redundant.

Chapter 3

At his little cottage at Pud End, Victor Gould pottered across the old croquet lawn to his summerhouse-cum-study overlooking the sea. From its window he could look down at the estuary and watch the fishing boats and yachts heading for the Channel. In the normal way he found great comfort sitting at his desk, but today there was no consolation to be had there. He had just received a very nasty shock and he needed time to think. Mrs Leacock, who came to clean the house and see that he was all right, as his wife Brenda put it, had left a note on the hall table to say that Mr Timothy had phoned to ask if it was all right for him to come down to stay for a few days.

It was not all right at all, in fact it couldn't have been less all right if Timothy Bright had deliberately chosen to make it so. It was the worst bit of news Mr Gould had received for a very long time and it had landed on the hall table just when he was about to enjoy himself, when something he had been looking forward to for a year was about to happen. He had been having a very pleasant time on his own (except for Mrs Leacock in the mornings, and he could avoid her) while his wife was taking an extended holiday in America visiting her relations there. Victor Gould was all for her visiting her relations so long as he wasn't asked to take part. It had been one of the trials of his married life that, in marrying Brenda Bright, he had married into her confounded family as well. Not that he had ever been welcomed there. From the very first the Brights had made it quite clear that he was not of their class or cultivation. Colonel Barnaby Bright, DSO, MC and bar, had gone so far as to attempt to dissuade his daughter in her bedroom the day before the wedding. 'My dear child,' he had begun, deliberately standing on Victor's trousers and raising his voice. 'You must see that the fellow is a bounder and a cad.' For a moment the naked Victor in the next room had preened himself. He rather liked being a bounder and a cad. The Colonel corrected himself. 'A sleazy, greasy bounder, the sort of dirty pimp and gigolo who hangs around hotel lounges in Brighton and sucks up to rich old women.'

In the dressing-room Victor Gould had flushed angrily and had almost sneezed. Brenda's reply had chilled him still further.

'I know all that, Daddy. I know he's awful and not one of us and that there is bad blood in the Gould family because Victor's Uncle Joe was cashiered from the Navy for attempting to bugger a stoker on a make-and-mend afternoon . . .'

For a moment Victor had been too shocked to listen. Uncle Joe's disgrace was news to him and his fiancée's familiarity with the term 'bugger' had surprised him almost as much as it had evidently mind-blown the Colonel.

'And of course he is all the things you say he is,' she continued, 'but that's why I need him. You do see that, don't you, Daddy?' (A gurgling sound from her father suggested he wasn't seeing anything at all clearly.) 'I need someone disgusting like Victor to give my life meaning.'

Naked and cold, Victor had tried to come to terms with this new role as her husband.

Colonel Bright was having difficulties too. 'Meaning? Meaning?' he bawled apoplectically. 'What the hell do you want meaning for? You're a Bright, aren't you? What more meaning do you need? You don't have to marry some filthy bounder to get meaning. The man's an absolute shit. He'll make your life a positive hell and go around having affairs with other fellows' wives and losing money on something loathsome like greyhound racing. Goddamit, the fellow doesn't even hunt.' This last was evidently the worst thing the Colonel could think of. But Brenda was not to be persuaded.

'Of course he doesn't, you old darling. He's far too yellow, and besides the poor dear wears a truss.'

'Dear God,' said the Colonel and Victor in unison. 'But the

22

damned man is only twenty-five. What the devil does he need a truss for at his age?'

It was a question Victor wanted an answer to as well. He'd never seen the inside of a truss in his life. Brenda's reply had stunned him too. 'I think it has something to do with his scrotum, Daddy,' she said coyly. 'Of course I don't know what yet. Perhaps after the honeymoon I'll be in a position to tell you.'

But Colonel Bright had no longer wanted to hear anything more about his prospective son-in-law. With a grunt of revulsion he had turned his heel, this time on Victor's shirt, and had stumped out of the bedroom. From that moment on he had avoided his son-in-law as far as was possible and had spoken to him only when forced to. And the family's attitude had never changed. Nor, he realized now, had Brenda's. At the time he had succumbed almost at once to her charms and the delicious moue she had made as she asked him if she hadn't been a clever little girliewhirl to get rid of Daddy so quickly. Only later when they had been married and Brenda had decided she'd had enough of sex herself and preferred counselling other people with sex problems did Victor fully realize the truth of her remark that she needed someone disgusting to give her life meaning. By 'meaning' she meant feeling morally superior. Not that Victor had cared. There had been compensations in his role as the morally inferior. He had been left free to have a notorious love life while Brenda had had the gratification of forgiving him. Victor found the forgiveness galling but could hardly blame her for it. His real quarrel remained with the Bright family. And now he was faced with the invasion of his house by his least favourite Bright, Timothy. To make matters worse he was expecting his own nephew Henry, who had just returned from a trip to South America and Australia.

'What a damned nuisance,' he muttered and looked out of the window in desperation. He had already tried phoning Timothy Bright's house in London but without a reply. As usual in his dealings with the Brights there was nothing he could do to prevent the fellow from coming. In the past he had worked out a set of tactics which had tended to keep them at bay by turning the central heating off just before they arrived and contriving a number of electricity black-outs when they were in the lavatory or bathroom. On the whole the system had been moderately successful, although his own reputation had suffered even more as a result. With Timothy Bright he would have to devise something more in the way of inconvenience. Victor Gould had no intention of having his own nephew's visit ruined.

In London Timothy Bright completed the arrangements for his trip to Spain. He had been to his doctor for something to calm his nerves and had been drinking much more heavily than usual. It was largely due to the fact that he was hardly ever entirely sober – the drink and the tranquillizers did tend to lessen his anxiety about piggy-chops – that his plans coincided with the realization that he had been hard done by in more ways than he had previously imagined. He felt particularly bitter about his own family. In Timothy's opinion they ought to have helped him by giving him money. Especially after all he had done for them in the City. Instead they didn't seem to care what happened to him. They'd let him land up in debt to the Markinkus brothers and they'd let the bank make him redundant. The Brights had always banked at Bimburg's, ever since the year dot, and if anyone could have used their influence to see he was kept on, they could. It hardly occurred to him that only their influence had got him the job in the first instance and had kept him in it for so long. From this constant self-pity his thoughts turned weakly to revenge.

If the family refused to help him, why should he do anything for them? From that point it was an easy slide to the idea of helping himself to what they owed him. It wouldn't be difficult. Rotten old Auntie Boskie, who was ninety or something, had given him her power of attorney to sell some shares when she was in hospital the year before and she had never cancelled it. And anyway she was in failing health and wouldn't notice anything. She wouldn't miss some other shares. Half of them weren't producing much in the way of dividends. And why shouldn't he use them? Especially if they saved him from piggy-chops. Auntie Boskie would give him the shares if she knew about piggy-chops, wouldn't she? It was hardly a question in Timothy's mind. He knew she would. Having overcome his very few scruples, Timothy Bright sold her shares, and then some of Uncle Baxter's, and by the time he left London had over £120,000 in cash on him. Of course he would pay it all back with interest when the present emergency was over. In the meantime he had something to fall back on if things went really wrong. With this precious idea in mind, and with the strange brown paper parcel Mr Smith had given him in one of his panniers, he set off for Cornwall.

He arrived to find Victor Gould sitting out on the lawn with his nephew Henry sipping their drinks in the evening sunlight. Timothy Bright felt aggrieved. He hadn't expected Henry to be there. He'd heard that Aunt Brenda had gone to America and he'd thought Uncle Victor would be on his own. Uncle Victor was known to the Brights as a curmudgeonly old fellow, no one Timothy knew much liked him, and it had never occurred to Timothy that he had any sort of social life of his own. Whenever he'd been down to Pud End to see Aunt Brenda, Uncle Victor had been in his summerhouse or doing something in the garden and had seemed to be some sort of appendage to his aunt, someone who ran errands and did the shopping for her and occasionally took his Wayfarer dinghy out or fished or something. That, after all, was one of the main reasons he had chosen Pud End as a place to stay. He could be quite sure that no one in the Bright family would go there while Aunt Brenda was away and, since Uncle Victor never had anything to do with the other Brights, they wouldn't learn where he was or what he was doing. And now Henry had barged in.

Timothy got off his bike and took off his helmet. 'Don't bother to get up,' he said. 'I'll get a glass and join you. I reckon I know where everything is.' He went into the house jauntily.

'See what I mean?' said Victor. 'He's absolutely insufferable.'

'Then why do you put up with him?' asked Henry. 'Tell him to go some place else.'

Victor Gould smiled bitterly. 'My dear boy, I can see you have no understanding of the complications and compromises that marriage forces on a man. Your aunt has family loyalties that are stronger than ... well ... than anything except some sort of maternal instinct. I could no more throw this lout out on his ear and live happily ever after with your dear aunt than a hippopotamus could flap its ears in a mud swamp and fly. I am doomed to endure the brute. Let's hope he's leaving tomorrow.'

But Timothy, who came out with a glass of Victor's best malt whisky, soon disabused him of this hope. 'Heard you were on your own, Victor,' he said. 'Thought I'd come down and cheer you up. Moody old bugger is our Uncle Victor.'

'Perfectly true,' said Victor. 'Very moody indeed.'

'I didn't know you rode a bike,' said Henry after a moment's awkward silence which Timothy hadn't recognized.

'Oh yes, frightfully good fun. Simply the only possible way to get about London these days, you know.'

It was a hellish evening. Timothy got drunk, didn't help with the washing-up after dinner, and talked all the time about the City and stocks and shares, topics which held not the slightest interest for the others. Worst of all he prevented Henry talking about his year off.

'Oh dear Lord, you can see what a shit he is,' Victor said on the stairs when finally he took himself off to bed. 'I really can't bear the thought of having him another day. I shall do something desperate.'

'Not a very pleasant specimen,' Henry agreed, and went up to his room thoughtfully. Poor old Uncle Victor was getting on in years and it was appalling that he should have to suffer this wretched yuppie in his house just to keep the peace with Aunt Brenda. Downstairs Timothy had turned the television on loudly.

'That's too much,' Henry muttered and went down to turn it down a bit. He found Timothy helping himself to a tin of Victor's

Perth Special tobacco. 'You know he has that specially made up for him,' Henry said.

'Yes, but he won't notice it. He's past it, you know. I mean I feel sorry for him,' Timothy said. 'He used to be a lot of fun, or some people say so, but he seems bloody sour and old to me. You going to have some?'

'I don't think so,' said Henry, but he took the tin all the same. And for the next hour he watched the television and listened to Timothy's maudlin conversation. By the time he went up to his room Henry Gould had formed some very definite opinions, the nicest of which he would have hesitated to express in words.

When he came down in the morning he found his uncle up and making himself some toast and coffee.

'I thought I'd be up and about before he deigns to favour us with his presence,' Victor said. 'I must say he left a hell of a mess in the other room and it looks as though he nearly finished the whisky. Let's hope it keeps him dead to the world for a bit. I thought we might take ourselves off for a walk along the coastal path and have lunch at the Riverside Inn.'

Henry looked out of the window at the fresh summer day. He and Uncle Victor were going to have a good time after all. After breakfast they set off, but just before they left Henry went up to his room, brought the tin of Old Perth Special Mixture down, and put it by the television set. The scheme he had in mind might not work, but if it did it would be Timothy Bright's own fault.

Chapter 4

It was late afternoon when Henry and Uncle Victor returned to Pud End for tea. They found Timothy Bright slumped in front of the television. The remains of his brunch were still on the kitchen table and he had evidently helped himself to a tin of genuine Beluga caviar he had found in the larder. He was not, however, in an apologetic or even grateful mood. 'Where have you been?' he asked almost truculently. 'I've been here on my own all day.'

Henry intervened before his uncle could explode. 'As a matter of fact we've been for a rather long walk. Along the cliffs,' he said.

Timothy missed the implication. 'You might have woken me. I could have done with a walk,' he said.

'You were dead to the world when I looked in at you this morning or I would have done,' Henry continued. 'Anyway you wouldn't have liked it much. Very windy and gusty.'

In the kitchen Victor was clearing up. 'Thank you for the tact,' he said when Henry came through. 'Almost certainly saved me from a murder charge. I know I'm at the age when one starts complaining about declining standards and so on but that young man really does convince me that things aren't what they used to be. A short – better still a long – spell of hard labour would surely do him a world of good. More to the point, it would certainly do the world some good.'

'I shouldn't be at all surprised if that's what he gets, Uncle Victor,' Henry said quietly as he began to wash the plates up. 'He's certainly up to something a bit shady.'

'Is he indeed?' said Victor with a touch more optimism. 'May one enquire how you know?'

'I sat up with the idiot last night, and listened to all his drunken boasting. He didn't tell me what the game is, but he was fairly

28

definite about being on to a quote good thing unquote, and in my experience that nearly always means something on the wrong side of the law.'

'How very interesting. You know, I should rather enjoy it if the police arrested him here. It would give me something to deter the rest of the Bright family from ever visiting us again.'

'On the other hand it would give Aunt Brenda something else to forgive you for,' Henry pointed out.

Victor winced. 'It's not a joke, my boy, not a joke at all. I hope that your wife has a thoroughly unforgiving nature, I hope for your sake, that is. You have no idea what a terrible deterrent forgiveness is. I'll never forget the time Brenda forgave Hilda Armstrong for . . . well, something or other. Of course she did it in public, at a Women's Institute meeting – or it may have been a parish council meeting. Most embarrassing for everyone. Must have been the parish council because I don't attend Women's Institute functions. Anyway it led to the Armstrongs being ostracized and, when old Bowen Armstrong didn't divorce her, he got poison-pen letters and filth like that. In the end they had to go back to Rickmansworth and pretend that life in the country hadn't suited Hilda's health. Actually she'd looked quite remarkably . . . yes, well, it only goes to show how very deadly forgiveness can be.'

'By the way, Uncle,' Henry said as they finished in the kitchen, 'I'd most strongly advise you not to touch any of that Perth Special tobacco. I know it's your favourite, but Timothy has been smoking it and . . .' He hesitated for a moment.

'And what?' said Victor.

'It may be a bit adulterated, Uncle V. I mean . . . Well, I just think –'

But Victor Gould interrupted him. 'Say no more. I think and hope I understand. And don't think for a moment I blame you. By the way, where did you find the cyanide?'

Henry laughed. 'Nothing as bad as that, I promise. It's just something I was given in Australia. I don't know exactly what it does because I don't use stuff like that but it's like a rather more powerful form of . . . Are you sure you want to know?'

'Perhaps not,' said Victor. 'I think I'll go and meditate in my study for a bit.'

He went back across the lawn to the summerhouse and sat in his favourite chair and thought how very pleasant it was to have a really amiable and intelligent nephew like Henry to help him cope with the crisis. And crisis was what having to cope with Timothy Bright amounted to. It was one of the mysterious aspects of human psychology that a family that could produce Brenda who, for all her faults – in Victor's opinion, saintliness was one of them – was intelligent and civilized, while at the same time spawning a creature like Timothy. Perhaps he was putting it the wrong way round and the peculiarity lay in the production of Brenda in a family composed otherwise of idle, snobbish and self-centred morons. Presently Victor Gould dozed off with the thought that he couldn't care less what Henry had put in his tobacco. If it got rid of the dreadful Timothy it couldn't be all bad.

In front of the TV set Timothy Bright was wondering what they were going to have for dinner. It was still early, of course, but he felt like a drink. If Henry hadn't been there in the room with him he would have gone over to the corner cupboard and helped himself, but with Henry there he somehow felt awkward about it. Instead he reached for the tobacco tin and began to fill his pipe as a way of showing he could do anything he liked if he really wanted to.

Opposite him Henry tried not to look. He had had no idea how much Toad to put in and only a very vague notion of its effect. He had never been into hallucinogenics and had only brought the *bufo sonoro* back to give to a friend who was doing research into mind-bending chemicals. All he had been told in Brisbane was that Toad was about the strongest LSD-type drug you could find and gave one hell of a trip. And a trip was just what Timothy Bright deserved. On the other hand he didn't feel inclined to sit there and

30

watch what happened. Definitely not. He got up and was about to go out when Timothy lit the pipe.

'I say,' he muttered, 'this baccy's a bit off, isn't it? Got a bloody odd smell.'

'It's Uncle Victor's Special blend,' Henry said. 'It may be a bit different.'

'You can say that again. Got an odd taste too,' said Timothy, and inhaled.

It was clearly a bad mistake. The tobacco was far too strong to be treated like a cigarette. He stared in a most peculiar way in front of him, then took the pipe out of his mouth and stared at that too. Something was obviously happening that he didn't fully understand. The 'fully' was entirely unnecessary. Timothy Bright didn't understand a thing. He took another puff and thought about it. The first impression – that he was inhaling from the chimney of some crematorium – had entirely left him. Timothy Bright smoked on.

He was in a strange new world in which nothing was what it seemed and familiar things had turned into fantastic and ever-changing shapes and colours. Nothing in this world was impossible; things moved towards him and then suddenly veered away or by some most extraordinary involution turned inside out and returned to their original shape. And the sounds were ones he had never heard before. The TV voices echoed in his seemingly cavernous mind and there were moments when he was standing, a puny figure, underneath the apse of his own skull. There were other voices in this great dome which was curved bone around, voices that reverberated like sunken thunder and ordered him to flee, to move, to run away while there was still time and before the great pig with the cut-throat razor came to exact vengeance on him. Timothy Bright obeyed the voices of his own inclinations and ran. He ran past Henry, ran wide-eyed and unseeing out into the garden to his Suzuki and a moment later that magical thing had left Pud End with a final spurt of gravel and was away down the country lane towards whatever he had to do and away from the pig with the razor.

Behind him Henry and his uncle stood on the croquet lawn and stared after him in awe.

'Good Lord,' said Victor as the sound of the bike died away. 'Was it my imagination or did he actually have some aura surrounding him?'

'I didn't see an aura,' said Henry, 'but I know what you mean. He's driving without lights, too.'

'At an incredible speed,' said Victor, trying to suppress the hope that was beginning to burgeon in his mind. Then they both looked up at the full moon.

'Of course, that may account for some of his actions,' Victor said. 'What in God's name is that muck made of?'

'Just some sort of toad,' said Henry. 'And I don't know that anyone is entirely sure. I suppose the nerve-gas scientists know exactly, but for all I know it may vary from toad to toad. I'll have to ask my biological chemist friend.'

'Well, I suppose we ought to have a drink,' said Victor. 'Either to celebrate or mourn, or possibly both. What a relief to have him out of the house.'

They went inside and turned off the television. 'I feel a bit guilty –' Henry began but his uncle stopped him.

'My dear boy, the damned fool helped himself to something that did not belong to him and there's the end of the matter. Doubtless in two hours time he will reappear and prove as noxious as he did just now.'

But Timothy didn't. He was already far to the north, travelling up the motorway at enormous speed and ignoring the rules of the road as if they did not exist. In what was left of Timothy's mind, they didn't. They had been replaced by a sense of the possible that defied all normal practice. He was not even aware of the motorway as such. What little mental capacity for analysis he had ever possessed had quite left him. He was on automatic pilot with the skill to ride a desperately fast motorbike without knowing in the least what he was doing. In short, with the Toad coursing through his bloodstream and doing extraordinary things to his synapses, Timothy Bright had regressed to the mindlessness of some remote, pre-human ancestor while retaining the mechanical skills of a modern lager lout. It would have been incorrect to say he was clean out of his mind, which was the observation of two traffic cops when the Suzuki clocked up 170 mph on their radar and they made the decision not to chase him on the grounds that they would only get involved in a particularly grisly retrieval operation requiring an infinite number of body bags. To Timothy Bright such a likely end never occurred. He was in the very centre of an enormous disco with flames and shadows dancing round him and terrors twining and unwinding in an intricate pattern of lights that were sounds and musical notes that transformed themselves into colours and endless necklaces of lights, before detaching themselves from the cat's eyes in the road and becoming the faces of Mr Markinkus and Mr B. Smith. If the Suzuki could have gone much faster at this point Timothy would have ensured that it did. He was now in the grip of demented terror which reached one almost insufferable climax only to have it succeeded by another. Underneath him the miles slid by unnoticed. Car and lorry rearlights swam towards him and were avoided like so many images on an arcade game with, to other drivers, a quite terrifying ease.

By ten o'clock Timothy had swung off the motorway onto side roads across a rolling upland of little towns and villages, wooded valleys and tumbling rivers. Here, acting on the instructions of his automatic pilot, he slowed down for corners and braked where necessary and swept up hills and onto moors where sheep miraculously crossed the road just ahead of him or just behind and there were few signs of habitation. Somewhere ahead of him lay safety from the demons in his skull and somewhere ahead was a paradisiacal land where there was infinite happiness. The images were ever-changing but the same message of escape in alternate forms sustained him for the drive. On and on he went into a world he had never known before and would never be able to find again. And all the time Timothy Bright remained unconscious of his actions and his surroundings. His hand on the throttle twisted this way and that, slackening the speed on the bends and accelerating on the straights. He didn't know. His inner experiences dominated his being. At some point during the night his bodily sensations joined forces with the mental images to convince him he was on fire and needed to take his skin off to escape being burnt. He stopped the bike in a wooded area by a stream and stripped off his clothes and hurled them down the bank before mounting the Suzuki again and riding on into his internal landscape entirely naked. Ten miles further on he came to the Six Lanes End where it joined the Parson's Road to the north. Timothy Bright shot across the intersection and took the private road belonging to the Twixt and Tween Waterworks Company. With a fine disregard for its uneven surface he shot the Suzuki up it. Cattle grids rattled briefly beneath him and he was up onto Scabside Fell beside drystone walls and open grassland. Ahead of him a great stone dam held back the waters of the reservoir. It was here that the night ride ended.

As he accelerated on what looked to him like the blue, blue sky an elderly sheep that had been sleeping on the warmth of the road grew vaguely aware of a distant danger and rose to its feet. To Timothy Bright it was merely a little cloud. The next moment the sheep was airborne and hurtling with the motorbike over the deepest part of the reservoir. In another direction Timothy Bright, still sublimely unconscious of his surroundings, shot through the air and landed in a coppice of young fir trees on the far bank. As he drifted limply through them and landed on the pine needles underneath, he knew no fear. For a while he lay in the darkness until the conviction that piggy-chops had begun drove him to his feet and out of the coppice. Now he was a bird, or would have been if the ground hadn't kept getting in the way. Three times he fell over on the tarmac and added to the damage he had already suffered. And once he got his foot stuck in the iron bars of a grid which he mistook for a giant clam. But this time the total disassociation produced by the Toad had begun to wear off.

34

Having escaped from the terrible grip of the clam he felt strangely cold.

He had to get home, though the home he had to get to had no clear identity. Home was simply where a house was, and ahead of him he could see a building outlined against the sky. In the half-world between mental agitation and partial perception he made his way towards it and found himself confronted by a solid stone wall and some iron gates. It was exactly what he wanted. He tried the gates and found them locked. Something dark was on the other side and might be looking at him. That didn't matter. Nothing mattered except getting into a warm bed. Timothy Bright grasped the wrought-iron gates and began to climb. He was going to fly from the top. On the other side a large Rottweiler waited eagerly. Trained from its infancy to kill, it was looking forward to the opportunity.

At the top of the gate Timothy Bright hesitated momentarily. He was a bird once again and this time he definitely intended to fly. Letting go of the spikes around him, he stood for a second with his arms outstretched. For a moment he was very briefly airborne. As he plunged downwards the Rottweiler, like the sheep on the dam, had a vague awareness of danger. Then 190 lb of yuppie dropped on it from a height of ten feet. As the great dog's legs buckled beneath it and the deep breath it had taken was expelled from its various orifices together with portions of its dinner, the dog knew it had made a mistake. Its jaws slammed together, its teeth locked on themselves and it was desperately short of breath. With a final effort to avoid suffocation, it tried to get its legs together. Splayed out on either side of its body, they wouldn't come. Only when Timothy Bright rolled to one side did it manage to break free. But the Rottweiler was a broken beast. With a plaintive whistle and a hobble it slunk round the corner of the house to its kennel.

Timothy Bright lay a little longer on the cobbled forecourt. He too had had the breath knocked out of him though to a lesser extent than the Rottweiler, but the urge to go to bed was stronger than ever. He got unsteadily to his feet and found the front door which flickered under a light in front of him. He turned the handle and the door opened. The hall light was on. Timothy moved towards the darkened stairs and climbed them with infinite weariness. Ahead of him there was a door. He opened it and went inside and found the bed. As he climbed into it someone on the far side stirred and said, 'God, you stink of dog,' and went back to sleep. Timothy Bright did too.

Chapter 5

In the conference dining-room at the Underview Hotel in Tween the Chief Constable, Sir Arnold Gonders, presided over a celebratory dinner for the Twixt and Tween Serious Crime Squad. Ostensibly the dinner was being held to mark the retirement of Detective Inspector Holdell, who had been with the Squad since it had first been set up. In fact the real celebration had to do with the decision of the Director of Public Prosecutions in London not to proceed with the trial of twenty-one members of the Squad for falsifying evidence, fabricating confessions, accepting bribes, the use of unwarranted violence, and wholesale perjury, which crimes had sent several dozen wholly innocent individuals to prison for sentences as long as eighteen years while allowing as many guilty criminals to sleep comfortably at home and dream of other dreadful crimes to commit.

The Chief Constable was particularly pleased by the outcome. He had spent the day in London and had had a private meeting with the Home Secretary and the DPP to hear the decision. As he put it to his Deputy, Harry Hodge, 'I told them straight. The morale of the Force is the priority. "Top Priority," I said. "And if you want to undermine that morale, you just go ahead and drag my lads into court. You won't have me as Chief Constable if you do and you'd better know that now." Well, they got the message and no mistake.'

Which was not exactly what had happened.

The decision had been taken two weeks before and even then it had needed the DPP's strongest arguments to persuade the Home Secretary that a trial would not be in the public interest. He had explained the problem over lunch at the Carlton Club. 'Start opening that particular can of fucking worms,' he said, 'and Pandora's Box will look like the good times.'

The Home Secretary had mulled this over with a piece of lamb's liver. 'You know, I'd never thought of it that way before,' he said finally, running a hand over his greasy hair. 'I suppose they have to.'

'Have to what?' asked the Director.

'Fuck. Must do, I suppose. Stands to reason.'

'Fuck what?' asked the DPP, who was beginning to think his own preference for prostitutes was being got at. For the life of him he couldn't remember one called Pandora.

'Other worms,' said the Home Secretary. 'All the same sex or both sexes, worms are. I suppose that's what bifurcated means.'

The DPP tried to pull his thoughts together. He couldn't see the significance of worms bifurcating. 'About the Twixt 'n Tween Serious Crime Squad,' he said. 'The thing is we've got Sir Arnold Gonders up there and, while I can't say he's my cup of tea, he pulls a certain amount of weight at Central Office. She appointed him and he's something of a favourite.'

'Really?' said the Home Secretary, with the private thought that in that case Sir Arnold Gonders must be extremely bent. 'Did his bit in the Miners' Strike against that shit Scargill, I suppose?'

'Absolutely. Never shrank back for a moment. Wanted to use armoured police horses against pickets and that sort of thing. And water canons with some sort of acid dye in them. Gets his instructions from God, apparently, like that other lunatic. Makes God sound fucking weird, if you ask me.'

The Home Secretary looked at him doubtfully. You never knew with DPPs these days. 'You've got a thing about fucking, haven't you?' he asked. 'Ever thought of bifucking?'

The Director of Public Prosecutions smiled unhappily. He was never entirely sure about the Home Secretary either. There had been some talk about cross-dressing.

Altogether it had been a most unpleasant lunch, but he had finally got the Minister to agree that the Twixt and Tween Serious

Crime Squad and the Chief Constable should be left in peace for sound party political reasons. These had to do with a property development company in Tweentagel which Sir Arnold had shown himself to be rather too well informed about during their private discussions over the phone. It had never crossed the Director of Public Prosecutions' mind that the ex-Prime Minister's family business arrangements were so involved. Sir Arnold's implied threat made him glad he hadn't dipped his hand into that particular barrel. In short, Sir Arnold Gonders knew far too much to be trifled with.

Now, sitting at the top table looking down over his lads, the Chief Constable preferred his own blunter version of events. It accorded more with the picture of himself he liked to have in his own mind, that of the kindly father to his men who would cheerfully sacrifice his own career to maintain their belief in themselves as the guardians of the law. Of course God came into the picture too. He would never have got anywhere in life without God being on his side all the time. Well, most of it anyway.

As he'd once put it to his Deputy, 'You ought to take up religion, Harry, you really ought. Beats Rotary any day of the week. I mean, it gives meaning, know what I mean. With God beside you, you know you're right. My golf handicap improved four strokes when I got religion. I'd been on twenty-two for almost as many years and suddenly I'm on eighteen. That's proof enough for me.'

The celebratory party was undoubtedly an excellent one. There was plenty of champagne and half a dozen cases of brandy had been donated by the main drug dealer for the area. It had been nicked from the cellar of a well-known connoisseur of fine wines and was known to be good. There was even a kissogram girl, naked except for painted convict's stripes, who had been paid for by the ex-Prime Minister's son with the message, 'To the dear old Bill. Keep it up, lads, and top the bastards.' This was much appreciated, although Sir Arnold, who, having started the evening on gin and tonics, had gone onto whisky, and had then been prevailed upon to drink a couple of pints of Newcastle Brown with some detective constables before progressing through the champagne to a particularly virulent Côtes de Provence and finally brandy, wasn't altogether sure about having naked women with stripes on them strutting about the room waving their fannies.

'Wouldn't have done in my young days,' he told Hodge. 'Still, it's only fun and it helps keep morale up.'

'Keeps other things up too, I dare say,' said his Deputy, but the Chief Constable chose not to hear. He was wondering whether he was up to putting his own thing into Glenda or not. Probably not.

In the meantime Chief Inspector Rascombe was making a speech. Sir Arnold lit another Montecristo No. 1 and sat back contentedly to listen. 'You can't expect a good detective like Rascombe to be a bloody orator as well,' he had told Hodge before the dinner, and Rascombe was proving him right.

It was only towards the end of his allotted ten minutes that the real meat of the speech became apparent. Until then the Inspector had concentrated on the excellent work the SCS, and particularly the retiring Detective Inspector Holdell, had done and the crimes they had 'solved'. But then he changed tack and spoke with surprising eloquence about the unbridled campaign of vilification the media was conducting against the finest body of men and women he had ever had the privilege to work with in defence of law and order. 'What the public have got to understand,' he said by way of conclusion, 'and what the fucking do-gooders are going to bloody learn, is that we are the Law' (cheers) 'and an Order means just that and, if they don't like it, they can piss in the pot or get out of the kitchen!'

The applause that greeted this analysis of the police role in society delighted the Chief Constable so much that he helped himself to another brandy and rose to his feet a truly happy man. In his own speech he praised Holdell for his dedication to making Tween a safer city which, since it was graded second in the league for violent crimes among all provincial cities, would hardly have reassured a sober and unbiased audience. One of the younger waiters did in fact have a coughing fit. But the Chief Constable went on, and on, and ended by reminding 'all you officers present that our island nation stands on the very brink of a new and terrible invasion, this time by organized international crime. Already the criminals – and we all know who they are – are trying to subvert our great traditions of justice and fair play by undermining the very foundations of morality which as we all know lie in family life. The so-called single-parent family – a non sequitur if ever I saw one because you can't have a mother without a father and vice versa – this so-called single-sex family is the dry rot of everything we Britons stand for. And I for one can tell you I am not having women with short hair and men with you-know-what and the out-of-town monkeys' (here he looked with facetious caution round the dining-room) 'with the big johnnies sticking their noses into the way we've always done things in this country.' He finished with his usual prayer to 'Almighty God, Father of all Things, help us in our struggle against the Powers of Evil, and those of impure heart who seek continually to hamper the Serious Crime Squads everywhere, to do Thy will. Amen.'

He sat down to the applause he expected and looked more favourably on the kissogram girls. Very favourably indeed. Oh yes, it was good for morale to have some properly sexed girls at a party like this. The tables had been pushed back and a space cleared and it was obvious there would be some dancing. Well, that was fine for the younger folk, but the Chief Constable had better things to do. In particular he was going to spend the rest of the night with Glenda and get her to show him some new tricks. That was one of the advantages of having the Old Boathouse up by the reservoir that his wife liked so much. Gave him the opportunity to get to see Glenda here in town. He had bought the boathouse at a very favourable rate when the Twixt and Tween Waterworks had been privatized and had spent a lot of money doing it up and modernizing it. Nice little bolt-hole was the way he'd seen it then but, now that Lady Vy had adopted it as her own, he tended to stay away as much as possible. And this weekend he had special reasons for staying out of the way. Vy had been over to Harrogate to pick up her so-called Auntie Bea and they'd be up at the boathouse by now and doing God alone knew what. Not that he cared any longer. Glenda was a good girl and knew how to give a man the sort of thing he liked. Yes, he'd go over to her flat and . . . He was just considering this happy prospect when Sergeant Filder came over and bent down. 'I'm afraid there's that fellow Bob Lazlett from the *Echo* outside asking for a statement, sir,' he said.

'At this time of bloody night? What sort of statement?'

'He says he's heard the prosecution has been dropped . . .'

The Chief Constable stubbed the cigar out angrily in the remains of his Camembert. 'How the fuck did he hear that? I haven't issued any statement and they said in London they were waiting to release one on Monday to miss the Sunday papers.'

'I wouldn't know, sir, but there's a whole pack of the buggers out there, including Channel Four and the BBC. I told them the dinner was only for Detective Inspector Holdell's going away but they wouldn't buy it.'

Sir Arnold Gonders pushed his chair back and stood up lividly. 'Harry,' he shouted at his Deputy, 'get those fucking girls dressed fast and see the lads don't go too far with their high jinks. No, better still, leave that side of things to Rascombe. You and me are getting out of here fast. I'm not having the bloody media photograph me this weekend. Let the sods rot. We'll go out the back way.' He went out into the foyer while the Deputy Chief Constable spoke urgently to the Chief Inspector. One glance over the balcony into the entrance hall below told Sir Arnold things were far worse than he had anticipated. The newsmen were everywhere, and it was only the presence of several uniformed policemen that was holding the mob back from swarming up the stairs.

Sir Arnold went back into the dining-room. 'Where's the back entrance?' he asked Sergeant Filder.

'They've got some of them round there too,' the Sergeant told him. Sir Arnold helped himself to another large brandy and handed the bottle to Hodge. He was tired, and he was buggered if he was going to face a horde of reporters and muckrakers in his present condition. The bastards would have it splashed that he was pissed.

'Right, Filder, see the management and get Hodge and me rooms here for the night,' he said. 'Those shits can spend eight hours in the street and more. As far as everyone is concerned Hodge and I haven't been here tonight.'

'I'm not sure that's such a good idea, sir,' Hodge told him. 'I'm told they've nobbled one of the waiters and he's told them about the kissogram birds.'

Sir Arnold stared bleakly into a publicity hell almost equalling that of some of the Crime Squad's victims. He knew only too well what the media could do to a man's reputation. He'd used them often enough.

He finished his brandy at a gulp. 'We've got to establish deniability,' he said, and called Rascombe over. 'We haven't been here tonight, right? Hodge and me weren't here. You organized this do for Holdell and, as far as you know, I'm still in London. Yes, I know they know we're here. They can't prove it if we all keep our traps shut. Right?'

'Right,' said Inspector Rascombe, who knew the drill.

'No interviews. No statements. Nixnie. A complete shutdown. Hodge and I haven't been here and, if that fucking hotel manager wants to keep his drinks licence, he'd better go along with the story. Make sure he knows which side his bread is buttered. Now then, Filder, call up an unmarked car and have it ready in Blight Street.'

'I can take you in mine,' said the Sergeant. 'It's back in the multi-storey.'

The Deputy Chief Constable looked anxious. 'But how are we going to get out of the hotel?' he asked.

'Well, there's always such a thing as a little diversion,' the Inspector told him. 'Couple of cameras broken and that bugger Bob Lazlett gets a few loose teeth. Can't be bad.'

'Be bloody disastrous,' said Sir Arnold. 'Nothing I'd like better than the little shit would break his neck but we don't do it for him.

Not tonight, any rate. Some dark alley and no one around would be different.'

Twenty minutes later, with the manager's eager compliance, a large van drove up to the service entrance, the tailboard went down and the conveyor belts began to unload the hotel's morning supplies. As it finished, Sir Arnold and Harry Hodge in white lab coats slipped over the tailboard and disappeared.

'What a bloody mess,' said the Chief Constable drunkenly. The brandy bottle was empty. 'I'm fucked if I'm going home now. Those shits will be besieging the house.'

'You can always come to my place,' said Hodge. But Sir Arnold was in no mood to come under the caustic eye of Mrs Hodge, thank you very much. And Glenda was definitely out of the question now. One whiff of that little number and an entire sewage works would hit the fan.

'I'll get Filder to take me up the boathouse. Those bastards come up there, I'll set the dog on them.'

It was nearly three when the Chief Constable finally climbed out of the van, slumped exhausted into the police Rover, and set out for Scabside Reservoir.

Chapter 6

It had begun to rain and the moon was gone by the time Sir Arnold Gonders stumbled out of the police car at the Old Boathouse. He was worn out, drunk and in a filthy temper.

'Will you be all right, sir?' the Sergeant asked as the Chief Constable stood outside the iron gates and finally found his keys.

'I would be if those fucking reporters hadn't wrecked the bloody evening,' he snarled and opened the gate.

'Yes sir, the media's a bloody menace,' said the Sergeant and drove off across the dam to the main road at Six Lanes End. Behind him the Chief Constable, having locked the gates again, was wondering why Genscher, the Rottweiler, who appeared to be limping, was wheezing so asthmatically.

'Mustn't wake her Ladyship, must we, old chap?' he said hoarsely and went across to the front door. After fumbling with the key he was infuriated to find he didn't need it. That bloody Vy again. She was always leaving the place unlocked. And he'd warned her time and again about burglars. 'I love that, coming from you, dear,' she'd retorted. 'The great Protector himself who's always going on about making the world safe for the ordinary citizen. And with Genscher in the yard only a madman would dream of coming in. Be your age.' Which was typical of the way the woman was always treating him.

Anyway he wasn't going to take chances of waking her now. Not that it would be easy with all those pills she took, and the booze. Standing in the hall Sir Arnold felt for the light switch and found fresh plaster. Vy had evidently had the switch moved. She was always getting builders or plumbers in and changing everything round. Not that he wanted the light. Mustn't wake Vy. Just to make sure, he took his shoes off and stumbled as quietly as he could up the stairs.

It was then that he heard the snores. He'd complained about her snoring before, but this was something totally different. Sounded like she was farting in a mud bath. One thing was certain. He wasn't sleeping in the same bed with that fucking noise. He'd use the spare room. He went into the bathroom to have a pee and couldn't find the light cord. Bloody builders hadn't put it where it ought to be. Sir Arnold undressed in the dark and then went out onto the landing and was about to go into the spare room when he remembered that Aunt Bea was probably in there. He wasn't going to risk getting into bed with that foul old bag. No way. He fumbled back along the passage, all the time cursing his wife. It was typical of her that the light switches had been moved. Always wanting everything to be different. Outside the bedroom door he hesitated again. Dear God, that was a fearful sound. Then it crossed his mind that something might be really wrong. Perhaps Vy had taken an overdose of those damned pills the doctor had prescribed for her depression. She could be hyperventilating. She was certainly doing something extraordinary. And wasn't snoring dangerous? He'd read that recently. For a moment a dark hope rose in the Chief Constable's mind. He was tempted to let her snore on. In the meantime he'd better take a Vitamin C and his half of Disprin.

Sir Arnold groped his way back to the bathroom and found the Redoxon. Or thought he did. A few moments later he knew he hadn't. The fucking things were Auntie Bloody Bea's denture cleaners. In the darkness Sir Arnold Gonders spat desperately into the basin and thought dementedly about his wife and her rotten relatives. And she had the gall to blame him for her nerves. They were the result, she claimed, of being married to a man with such a close relationship with all those dreadful criminals he worked with. She'd been ambiguous about which criminals she'd meant, but he had always been conscious that she and her family believed she had married beneath her and really couldn't have done anything else – short of marrying one of the classier Royals. The Gilmott-

46

Gwyres were appalling snobs. On the other hand she also felt very badly about his relationship with God, and if God Almighty wasn't socially upmarket, Sir Arnold Gonders would like to know who was.

Unfortunately Lady Vy's nerves had recently been made very much worse by some clown in the Communications Repair Section who had twice programmed her car phone so that it had put her through to some very shady establishments down by the docks. The next time Vy had used the phone she had been answered by the sod who ran The Holy Temple of Divine Being or on occasion, the second occasion in her case, The Pearly Gates of Paradise. Lady Vy, trying to get through to her sister who was supposed to be still alive, had been horrified to find a clear indication that her husband actually did phone God and that the blighter was manifestly an Oriental bent on offering her 'any sexual application, herb or vibrating what-not that will bring you Heavenly satisfaction. Money-back guarantee. Massage and manual assistance also available.' Her reaction to this first call had been to write off her Jaguar and two other cars by going down the up slipway onto the M85. On the second occasion, three weeks later, she told God, or whoever was in charge of The Pearly Gates of Paradise and it could be the Angel Gabriel himself for all she cared, to fuck off, you shit. As a result she had had a terrible crisis of conscience before she'd even got home at the thought that she might indeed have been speaking to God. 'You're always having talks with the bloody man,' she had screamed hysterically at Sir Arnold, 'and for all I know . . . But why me? Why pick on me of all miserable sinners?'

It had all been most harrowing and Sir Arnold had counted himself lucky that he knew exactly who she had been talking to – Glenda used some of the bastard's gadgets – and had told the swine he'd put him out of business and circulation for a long time if he ever played God again. This hadn't helped Lady Vy. She had never been the same woman since and had threatened him with divorce if he ever said God was love again in her hearing. Sir Arnold had blamed that bloody Indian, and his wife had blamed herself for ever marrying a policeman. In the end her doctor had persuaded her to consult a psychiatrist who had advised her that she was suffering from a very natural condition in women of her age and from lack of sexual satisfaction. The Chief Constable, who had had his men bug the psychiatrist's office in the hope that she'd admit to committing adultery, had temporarily agreed with this diagnosis. The woman was obviously depressed and lacked sexual satisfaction and he'd sometimes wondered what the result would have been if she had been subjected to the sort of test female shot-putters in the Olympics were given. The psychiatrist's next suggestion, that she must insist on her conjugal rights at least twice a week together with Vy's raucous laughter and protest that he couldn't get an erection once a year let alone twice a week, was far less to his liking. The confounded woman's appeal for him had always sprung from her social connections rather than anything approaching sexual fancy. In fact even before the Lord had shown him the error of his ways he had been far more attracted by lithe and girlish figures like Glenda's and not by Vy's muscular and ill-proportioned torso. All the same, spurred on by her diabolical laughter and by massive doses of Vitamin E, he had done his damnedest to satisfy her marital needs. Fortunately the anti-depressants combined with her nightly intake of gin to render her too doped to want sex or even to know when she hadn't had it. Still, Sir Arnold didn't want to lose her entirely – she had influence through her father, Sir Edward Gilmott-Gwyre, and she gave him a social acceptability he would otherwise lack. But now, to judge by the hideous snores, she was in serious trouble.

He pushed himself away from the bathroom wall and staggered down the passage again and had opened the bedroom door before another alarming thought hit him. He'd never heard her make a noise like this. And naturally she had thought he'd be staying in Tween as he usually did after a heavy night. Perhaps that horrible butch Aunt Bea was sleeping in his bed. If she was, the old slut was in for a nasty surprise. He might not like his wife, but he was damned if he was going to have a lesbian take his place in his own bedroom. The Chief Constable moved towards the bed very cautiously with his hand out and as he groped about towards those snores, his fingers touched some hair. In the darkness Sir Arnold Gonders froze in his shambling tracks. That wasn't Vy's hair – he'd know her curls anywhere – and it wasn't Bea's either, hers was short and straight. The stuff he'd just felt was long and greasy. It was a man's hair and, come to that, those were a man's snores. There was no mistaking the fact. There was no mistaking something else either. The smell.

He knew now why Genscher was limping and wheezing. He also knew that he was dealing with an exceptionally dangerous intruder. All his life he'd known something like this was going to happen if Vy left the bloody door open – in his drunken and exhausted state he wasn't thinking at all clearly. The possibility of the house being taken over by the IRA flashed through the Chief Constable's disordered mind. He had to get to his gun in the bedside drawer, the gun and the panic button. With the utmost caution he felt for the bedside table and began to ease the drawer open. The damned thing was stuck. He pulled harder and the thing came a short way out with a loud squeak. The next moment there was a movement on the bed. Sir Arnold hesitated no longer. If he couldn't get to his gun . . . his hand groped around inside the drawer but there was no gun and no panic button. Grasping the wooden bedside lamp by its top he swung the base down onto the snores. A horrid thud, the bulb in the lamp shattered, the plug came out of the wall socket and the snores stopped. In the darkness Sir Arnold stepped back to the main light switch by the door, trod on a piece of broken bulb, cut his foot and swore.

By the time he'd managed to turn the light on it was fairly clear that things were more dreadful than even he had anticipated. For one thing Lady Vy was awake – she had been kicked into a semblance of life by the reflex convulsion of Timothy Bright's legs – and without her contact lenses was having difficulty telling who was who. Beside her in the bed what she imagined was Sir Arnold lay bleeding horribly from a scalp wound while a naked man with

49

some sort of club in his hand was swearing horribly over by the door. To Lady Vy's boozy anti-depressed mind it seemed obvious she was about to be raped and murdered. Acting with remarkable speed for a woman in her condition, she scrabbled for the Chief Constable's revolver which she'd kept handy in her own bedside drawer. It was her ultimate line of defence and she meant to use it. Her first shot hit the mirror in the Victorian wardrobe to the murderer's right. Lady Vy tried to aim more carefully for the second and as she did so she was vaguely conscious that her attacker was yelling at her in a faintly familiar voice. 'For fuck's sake put that fucking gun down –'

The second shot missed him on the other side and, having gone in one side of the hot-water boiler and out the other, ricocheted round the en-suite bathroom. There was no need for a third shot. Sir Arnold had scampered through the door and slammed it behind him. Lady Vy reached for the panic button which had been installed to alert every police station within a radius of fifty miles that the Chief Constable's weekend residence had been entered by intruders.

To Sir Arnold Gonders the next half hour was a foretaste of hell. As the siren on the roof began to wail and the entire building was brilliantly floodlit by halogen lamps in the garden while simultaneously a dozen police stations were alerted to a Top Priority Emergency, he knew that his career was on the brink of an abyss. He hurled himself down the darkened staircase and was halfway to the telephone in his study when the hall lights came on and he was confronted by the elderly Scots housekeeper in her dressing-gown.

'Och Sir Arnold, do you ken wha's ganging on?' she asked.

The Chief Constable brushed her aside with the bloodied bedside lamp. The stupid old cow, of course he didn't know what was going on. Once in his study he dropped the lamp on a valuable Persian rug and grabbed the phone. The number, the coded number to cancel the alert? What the hell was it? Finally, in desperation, he dialled 999 and was asked which of the Emergency Services he required. It was a rather more relevant question than he realized at the time, though the house had yet to catch fire.

'Police,' he barked and was put through to a recorded message asking him to be patient as Police Services were stretched to the limit. Sir Arnold knew that. He had dictated the message to his secretary himself.

'While you are waiting to be attended to,' the soothing female voice went on, 'we at Twixt and Tween Police Services would like you to know about the ancillary assistance we are able to offer the public. Officers are always on hand to conduct Road Safety Classes at schools of all levels, Primary, Secondary, Further and Independent. We also hold regular classes in Self-Defence for Senior Citizens and Persons of the Female Gender. These are available at –'

'Fuck off, you bitch,' shouted the Chief Constable and slammed the phone down. A new and even more awful possibility had just entered his mind. Vy and a young man in bed . . . A toyboy! He had to think of some way of stopping scores of policemen converging on the house in which he had almost certainly murdered his wife's lover. But first he had to find a way of turning that infernal siren off. Livid with a fresh terror he dashed back across the hall to the kitchen in search of the fuses and was blundering about in the pantry where they had been. The fucking things had been moved. That Vy and her electricians. And what was the point of having Emergency Services if you couldn't get through to the sods. The other inhabitants of the house weren't helping. As he turned back towards the study with the intention of blasting that bleeding siren on the roof into silence with his shotgun he came face to face with Auntie Bea.

'Has something dreadful happened?' she enquired, at the same time studying his anatomy with only slight interest and considerable disgust. 'I thought I heard shots and then all those incredible lights came on and that dreary siren. Can't you switch it off?'

'No,' said the Chief Constable. 'And nothing serious has happened.'

'Well, I certainly can,' said Auntie Bea. Behind her in the study the phone had begun to ring. For a moment they grappled in the doorway and then the Chief Constable broke loose and hurried to the study. In the kitchen Bea found the mains switch and the siren wailed down. She came back with the housekeeper and stood in the study doorway. The Chief Constable had answered the phone.

'This is Harry Hodge, the Deputy Chief Constable here,' said a strangely controlled voice.

'I know that. I know exactly who it is,' Sir Arnold yelled back.

'Good, good,' said the voice, still exercising an unnerving calm. 'Are you all right? I repeat, are you all right? Take your time replying.'

Sir Arnold didn't. It was bad enough standing in the study bollock naked with a middle-aged woman in a startling kimono staring at him and at the blood on the floor . . . 'Of course I'm fucking well all right. The button got pressed accidentally is all.'

'Good, very good,' said the Deputy Chief Constable, maintaining his cool. 'I quite understand. Now are you all right? I repeat, are you all –'

'Listen, Hodge, what do you mean you understand? I'm standing here starkers and you . . .' Here he turned on Auntie Bea. 'Fuck off, for Chrissake.'

'Try and keep calm,' said the wretched Hodge in the same nerveless tone. 'Everything is under control. Now then. Are you all right? I repeat –'

'You ask me again if I'm all right, Hodge, and so help me God I'll break your fucking neck. I've told you I don't know how many times I'm all right. How many more times have I got to tell you?'

Over the line he could hear the Deputy Chief Constable asking more or less the same question. Sir Arnold remembered the drill. 'Hodge,' he said, with a new controlled calm that was as peculiar in its own way as that of his Deputy, 'Hodge, I am all right. I repeat, I am all right. Repeat. I am all right.'

'Well, that's all right then,' said Hodge almost regretfully. 'It was a false alarm then? Shall I call off the QRS lads?'

52

'The who?' The past few minutes had slowed the Chief Constable still further.

'The Quick Response Squad,' Hodge said, a new doubt creeping back into his voice.

'Those swine?' yelled the Chief Constable. 'Of course call them off at once. Why do you think I phoned you?'

'Phone me, sir? Phoned me? I don't want to question your judgement at a time like this but in actual fact I phoned you. Are you sure you are quite all right?'

The Chief Constable made a supreme effort. 'Hodge, please believe me when I say I am perfectly all right, all right, all right. Got it? I am entirely all right and I want to get back to bed.'

'If you say so, sir. All the same, it seems a pity not to take the opportunity to use this as a training exercise.'

'No. Repeat, no. Repeat, no, on no account. Over and fucking out.' And putting the phone down the Chief Constable turned back to even more immediate problems.

Chapter 7

The first problem was to get back into the bedroom and have it out with Vy. She was to blame for what had happened. Any reasonable husband coming home and finding some filthy young gigolo in bed with his wife would have acted in a similarly violent manner. In a way what he had done had been rather complimentary to her and showed the right amount of jealousy. There was certainly no need for her to have behaved in that irrational way with the gun. He might have been killed and then where would she have been? On the other hand he had no intention of going back into the bedroom until she'd promised not to do anything dangerous again. Outside the bedroom door he stopped. 'Darling, darling,' he called softly. 'It's me. You know. Me. Pooh Bear and Wiggly Toes and . . .'

Inside the bedroom Lady Vy had found her contact lenses and the nature of her mistake. 'Oh, for God's sake, not at a time like this. Not with –'

Sir Arnold hurled himself through the door. Gun or no gun, he had to stop her before she said any more. 'Hush,' he yelled in what he supposed was a whisper. And then, more for the benefit of the two women downstairs than for Lady Vy herself. 'Now, dear, you mustn't blame yourself. We all make mistakes.'

'Blame myself? Blame myself? I wake up to find you beating someone to death with a bed lamp and –'

'No, dear, no, that's not quite true,' he said in a whisper that was practically a bellow. Then, sotto voce, 'Walls have ears, for Chrissake.'

Lady Vy looked at him dementedly. 'Walls have ears? You stand there in the altogether and tell me in some godawful whisper that walls have ears? Are you clean off your trolley?'

Sir Arnold signalled frantically towards the door. 'We don't need any witnesses,' he said in a conversational tone.

'You may not,' said Lady Vy. 'In fact I'm sure you don't, but as far as I'm concerned –'

Sir Arnold crossed to the bed and drew back the sheet that was covering Timothy Bright's naked body. 'Shut up and listen to me,' he hissed. 'I come home and find you tucked up with this. With some foul toyboy you've been having it off with in my fucking bed and the sod has the gall to sleep here and snore '

He stopped and stared down at Timothy's scarred knees, hands and arms, not to mention a seriously bruised chest and mangled face, and revised his opinion of Vy. If passionate love was what the poor devil and Vy had been making, he was exceedingly glad he had never succeeded in arousing her sexually to such extraordinary lengths. For a fraction of a second it occurred to him that his wife had been seeing too many Dracula movies. Or cannibal ones. Only the lack of blood on her face-cream convinced him otherwise. He preferred not to look at the brute's head. The scalp wound was still leaking blood onto the pillow. In any case Lady Vy had his attention now.

'What do you mean "toyboy" and "having it off", you vile creature?' she spat with a hauteur that was almost genuine. 'Do you think I would dream of sleeping with a . . . a callow youth, a mere child?'

Sir Arnold looked back at the bloke on the bed. It had never occurred to him that his wife could think of someone in his late twenties as a mere child. Or callow, whatever that meant. It didn't seem natural, somehow. He tried to get back to the issue. 'What do you expect me to think? If you came home unexpectedly at whatever hour it was in the middle of the night and found a naked girl in bed with me, what would you think?'

'I'd know perfectly well you hadn't been having normal sex with her,' Lady Vy hurled back at him. 'I suppose fellatio might do something for you but you can count me out. It's too late in my life for that sort of thing.'

Sir Arnold ignored this obvious attempt to sidetrack him. 'All right,' he demanded. 'Who is he? Just tell me who he is.'

'Who he is?'

'I think I've got a right to know that much.'

'You're asking me . . . ? I don't know.'

'You don't know. You must know. I mean . . .' Sir Arnold goggled at her. 'I mean you don't have some little shit in bed with you without finding out who he is. It's . . . it's . . .'

'If you really must know I thought it was you,' said Lady Vy with revived hauteur.

The Chief Constable gaped at her open-mouthed. 'Me? One moment you say I can't get it up without a mouth job and the next I'm the blighter who has just fucked you rigid.'

For a moment Lady Vy looked as though she might go for the revolver again. 'I keep telling you,' she shouted, 'nobody did anything. I didn't even know he was there.'

'You must have known. People don't just climb into bed with you and you don't know.'

'All right, I suppose I was vaguely aware of someone getting into the bed but naturally I thought it was you. I mean he stank of dog and booze. How the hell was I to know it was someone else?'

Sir Arnold tried to draw himself up. 'I do not stink of dog and booze when I come to bed.'

'Could have fooled me,' said Lady Vy. 'Come to think of it, it did.' She groped over the side of the bed for the gin bottle. Sir Arnold grabbed it from her and swigged. 'And now,' she continued when she'd got it back, 'now you've gone and murdered him.'

'Not murdered, for God's sake,' he said, 'manslaughter. Quite different. In cases of manslaughter judges frequently –'

Lady Vy smiled horribly. 'Arnie dear,' she said with a degree of malice that had been fermenting for years, 'it doesn't seem to have got through to the thing you call your brain that you are finished, finito, done for and all washed up. Your career is over. All those lovely directorships with big salaries for favours received, all those nice jobs the good old boys like Len Bload were going to hand you for running the Property Protection Service you call your constabulary, all gone bye-bye now. You're up above the Plimsoll line in excreta, as Daddy used to put it. And it doesn't matter what some senile old judge, hand-picked by the DPP to keep you out of prison, says. You're all washed up, baby.'

Sir Arnold Gonders heard her only subliminally, and in any case he didn't need telling. There were some crimes even a Chief Constable couldn't commit with anything approaching impunity, and one of them had to be battering a young man to death with a blunt instrument in his own bed. To make matters worse he couldn't look to the ex-prime minister for help. She wasn't in power any longer.

He took Timothy Bright's wrist and felt for the pulse. It was, all things considered, surprisingly strong. The next moment he was rummaging in the wardrobe for a torch.

'What are you going to do now?' Lady Vy demanded as he shone the light into one of Timothy's eyeballs and looked at his iris.

'Drugged,' he said finally. 'Drugged to the top of his skull.'

'Perhaps,' said Lady Vy, turning a bit weepy now. 'But look what you've done to the top of his skull.'

Sir Arnold preferred not to. 'Take a urine test off this one and it would burn a hole in the bottle,' he said.

'Are you sure? I mean it seems so unlikely.'

The Chief Constable put the torch down and turned on her. 'Unlikely? Unlikely? Anything more unlikely than coming home to . . . Never mind. Look at his knees, look at his hands. What do they tell you?'

'He seems rather well . . . well-proportioned now that you come to mention it.'

'Fuck his proportions,' snarled the Chief Constable. 'The skin has been scraped off them. The bugger's been dragged along the ground. And where are his clothes?' He looked round the room and then, putting on a dressing-gown, went downstairs.

There were no clothes to be found. By the time he got back to the bedroom the Chief Constable knew what had happened and was trying to come to terms with the prospect before him. 'This is a set-up, that's what it is. I'm being framed. Those press bastards will arrive any minute now and –'

'Oh God, we've invited people over for drinks at twelve,' Lady Vy interrupted, her social priorities coming to the fore. 'With that MP you're so friendly with. Do you think . . .'

The Chief Constable stared into another abyss. 'We've got to move quickly,' he said. 'This bastard isn't going to be here when they come. He's going down to the boiler-room.'

It was Lady Vy's turn to stare into hell. 'But it's oil-fired. You can't possibly dispose of him in the boiler. How can you think of such things?'

'I didn't, for Chrissake. I'm not going to burn him. I'm going to put him on ice until the heat's off, that's all.' And leaving his wife trying to cope with these weird contradictions, Sir Arnold hurried downstairs again. When he returned he had some parcel tape and two plastic bin liners.

'What are you going to do?' Lady Vy asked. Sir Arnold left the room again and this time rummaged in the bathroom. He returned with a length of Elastoplast. Lady Vy goggled at him. 'What . . . What are you –'

'Shut up and make yourself useful,' he snapped. 'We're going to tie this bastard up so tightly he won't know where the hell he's been.'

'My dear Arnold, you don't really think I'm going to assist you in this horrible scheme.'

The Chief Constable stopped trying to get Timothy's legs into a bin liner and straightened up. 'Listen to me,' he said with a terrible intensity. 'I don't want to hear any more of your "dear Arnold" toffee-nosed crap. And you'd better get this straight. If I go down the social sewer because of this, don't think you're going to stay clean, because you aren't. This time you're going to dirty your hands.'

Lady Vy tried to draw herself up. 'Well, really. Anyone would think I had something to do with his being here.'

'Seems a reasonable assumption. And I'll fill it out for you. You and your Auntie Bea are into S and M. Pick him up some place – he looks as if he might come from Harrogate – and you fill him with intravenous crack or Sweetie B gives him a spinal tap of Columbian ice with that hypodermic of hers and you drag him here and have some fun. Get the picture?'

Lady Vy was beginning to. 'You'd never dare. You'd never dare do anything . . . I mean Daddy –'

'Try me,' said Sir Arnold. 'Just try me. And your bloody Daddy is going to like his picture in the fucking *Sun* with a headline EARL'S DAUGHTER IN LESBIAN LOVE TRAP and all about you and the butch-dyke with her heroin habit and . . .'

'But Bea's an aromatherapist and stress counsellor. She's –'

'Just made for the *Sun* and the *News of the World*, she is. And the aroma she's going to be giving off unless you start helping is going to make this dogshit smell like Chanel No. 5. Now then, hold this bloody bag open while I get his legs in.'

But it was obvious that Timothy Bright was too large and intractable for the garbage bag. In the end they dragged the sheets off the bed and rolled him up in them. Sir Arnold picked up the parcel tape and set to work with such thoroughness that the thing they dragged with immense difficulty down to the cellar looked like a mummified body with holes for its nose. Finally they dropped Timothy into the very darkest corner of the cellar beyond the old stone wine racks.

'That ought to keep the bastard quiet for a bit,' said Sir Arnold only to have his hopes dashed as Timothy Bright shifted on the floor and groaned. For a moment the Chief Constable hesitated. Then he handed Lady Vy the torch and turned to the steps.

'Just see he doesn't move,' he said and hurried up to the kitchen. He returned with a plastic basting syringe, a measuring glass, and a bottle of whisky.

'Oh my God, what are you going to do now?'

'Shut up,' said the Chief Constable. 'And hold that torch steady. I don't want to get the measures wrong.'

'What's that syringe thing for?' asked Lady Vy.

'Well, it's not for basting chickens,' said Sir Arnold. 'It's for giving the bastard something to keep him quiet. Like two ounces of Scotch every two hours with a couple of your Valiums and some of those pink pills you take at night. That way the bugger won't know where he is or has been or what time of day it is.'

Lady Vy looked at the bundle on the cellar floor and doubted if the whisky was necessary. The other sedatives certainly weren't. 'Give him those pills and he won't know anything ever again,' she said, 'and I don't think you ought to pump Scotch into him with that thing. He'll almost certainly choke to death.'

'I'm not going to pump it in. Dribble it, more likely. OK?'

But Lady Vy was staring at him. 'You're mad. Absolutely raving. You propose to dribble two ounces of whisky mixed with Valium . . . Dear God.'

'No,' said the Chief Constable firmly. 'And at this moment in time I don't want to be told. Now then, hold this thing.' He held the plastic syringe up.

'I am not holding anything,' said Lady Vy just as firmly. 'You can do what you like but I am not going to be an accessory to murder.'

'Oh yes you are,' said the Chief Constable with a terrible look on his face. Lady Vy held the syringe.

Five minutes later Timothy Bright had successfully taken his first dose of Valium and whisky. Lady Vy's pink anti-depressants hadn't been added to this lethal brew after all.

'That should guarantee he doesn't wake up for a bit,' said Sir Arnold as they climbed the cellar steps. 'Keep him unconscious until I've had a chance to come up with something.'

He locked the cellar door.

For the rest of the night he tried to sleep on the couch in his study. As he tossed between brief sleep and appalled wakefulness, he searched his memory for a particularly vindictive villain who could have set this trap up. There were just too many criminals with a grudge against him. And how come the press gang hadn't turned up on the doorstep? Presumably because he'd called the Quick Response Squad off. The squad's arrival would have been the excuse for a massive publicity invasion. But they needed the QRS boys to lead them to the Old Boathouse. Sir Arnold was glad it was so isolated. All the same, something was fucking weird. He'd phone around in the morning to see if anyone had been tipped off for a spectacular happening. No, he wouldn't. Silence, absolute, complete and total silence was always the best response. Silence, and with God's help he would find a way out of this nightmare. Just so long as the bastard didn't die.

Between clean sheets in the big bedroom upstairs Lady Vy cursed herself for a fool. The water from the punctured hot-water tank had crept under the door of the bathroom and was soaking through the carpet into the floor. She should have listened to Daddy all those years ago. He had always said you had to be a sadistic cretin to be a successful policeman, and he'd been spot on.

Chapter 8

At Pud End Henry Gould woke with the horrid sensation that he had done something terrible. It took him a moment or two to remember what it was, and when he did he was genuinely worried. 'Oh Lord,' he muttered as he got up hurriedly, 'what an asinine trick to pull.' When he went downstairs it was to find his uncle sitting over his breakfast coffee in the old farm kitchen with the radio beside him. He was looking particularly cheerful for a man who had almost certainly just lost a nephew. Henry had no doubt about that. In the sober light of the morning he felt sure his cousin must have been killed. No one stoked to the synapses with *bufo sonoro* could possible ride an enormously powerful motorbike for any distance and live. Toad was the most powerful mind-bender.

'No need to look so gloomy,' Victor told him. 'I've been listening to the local radio since six but they've made no mention of any accident involving a motorcycle, and they always do to encourage the others. Timothy is probably sleeping it off in some hedgerow. That sort always have the devil on their side.'

'I certainly hope so. Goodness only knows what that Toad stuff is. From the way it worked I'm surprised he could get on the bike, let alone ride the thing.'

But it was later in the morning when Victor Gould went up to air the spare room that he realized Timothy Bright had left a brown paper package and a large briefcase. He carried them through to the cupboard under the stairs and deposited them there with the thought that Timothy would certainly be returning to claim them. It was a fairly dreadful thought but at least he was temporarily absent.

Timothy Bright would have shared Henry's consternation had he been in any condition to. As it was he slept on happily unconscious of his situation and with the remains of the Toad doing new things to his neurons now that it had been freshened up with Valium and whisky. He was fortunately unaware that he was strapped up inside two bloodstained sheets and a pillow case wedged into a distant corner of the Old Boathouse cellar, and that he himself looked very much like one of the sacks of coal that had once occupied a space there.

Above his head and out in the garden the guests at the Gonders drinks party wandered about clutching glasses of a rather acid white wine that had been sold by Ernest Lamming to Sir Arnold as 'a first-rate little Vouvray' which had a certain accuracy about it though the Chief Constable now wished he hadn't bought quite so much of the stuff. In particular he wasn't feeling at all like drinking anything very much himself. He'd had three hours disrupted sleep and had woken with the feeling that he had not only drunk far too much but that he must have been hallucinating during the night. What appeared to have happened, namely that he had probably murdered some bastard who had been sleeping with Vy, couldn't possibly have been the case. In fact all the events of the night had such a nightmarish quality about them that he would willingly have spent the entire day in solitude trying to figure out what the hell was going on. Instead he was forced to adopt a bonhomie he didn't in the least feel. Anyway he wasn't drinking that battery-acid Vouvray. He'd stick to vodka and tonic and hope it helped his head.

It was an indication of the remarkable social changes that had taken place in the eighties that the guests were such a very unmixed bunch. In earlier days there would have seemed something distinctly suspect about a Chief Constable who had quite so many friends in the property development and financial worlds and so very few among what had once been known as the gentry. This was particularly true in Twixt and Tween. The county had once been famous for the great industries and shipyards of Tween and the grouse moors and huge estates of the great landowners of Twixt. At the Gonders party there were none of the old ironmasters, and the only industries represented were service ones. None of the landowners would have mixed at all happily with the guests at the Old Boathouse. Then again there were no trade unionists. Sir Arnold Gonders had learnt the political catechism of Thatcherism very well indeed: only money mattered and preferably the newest money that talked about little else and cared for nothing. There were a great many people from the TV and showbiz world. 'Communication is the real art of a Chief Constable,' Sir Arnold had once pontificated. 'We must keep the people on our side.' It was a revealing comment suggesting that society was irremediably divided.

Certainly in the Twixt and Tween Constabulary area if people did not know which side Sir Arnold Gonders was on, a glance at the guest list would have given them some insight. Len Bload of Bload and Babshott, Public Relations and Financial Consultants to the County Council, was there with his wife, Mercia, the ex-model and masseuse who had risen to a directorship of B and B. Len Bload always addressed the Chief Constable as 'My boy,' and obviously looked on Sir Arnold as an active member of his team. 'We've all got to look after one another is the way I look at it, my boy. We don't who will? Tell me that,' Len Bload had said more times than Lady Vy could bear to recall. She also disliked women who talked quite so openly about hand sex as Mercia Bload. Then there were the Sents. If she disliked the Bloads, she positively detested the Sents. Harry Sent was a dealer. 'Don't ask me in what. Everything. You name it, I got it. Some place I got to got it. You know my motto? "I'll have it Sent." Get it? I'll have it. Sent. Great logo I got out of Lennie for free. You know why?' Lady Vy certainly didn't want to but noblesse was supposed to oblige. 'Because one time I'm screwing Heaven I got to think of Mercia to get it up at all. Ain't that so, Heaven?' Mrs Sent smiled sourly and nodded. 'I fuck better with that photo of Mercia in a bikini on the pillow, right?' A shadow of something approaching pain crossed Olga Sent's face. Lady Vy would have sympathized with her – the misery of being called 'Heaven' by a man as gross as Harry Sent would have broken a weaker woman – if she had not once heard Mrs Sent describe her as 'that Gonders cow. So snobbish and no money with it. Drop dead is what I wish for her.' Lady Vy had complained to Sir Arnold at the time about the remark but all he'd said was, 'Got to keep in with the locals, you know.' Which was a bit rich, considering old Sent claimed to have escaped from Poland to fight with the Free Polish Army. And someone had once accurately described Olga as looking like a concentration-camp guard who should have been hanged for Crimes against Humanity.

On the other hand there were a great many people in the county who had come only once to the Chief Constable's parties, and had found reasons never to come to another. Sir Percival Knottland, the Lord Lieutenant, was one such absentee. He still hadn't got over meeting at a Gonders party a man who had advised him to invest in a particular pizza chain 'because there's a lot more than cheese and anchovies involved, you know what I mean.' The Lord Lieutenant thought he did and had complained to the Chief Constable, but Sir Arnold had assured him confidentially that the fellow was all right. 'To be frank, he is one of our top grasses. Couldn't do without him. Got to keep him sweet.'

'But he advised me to invest in Pietissima Pizza Parlours,' said the Lord Lieutenant. 'Something about there being icing on the cake. Did I know what he meant? It sounded most suspicious to me. Shouldn't you be investigating this pizza company very carefully?'

The Chief Constable had taken his arm confidentially. 'Between ourselves, I have. Solid investment as far as I can tell. I put ten thousand in myself. Should double your money in six months.'

'And you really don't think these Pietissima Parlours are being used to distribute drugs?' the Lord Lieutenant asked.

'Good gracious, I hope not. Still, I can't guarantee it. Everybody's into that game nowadays. I'll ask my drug lads, but I shouldn't worry. Money is money, after all.'

The Lord Lieutenant had been so appalled that he had written to the Prime Minister only to get an extremely brusque letter back telling him in effect to stick to his role as Lord Lieutenant – a role which, it was implied, was entirely ceremonial and redundant – and leave the work of policing the community to the professionals like Sir Arnold Gonders who was doing such an excellent job etc. The Lord Lieutenant had taken the advice and had steered well clear of the Chief Constable ever since.

So had Judge Julius Foment, whose faith in the British police had been shattered by the discovery that he had been relying on the evidence of detectives in Twixt and Tween to sentence perfectly innocent individuals to long terms of imprisonment for crimes the police knew perfectly well they could not possibly have committed. As a child refugee from Nazi persecution the Judge had been horrified by the change that had come over the British police. He had even thought of selling his own house on the far side of the reservoir when the Gonderses moved into the boathouse. He hadn't, but he did not even reply to their invitations.

There were other people who stayed away. They were the genuine locals, the farmers and ordinary people in the villages round about who could be of no advantage to the Gonderses or their guests but belonged to an older and more indigenous tradition. Of these the most antipathetic to the human flotsam on the Gonderses' lawn that Sunday were the Middens, Marjorie Midden at the Middenhall and her brother, Christopher, who farmed thirty miles away at Strutton.

From the first Sir Arnold had found himself up against Miss Midden. She lived in an old farmhouse behind the rambling Victorian house known as the Middenhall where she had lodgers. She had opposed him over the fencing of the common land known as Folly Moss on the grounds that it had provided free grazing for the villagers of Great Pockrington for a thousand years. Sir Arnold's argument that there was only one family living at Pockrington now and that the man worked in the brickyards at Torthal and had no interest in grazing anything on Folly Moss was met by Miss Midden's retort that there had once been two hundred families at Pockrington and the state of the world being what it was who was to say there might not be as many families there in the future.

'Jimmy Hall may mean very little to the Chief Constable,' she had said at a public meeting, 'but he represents the rights of the common man to the common land. Rights have to be fought for and are not going to be set aside while I'm around.'

Sir Arnold had tried to argue that he only wanted to put barbed wire up to keep other people's sheep out and that Jimmy Hall could use the land if he wanted to. It was no good. Miss Midden had answered that barbed wire too often defined the boundaries of liberty and set unwarranted limits on people's free movement. The common land had remained unfenced.

There were other grievances. One of his patrol cars had chased a vehicle that was obviously being driven by a drunk down the drive into the Middenhall estate. An elderly man who was seen stumbling across the lawn was pinioned to the ground and handcuffed. Anywhere else in the Twixt and Tween area that sort of police action would have roused no comment. On several housing estates on the outskirts of Tween it might just have provided the local youths with an excuse for a punch-up with the cops, but that was to be expected. What came as an unnerving shock to the Chief Constable was for a supposedly law-abiding member of the middle classes to use the law to make a mockery of two of his officers in court when the whole thing could have been avoided by a quiet word with him.

But Miss Midden hadn't done that. Instead she had pursued a vendetta with the two constables most unreasonably. After all, they had merely taken the supposed driver back to the Stagstead Police Station when he had refused a breath-test (and had already assaulted them both in pursuance of their duty) and the police doctor had taken a blood sample which had clearly shown that the defendant's blood alcohol level was way over the limit. As a result the defendant, Mr Armitage Midden, an elderly white hunter who had recently returned from Kenya where he had been known as

'Buffalo' Midden, had been charged with dangerous driving, driving with a faulty rear light, assaulting two police officers, and drunken driving. Bail had been granted the next day when the said Mr Midden had spent a salutarily uncomfortable night in the cells and had been driven back to the Middenhall by Miss Midden herself. She had been thoroughly unpleasant to all the officers in the Stagstead police station.

But it was only when the case came to court that the police learnt the defendant was (a) without a licence to drive, (b) had such an aversion to motor cars that he had once walked from Cape Town to Cairo, and finally (c) had earned his formidable reputation as a superb shot by being a lifelong teetotaller. In short, it had been an excruciatingly embarrassing case for the Chief Constable, the two arresting officers, and the police surgeon, and had done nothing to enhance the reputation of the Twixt and Tween Constabulary. Miss Midden had gone to her cousin, Lennox, and had insisted he brief an extremely sardonic and experienced barrister from London. And quite clearly she had instructed him to put the police conduct in the most protracted and worst possible light. The barrister's cross-examination of the police witnesses had been particularly painful for the Chief Constable, who had inadvisedly allowed himself to be called to give evidence in support of his own constables and the Twixt and Tween Constabulary. Looking back on the case Sir Arnold considered he had been deliberately inveigled into appearing and made to look an idiot and worse. He had testified to the police surgeon's absolute probity before the case was stopped by the judge. And finally there had been Buffalo Midden's splendid war record – he had been awarded the DSO with bar and the MC for conspicuous bravery in Burma. In the public gallery Miss Midden had enjoyed her triumph. The Chief Constable had been careful not to look at her but he could imagine her feelings. They'd been the very opposite of his.

But now he was not concerned with Miss Midden's arrogance. In the middle of the party his thoughts kept returning to the fellow

68

in the cellar. He was particularly irritated and alarmed by Ernest Lamming who kept insisting that Sir Arnold had a splendid selection of wine and who wanted to see it was being kept in the proper conditions.

'I mean I don't sell plonk. Only the genuine article and there's some lovely stuff you got like that '56 Bergerac and the '47 Fitou. That's worth a bob or two now if you've been looking after it properly. I mean I want to see you got those bottles on their sides and all that. If you've got them standing up, the corks will dry out and your investment is down the plughole.'

'Actually I moved it back to the Sweep's Place house,' Sir Arnold told him. 'I didn't like to leave valuable wine like that out here with the house being empty all week.'

'But you haven't even got a cellar there,' said Lamming. 'Out here was just right for it. The cellar here was specially built to keep the champagne and suchlike the waterworks millionaires drank when they came out on a spree at the end of the last century.'

Sir Arnold had been saved by the intervention of one of the new waterworks millionaires, Ralph Pulborough, whose salary had just been increased by 98 per cent while water charges had gone up 50 per cent.

'Now look here, Ernest, fair dos and all that. I don't want to hear any more snide remarks about water rates and so on,' he said, 'and I object to being called a waterworks millionaire. I was a millionaire long before I went into water, and you know it. If you want efficiency you have to pay for it. That's the law of the market. It's the same with that plonk you sell.'

'I do not sell plonk,' Lamming retorted angrily. 'You won't find a better bottle of Blue Nun this side of Berlin than what I sell. And your water's nothing to write home about. There was a dead sheep floating out there by the dam when I drove over just now. And the tap water is so bad we've had to install a reverse osmosis diaphragm for Ruby to have a clean bath.'

'My dears, a reverse osmosis diaphragm,' minced Pulborough,

'how very appropriate for her. Did it hurt very much at first? I simply must ask her.'

Sir Arnold hurried out of earshot and went in search of Sammy Bathon, the TV interviewer and entrepreneur, who had recently established a chain of betting shops with the help of the Government's Aid to Industry Scheme. Sammy Bathon was a chap with his ear close to the ground and, if anything had been going the rounds about a Press coup that failed last night, he'd be the one to know.

He found him discussing the advantages of cryogenics with the Rev. Herbert Bentwhistle. 'Sure, sure, Father, I'm not knocking the Holy Book but where does it say anything about leaving things to chance? So I have eternal life without liquid nitrogen by being a good boy. I prefer my way. Bigger chance for Sammy with the nitrogen maybe.' He winked at Sir Arnold but the eye behind it did not suggest any secret information about the intruder.

It was a remark he caught as he passed the group round Egeworth, the MP for West Twixt, that interested the Chief Constable most. 'She's a confounded nuisance, Miss Midden is,' Egeworth was saying. 'Spends half her life preventing developments that would serve the community. I wish to God someone would shut her up.'

'You mean she's been poking her nose into the housing scheme at Ablethorpe?' someone said. 'You preserve a few trees and lose the chance of a development grant. Where's the sense in that?'

'That's the trouble with these so-called old families. They seem to think the past matters. They don't think of the future.'

Sir Arnold went into his study and shut the door. He was exhausted and he had to think of his own future. The vodka had been of only temporary help. Why wouldn't they hurry up and go so that he could get some shut-eye and give that bastard his next dose of whisky and whatever? He sat down and thought about Miss Marjorie Midden. Her and that Major MacPhee. If only he could find out if it was one of her weekends away birdwatching or visiting gardens. The Midden would be an ideal place to dump that sod in the cellar. There were all those old weirdos living at the Middenhall and, while he wasn't prepared to venture down the drive to the Hall itself, the Midden farmhouse where the old cow lived with Major MacPhee was conveniently isolated. It would be nice to get her to take the rap for the young toyboy. It was a lovely idea. In the meantime he'd just make a phone call.

He dialled Miss Midden's number. There was no reply. He'd call the Middenhall later to check she was really away. As he passed the kitchen door he heard Auntie Bea talking to Mrs Thouless the housekeeper. 'I really don't see why Arnold had to say that he'd taken the wine to Sweep's Place when it's patently untrue. And as for a '47 Fitou! Can you imagine how frightful it must be?'

Fortunately the housekeeper was deaf. She was talking to herself about glass and blood all over the bedroom floor and the mirror broken and all that water. Sir Arnold hurried upstairs to check that there were no bloodstains on the wall about the bed. There weren't, and the marks on the carpet were all his own. He was also glad to see that Vy had passed out on the bed. She had spent the party drinking gin and Appletiser and pretending it was champagne. It hadn't worked. The gin had won.

Chapter 9

By the time he had seen all the guests leave, Sir Arnold's exhaustion was almost total. Only terror kept him going – terror and black coffee. But during the afternoon a new stimulant entered the picture. It came with the realization that whoever had brought that filthy lout to the house and his bed must have had an accomplice on the inside. All the facts, in so far as he could marshal them, pointed to that incontrovertible conclusion. Sir Arnold in his awful condition certainly couldn't controvert it. He clung instead to certain facts, the first of which was that someone, and if he could lay his hands on that someone . . . some shit had unlocked the iron gates to let some other shits in with the young bastard now in the cellar and, when they had left, had locked the gates again. There was no other way they could have got in. The walls and the steel-shuttered windows on the reservoir side of the house made any other route impossible. When it came to self-protection, the Chief Constable did himself well.

That was the first point and it was confirmed by the second, the pitiful state of the Rottweiler. If Sir Arnold felt awful – and he did – the dog was in an even worse state. True, its legs had recovered and it could walk – well, at any rate hobble – but in nearly every other respect it had the look of an animal that had made the mistake of taking on a thoroughly ill-tempered JCB. Its jaws were in a particularly nasty state and, when once or twice it tried to bark or make some sort of audible protest, it merely achieved what looked like a yawn. No sound issued from its massive throat, though when it hobbled, it wheezed. In more favourable circumstances Sir Arnold would have got his wife to call the vet, but that was out of the question. Circumstances were the least favourable he had ever known and he had no intention of allowing any damned vet to come poking around the place. He had even less of allowing Lady Vy or that beastly Bea to go anywhere. Genscher would have to suffer in silence. All the same, the dog provided further evidence that Bea had helped the swine who had put that lout in his bed. The dog knew her and had evidently come to like the cow. In his disgusted opinion it ought to have savaged her the first time she set foot on the premises. Instead it had trusted her. Sir Arnold wasted no sympathy on the animal. It had only itself to blame for its present condition. The damned woman must have taken a crowbar to the brute.

Following this line of reasoning, he wondered what she had taken to Lady Vy. Probably a near-lethal dose of anti-depressants. Like twice her normal dose. And this on top of her usual bottle of gin. Well, two could play that game, and he wasn't going to have anyone interfering with his plans for the disposal of the bloke in the sheets.

He was now left with the practical problem of getting the bloke out of the cellar and depositing him somewhere else. Once that had been achieved successfully any attempt to blackmail him would be a right give-away. That bloody Bea wouldn't be able to say a thing. The opportunity would have passed. It was a nice thought.

Sir Arnold applied his mind to the solution of this problem. First the place would have to be somewhere near enough for him to be able to get there and back in an hour. Sometime between 2 a.m. and 3 would be ideal. And this time Auntie Bea would be the one to have something to make her sleep. Say 80 mg of Valium in her tonic. That would undoubtedly do the trick. Or in the gin? No, tonic was better. She would drink more of the tonic. He went through to the sitting-room and got a bottle and made up the potion. And it wouldn't hurt if Vy got a dose too. He didn't want her interfering in his plan or even knowing what it was. He knew his wife. She had an infinite capacity for forgetting the unpleasant facts of her experience and for concentrating on only those things that gave her pleasure. With the help of enough gin she could forget any sort of crime. He wasn't going to worry about Vy.

His thoughts, such as they were, reverted to the Middenhall. If only he could be absolutely sure Miss Midden had gone away and the old farmhouse was unoccupied it would make the ideal spot to dump the bastard. It was close enough to be convenient and at the same time far enough away to remove all suspicion from the Old Boathouse. Best of all was the proximity of all those very dubious Midden family eccentrics in the Hall itself. In a way it would be easier to dump the fellow in the garden there but there was always the danger he might die of exposure in the night air. No, he'd have to go inside a building, preferably a house, where he'd definitely be found fairly quickly. And the farmhouse was sufficiently close to the Middenhall proper to cast suspicion on its strange inhabitants. Let Miss Midden come home and find that little lot in her bed and it would be very interesting to get her reaction.

In spite of his fatigue the Chief Constable almost smiled at the thought. Once again he phoned the farm and got no reply. He tried the Middenhall itself and asked for the Major. 'I'm afraid he's away for the weekend,' a woman told him.

Sir Arnold took his courage in his hands. 'Then perhaps Miss Midden is available,' he said.

'She's not here either. They won't be back till Monday or even Tuesday.'

'Oh well, it can wait,' said the Chief Constable and, before the woman could ask who was calling, he put the phone down.

Now all that remained was to move the Land Rover down to the old byre so that he wouldn't be heard from the house when he started it up. Having done all the essential things, Sir Arnold settled down to get some rest.

In fact there was no need to wait until 2 a.m. to make the move. At ten o'clock Auntie Bea said she was dead tired and wandered off to bed and Lady Vy followed, looking very weirdly pink. Sir Arnold hoped he hadn't overdone the Valium in the tonic. Well, it couldn't be helped now. He went down to the cellar and gave the unwanted visitor his final shot of whisky before trying to move the body up to the ground floor.

74

It was at that point that he realized he was dealing with a dead weight. It had been easy enough to get the fellow down to the cellar. For one thing Vy had helped him and for another it had all been downhill. Getting the brute up again was another matter altogether. Sir Arnold tugged Timothy Bright halfway up the cellar steps, and dropped the load twice to avoid having a heart attack. After that he changed his mind about the route out. If he dropped the blighter again he might well kill him, and if he went on trying to get him up the steps he would almost certainly kill himself.

Having got his racing pulse almost back to normal, Sir Arnold stood up and went over to the hatch. Originally it had been used to roll beer barrels down into the cellar. He would have to use it now to get the bloke up. Sir Arnold pulled the ropes and undid the bolts. Then he went upstairs and round to the yard and opened the hatch from above. Beside him Genscher wheezed strangely and sniffed. The poor creature was still in a bad way. But Sir Arnold hadn't got time to worry about the Rottweiler's problems. He had far more important ones of his own to consider.

He fetched a rope from the garage and dropped one end down the hatch into the cellar. Then he went back down into the cellar and dragged the body over to the beer ramp under the hatch. Here he tied the rope round the fellow's waist. So far so good.

He was about to go up the steps when to his horror he heard footsteps on the floor above. Switching off the light, he stood in the darkness sweating. What the hell was happening? That bloody Bea couldn't be prowling round the house now. It wasn't possible. He had watched her sink three gin and tonics and there'd been all that Valium in the tonic bottle. The woman must have the constitution of the proverbial ox to stay awake with that lot inside her. Or perhaps the cow had realized her drink had been doctored and had taken something to counteract it. She was obviously far brighter than he had supposed. And the door of the cellar was open. She was bound to spot it.

Upstairs, Aunt Bea blundered across the kitchen in search of some bicarbonate of soda, anything to stop her head spinning. She hadn't felt this drunk in a long time, and to make it all the more peculiar she'd only had three small gin and tonics and had drowned the gin in tonic too. At this rate she'd have to give up drinking altogether. There must be something terribly wrong with her liver. As she blundered into the kitchen table and clutched at the back of a chair and finally sat down, she was an extremely puzzled woman. She was even more puzzled by an over-riding desire to sing. She hadn't had that urge for ages and usually did it in the privacy of her own flat, and in the bathroom at that. It was all very well being a powerful woman and generally rather masculine in many ways, but it was no great help having the voice of an extremely bad soprano. But now for some unknown reason she felt like singing 'If you were the only girl in the world and I was the only boy.'

As the sounds reached the Chief Constable in the cellar and were translated into an overture, a new and frightful thought occurred to him, that the ghastly Auntie Bea was making some disgusting proposition to him – one that he rejected out of hand. She evidently knew he was in the cellar but, if she thought he was going to play the girl to her being the boy, she had another think coming. And she couldn't possibly be singing to anyone else in the house. Mrs Thouless was as deaf as a post and Vy was without question dead to the world. As if to confirm him in this insane notion that he was being courted by an unabashed lesbian, and if she had looked any different the normally passive Sir Arnold might have welcomed the experience, Auntie Bea got up and crossed to the cellar door and peered down the steps. 'If there is anyone down there, you can come up now to Auntie Bea and give me the tongue of day,' she whispered. The Chief Constable curdled in the corner. He had many fantasies in his life, but that was definitely not one of them. 'All aboard the Auntie Bea. Last orders and rites. The rest is silence.' And having uttered these ominous words, she shut the cellar door and locked it.

In the darkness Sir Arnold Gonders listened to her retreating footsteps and cursed the day his wife had brought the beastly woman into their life. Either she was taking the piss out of him or

76

she was clean out of her skull. Whichever she was he had to get himself out of the fucking cellar, one, and two, drag the blighter up after him. The only way out now was up the planks of the beer-barrel ramp. By the light of the moon shining occasionally through the scudding clouds he tried climbing the plank by gripping the edge with his hands and moving one of his feet at a time. Halfway up he slipped and was left clutching the plank to himself like a mating toad. With infinite care to avoid splinters he let himself down and considered the problem again. What he needed were some non-slip soles or, since they weren't available, something he could attach to the plank that wouldn't slip. For a minute he thought of using Timothy Bright as a temporary ladder and had got so far as to prop him against the plank when he decided that wasn't very clever. Unless he tied the fellow on . . .

Sir Arnold cancelled the project and went back with his torch to look for something to stand on. He found it at the back of one of the stone wine racks in the shape of a battered suitcase which contained ancient copies of *La Vie Parisienne* and which had once belonged to a waterworks employee who had evidently whiled away his spare time with photographs of unclad French women of the thirties. Sir Arnold had kept them for his own amusement but now the suitcase was going to be put to a better purpose.

Five minutes later he was out into the cool night air and grasping the rope attached to the body in the cellar. He stood for a moment to consider the problem. It was amazing how quite simple tasks became problematical when they had to be put into effect. One thing he wasn't going to do was have the rope slip back through the hatch if he had to let go. Walking across the cobbled yard he tied the end to the leg of a bench in his workshop. As he straightened up he began to realize that pulling the body wasn't going to be at all easy. He wished now he hadn't left the bottle of whisky in the cellar. He could do with a stiff dram before attempting the big pull. He went round to the French windows and was grateful to find that Auntie Bea hadn't locked them too. In his study he poured himself a large Chivas Regal and drank it down. Yes, that felt better.

Back in the yard he grasped the rope and began to pull. Slowly, the body crept up the planks and Sir Arnold was beginning to think he had done it when his feet slipped on the cobbles and with a nasty thud Timothy Bright fell onto the floor of the cellar again. As the Chief Constable fought to get his breath back Genscher whined beside him. Sir Arnold looked down at the huge dog and was inspired. He had found the perfect method of getting the damned lout up and out. He went into the workshop and found several rolls of insulating tape.

'Genscher old boy, come here and make yourself useful,' he called softly. 'You're going to be my dumb chum.'

Five minutes later the Rottweiler was. With twenty metres of insulating tape strapped tightly round its jaws and the back of its head it was incapable of whining and its breathing had taken on a new and stressful wheezing.

'Now then,' said Sir Arnold, 'just one more thing.' And he tied the rope to the dog's collar. Then he stepped back and took a deep breath before unleashing all the rage against circumstance that had built up in him since he had been hounded by the press at the Serious Crime Squad celebrations. As he kicked Genscher's so far unscathed scrotum the great beast bounded forward, desperately trying to come to terms with this appalling visitation and the changed relationship with a master who had previously treated it almost kindly. In the cellar, happily oblivious to the fate waiting for him, Timothy shot up the ramp and through the hatch onto the cobbles and was dragged across the yard by the desperate dog. As Genscher hurled himself away from his own backside, Timothy followed and was dragged into the workshop where he collided with the leg of the bench, bounced off it and was finally wedged under the front off-side wheel of Lady Vy's Mercedes.

Outside Sir Arnold tried to undo the rope. The Chivas Regal had got to him now and he was conscious that the family pet no longer trusted him. 'It's all right, Genscher old chap,' he whispered hoarsely but without effect. The Rottweiler was not a very bright dog and it certainly wasn't a fit one but it knew enough and was fit enough to keep out of the way of owners who muzzled a dog's jaws with half a mile of insulating tape and then kicked it in the balls. As the Chief Constable stumbled about the yard in pursuit, Genscher made for the only bolt-hole it could find and shot through the hatch. Behind it the rope tautened and for a moment it seemed as though the body in the sheets would follow it. But Timothy Bright was too tightly wedged under the Mercedes and the rope had wound itself round an upright in the garage. As the Rottweiler began to strangle to death halfway down the chute, Sir Arnold acted. He wasn't going to lose the fellow whatever happened. Groping among the tools on the bench he found a chisel and, kneeling on the ground, stabbed at the rope. Most of his attempts missed but in the end the rope parted and a dull thud in the cellar indicated that the Rottweiler had dropped the remaining five feet to the floor. Sir Arnold got to his feet and began to haul the body from below the Mercedes.

He collected a wheelbarrow and, wedging Timothy across it, slowly wheeled him down to the Land Rover in the byre. Twice the body fell off and twice he replaced it, but in the end he was able to heave it up into the back of the vehicle. Then he checked his watch. It was almost one o'clock. Or was it two? It didn't matter. He didn't give a fig what time it was any longer so long as that old bitch Miss Midden was well and truly away from the farm. The Chief Constable was pissed and mentally shagged out and only his sense of self preservation kept him going. He wasn't going to waste time getting the wretched fellow out of the sheets here. He'd do that once he'd unloaded the bugger at the Midden. Sir Arnold climbed back into the driving seat and eased the handbrake off. The Land Rover coasted slowly down the hill away from the Old Boathouse and the reservoir. When he was out of sight he let in the clutch and started.

Twenty-five slow minutes later, still driving without lights, he turned up towards the Midden and got out to open the gate. For a moment he hesitated. There was still time to dump the bugger somewhere else. Once in through the gate there could be no turning back. And a little way down the road to his right was the Middenhall itself. The entrance to the estate was only a quarter of a mile further on. Sir Arnold could see the beech trees that marked the wall of the estate. No, even at this late hour there might be weirdos up and about in the grounds. It was here or nothing. He pushed the gate open and drove up into the back yard and then under the archway to the front of the house. There he sat for a moment with the engine running but no lights came on in the house. Ahead of him was another gate and the track that had once been the old drove road to the south. It was unpaved and led across the fell but it would provide a very useful route away from the house when he had finished. The Chief Constable switched off the engine and got out and listened. Apart from the hissing in his right ear, which he attributed to too much whisky, the night was silent.

He went round to the back of the Land Rover and put on a pair of washing-up gloves. Then, moving with what he supposed was stealth, he crossed to the front door and shone his torch on the lock. It wasn't, he was glad to find, a Chubb or even a complicated Yale-type lock. It should be easy enough to break in.

In fact there was no need. The door was unlocked. Typical of a woman, thought the Chief Constable, before realizing that the door might be unlocked but it was also on a chain and he still couldn't get in. Another thought struck him. Perhaps Miss Midden was still there. It was possible she had changed her mind about going off for the weekend. He should have thought of that earlier. Sir Arnold backed away from the front door and went back through the archway to the back yard. It was here Miss Midden garaged her car. He looked in the old barn across the yard and was relieved to find it empty. After that he tried the back door, but that was locked and with a Chubb too. No chance of breaking in there. He went round the windows, trying them all. They were of the old-fashioned sash type and on one the catch was broken. Sir Arnold Gonders slid the window open and clambered through. His torch showed him that he was in the dining-room. A large mahogany table with chairs all round it and a bowl of faded flowers in the middle and a large old sideboard with a mirror above it. To his left a door. He crossed to it and found himself in a room with a bed, a desk, an armchair and a bookcase. A pair of men's shoes and slippers and a dressing-gown. He was evidently in Major MacPhee's room. Nothing could be more convenient. With renewed confidence he opened the window and returned to the Land Rover. Ten minutes later Timothy Bright was out of the bedsheets and the Chief Constable had dumped him, with some difficulty, through the open window into the Major's bedroom.

It was at that moment he saw headlights bridge the rise on the road. He wasn't waiting to find out who was coming up from Stagstead at that time of night. Acting with surprising swiftness for a drunk and exhausted man, he rolled the unconscious Timothy under the bed and climbed out of the window and shut it. Then he hurried round to the Land Rover, opened the gate onto the drove road, went through and shut the gate again before remembering he'd left the front window open. For a moment he hesitated, but the headlights were much closer now. As they turned up towards the farmhouse Sir Arnold drove slowly and without lights across the fell, guided by the bank of old wind-bent thorn trees on one side. Only when he reached the Parson's Road and was out of sight of the Midden did he turn the lights on and drive normally back to the Old Boathouse. Behind him the night wind fluttered the curtain in the open window.

Chapter 10

As she drove the old wartime Humber she had inherited from her father back to the farmhouse Miss Midden was in a filthy mood. She had been looking forward to a weekend on the Solway Firth, visiting gardens and walking. But her plans had been ruined by Major MacPhee. As usual. She should have had more sense than to allow him to go to Glasgow by himself. The city always did terrible things to the silly little man, both mentally and then physically. This time he and the city had excelled themselves.

'You're a perfectly filthy mess,' she had told him when she found him at the Casualty department of the hospital. 'I can't think why I put up with you.'

'I'm awfully sorry, dear, but you know me,' said the Major.

'Unfortunately. But not for much longer if you go on like this,' she had replied. 'This is your last chance. I can't think what gets into you.'

In fact, of course she could. A large quantity of Scotch whisky. And as usual when he went to Glasgow the Major had drunk himself into a disgusting state of daring in more awful pubs than he could remember and had then chosen a particularly explosive bar filled with young Irishmen in which to announce in a very loud voice that what was needed to solve the problems of Ulster was to bring back the B Specials or better still the Black & Tans. The Irishmen's reaction to this appalling suggestion had been entirely predictable. In the battle that followed Major MacPhee had been thrown into the street through a frosted-glass window that had until then borne the inscription WINES & SPIRITS, only to be hurled back into the pub by an enormous Glaswegian who objected to his girlfriend being physically accosted by small men with ginger moustaches. After that the Major had discovered the real meaning of 'rough trade' as thirty-five drunk Irishmen fought over and around him for no very obvious reason. In the end he had been rescued by the police, who had mistaken him for an innocent bystander and had rushed him to hospital. By the time Miss Midden found him there he had several stitches above his left black eye and all hope of continuing the weekend at the Balcarry Bay Hotel had vanished. No respectable hotel would have accepted the Major. His trousers were torn and he had lost the collar of his shirt and one shoe.

The doctor in Casualty had been entirely unsympathetic. She had been working all hours of the weekend and didn't take kindly to people like Major MacPhee. 'You're very lucky to be alive,' she told him. 'And the very next time you are brought in here like this I shall consider a psychological examination. There are too many alcoholic nutters like you on the streets of this city.'

Miss Midden agreed with her. 'He's really despicable,' she said, only to find that the doctor assumed she was the Major's wife.

'If you feel like that, why don't you divorce him?' she asked and, before Miss Midden could find words to express her outraged feelings, the doctor had gone off to tend to a youth who had been hit over the head with a broken bottle.

As they drove out of the city Miss Midden gave vent to her fury. 'You really are a truly horrible person,' she said, 'and mad. You've ruined my weekend by behaving like . . . like, well, like the sort of person you are.'

'I'm really sorry. I honestly am,' the Major whimpered. 'It's just that as soon as I find myself in a saloon bar, or better still a public one, I get this terrible urge.'

'We all get terrible urges,' said Miss Midden. 'I have one at the moment and I might very well act upon it if I didn't think you'd get some perverse pleasure out of it. You evidently have a death wish.'

'It isn't that,' said the Major through swollen lips. 'The urge comes on me all of a sudden. One moment I'm standing there with my foot on the rail and a small treble malt in my hand and some nice fellow beside me and then out of the blue I have this irrepressible urge to walk up to the biggest oaf I can see and tell him to shut his gob. Or something that will make him try to think. It's wonderful to see a really strong, powerful thug come to life. The look on his face of utter bewilderment, the growing gleam in his eyes, the way he bunches his fists and shifts his shoulders for the punch. I must have seen more really big men throw punches than half the professional boxers in the world.'

'And look what it's done for you. It's a wonder you haven't got brain damage. If you had a brain to damage.' For a while they drove on in silence, Miss Midden considering how strange it was that she had been left the Middenhall with its curious collection of inhabitants, and the Major nursing a separate grievance.

'You could always have left me behind at the Infirmary. I rather liked it there.'

'And have you come home with some foul disease? Certainly not. That hospital looked most insanitary.'

'That's only in Casualty. Casualty is always like that on a Saturday night. It's so busy.'

Presently, as they crossed the border, Major MacPhee fell asleep and Miss Midden drove on, still mulling over her curious circumstances. For one thing, in spite of his occasional outbreaks, she continued to put up with the miserable Major. He was useful about the place and shared the housework. He was also a quite good cook, though not as good as he claimed. Miss Midden did not disillusion him. The poor wretch needed all the pretence he could muster. And his bouts of drunken masochism in Glasgow were, she supposed, part of the camouflage he needed to cover his cowardice. He really was a most despicable creature. But, and in Miss Midden's eyes it was an important 'but', he polished his little brogues every day and took pains over his appearance to the point of wearing a waistcoat and sporting a fob watch. That it was a silver one, while the chain across his stomach was gold, touched her by its pathos. Yes, he was particular about his appearance, grooming his little moustache and surreptitiously dyeing his hair. Even his suits were as good as he could afford and to make them look as though they had been tailored for him he had learnt to take them in at the waist.

From Miss Midden's point of view it was a useful affectation. The Major had to conform to the shape of his jackets, which meant that he ate very little. Even so he had developed a little paunch and recently he had begun to wear a dark blue double-breasted blazer on which he had sewn the brass buttons of a Highland regiment he had found in a junk shop in Stagstead. The regiment had been disbanded long before the Major could possibly have joined the army. Miss Midden knew this and had been tempted to ask him why he didn't buy himself a kilt as well, but she hadn't the heart to. There was no need to hurt his pride, he had so little of it. And in any case he had such miserably thin legs . . . No, it was better not to say anything. All the same there were times, and this was one of them, when she wished she was rid of him. She had illusions of her own to protect and his grubby fantasies, his little store of magazines which he kept locked in a briefcase, sometimes seemed to leak out into the atmosphere and fill her with a sad disgust.

On the other hand for all his faults Major MacPhee was not a Midden, and with so many family members, or people who claimed to be relatives, living down at the Middenhall his inability to demand anything of her was a distinct advantage. As she put it to Phoebe Turnbird over at Carryclogs House, 'Of course he's a very silly little man and, if he was ever in the Army he was probably a corporal in the Catering Corps, but at least I can throw him out whenever I want to which is more than I can say for the people at the Hall. I'm lumbered with them. I sometimes dream the place has burnt down and I can get away. Then I wake up and it's still there in all its awfulness.'

'But it's a lovely house . . . in its way,' Phoebe said, but Miss Midden wasn't to be fooled or patronized. Carryclogs House was beautiful, the Middenhall wasn't.

'If you think it lovely . . . well, never mind,' Miss Midden had said and had stumped off across the fell, whacking her boots with the riding crop she always carried.

Now, driving back through the night following the narrow lanes she knew so well and disliked on this occasion so intensely, she cursed the Major and she cursed her role as mistress of the Middenhall. Most of all she cursed the Middenhall itself. Built at the beginning of the century by her great-grandfather, 'Black' Midden, to prove to the world that he had made a fortune out of cheap native labour and the wholesale use of business practices which, even by the lax standards of the day in Johannesburg, were considered more devious and underhand than was socially acceptable, the house ('pile' was the more appropriate term) was proof that he had no taste whatsoever. Or, to be more accurate, that he did have taste but of a sort that could only be described as appalling. To describe the Middenhall itself was well-nigh impossible. It combined the very worst eccentricities of every architectural style Black Midden could think of with a structural toughness that was formidable and seemingly indestructible. To that extent it accurately reflected the old man's character.

'I want it to be a monument to my success in life,' he told the first architect he employed, 'and I haven't got where I am today by being nice and namby-pamby. I've come up the hard way and I mean to leave a house that is as hard as I am.'

The architect, a man of some discernment, had his own ideas about how his client had 'come up' and supposed correctly that the lives of his employees must have been exceedingly hard. Accordingly he had presented a design that had all the charm of a concrete blockhouse (Black Midden had built a great many blockhouses for the British during the Boer War). The old man had rejected the design. 'I said a house, not a bloody prison,' he said. 'I want towers and turrets and stained-glass windows and a huge verandah on which I can sit and smoke my pipe. And where are the bathrooms?'

'Well, there's one here and another there –'

'I want one for every bedroom. I'm not having people wandering about in dressing-gowns looking for the things. I don't care what other people have. I want something better. And different.'

The architect, who already knew that, went away and added towers and turrets and stained glass and a vast verandah and put bathrooms in for every bedroom. Even then Black Midden wasn't satisfied. 'Where's the pillars along the front like they have in Greece?' he demanded. 'And the gargoyles.'

'Pillars and gargoyles?' the architect said weakly. He had known he was dealing with a difficult client but this was too much. 'You want me to add pillars and gargoyles?'

'That's what I said and that's what I meant.'

'But they hardly go together. I mean . . .' protested the architect, a devotee of Charles Mackintosh.

'I know that. I'm not a damned fool,' said Black Midden stoutly. 'The pillars are for holding up the front of the house and the gargoyles are for spouting the rainwater off the gutters.'

'If you say so,' said the architect, who needed the money, but who was also beginning to wonder what sort of damage this appalling building was going to inflict on his reputation, 'but there is a slight problem with the verandah. I mean if you want pillars and a verandah –'

'And I do,' Black Midden insisted. 'It's your business to solve problems. And don't put the pillars in front of the verandah. I want to sit there and enjoy the view. I don't want it spoilt by a whole lot of damned great pillars in front of me. Put them behind.'

The architect had gone away and had spent a fortnight desperately trying to find a way of meeting his dreadful client's requirements while at the same time teetering on the verge of a nervous breakdown. In the end he had produced a design that met with the old man's approval. The Middenhall had gargoyles and stained glass. Every bedroom had a bathroom, the columns were behind the vast verandah, and there were all the towers and turrets, balconies and loggias imaginable. Nothing matched, and everything was immensely strong and consequently quite out of proportion. Black Midden was delighted. The same couldn't be said for the rest of the Middens. The family had never had any social pretensions and had been quite content to be small farmers or shopkeepers or even very occasionally to enter the professions and become doctors or solicitors. They had liked to think of themselves as solid, respectable people who worked hard and went to Chapel on Sunday. Black Midden destroyed that comfortable reputation. His excesses were not confined to building a ghastly house. A succession of too well-endowed mistresses, some of whom couldn't by any stretch of the imagination be called white, had been brought to the Middenhall, always in open carriages so that their presence couldn't be ignored, and had disported their excessive charms on the lawns and, on the most memorable occasion, by swimming naked in the lake at a garden party which the Bishop of Twixt had most inadvisedly agreed to attend.

'Well, that stupid old bugger isn't going to forget me,' Black Midden had commented at the time, and had gone on to make absolutely sure that no one else who came to the Middenhall would ever forget him by lining the drive with a series of sculptures in the hardest Coadstone, each of which depicted some ostensibly mythical event with a verisimilitude that was revoltingly authentic except in size. At the top of the drive a twenty-foot Leda was all too obviously enjoying the attentions of a vast swan, while further down the Sabine women were getting theirs from some remarkably well-hung Roman soldiers.

All this had pleased Black Midden immensely. Other people felt differently. Having planned a celebration party to mark the completion of the statues he was thwarted when the entire outdoor staff had gone on strike and the cook and the indoor women had left without notice. For a year Black Midden had held out against local opposition to the revolting statues by importing staff from outside the county at enormous cost. Finally, ostracized by every one of his own relatives and by the rest of the county, he had retired to Lausanne only to die of monkey-gland poisoning in an attempt to restore his virility in 1931. By then the statues had been dismantled by a blasting squad from the quarries at Long Stretchon in the course of which a number of windows in the Middenhall had also been blown out, largely, it was thought, thanks to the attempt of his nephew, Herbert Midden, to bribe the demolition men into blowing up the entire house. Black Midden's revenge was revealed only with the reading of his will, drawn up by the most experienced lawyers in London. He left the house, demesne, lands, and estate, together with his entire fortune, to the youngest Midden over the age of twenty-one in each succeeding generation with the proviso that the Middenhall be kept in unaltered condition and a room be provided for any Midden who wished to have one.

At the time these terms had not seemed too burdensome. No sane Midden would want to live in the awful house and the income from the Midden Trust was considerable. By the time Miss Midden inherited the place things had changed.

Chapter 11

At first the change had been almost imperceptible, so much so that some Middens – Lawrence Midden the bank manager in Tween was one – maintained that with their disreputable uncle's death things had gone back to normal.

'Of course, there is that indestructible palazzo,' Lawrence admitted, giving vent to his feelings about foreigners, art, and extravagance at the same time, 'but the Trust provides for its upkeep and I am told that there are ample funds.'

'In Liechtenstein,' said Herbert bitterly. 'And who are the Trustees? Do we know anything about them? No, we don't. Not one damned thing except their address, and it wouldn't surprise me to learn that it is a post box. Or poste restante, Hell.'

It was true. Black Midden's funds had been so discreetly dispersed into numbered and hidden accounts all over the world that, even if the Middens had tried to find out what their total was and had got past the barrier of secrecy erected in Liechtenstein, they would never have found out. But the quarterly payments arrived regularly and for some years it had been possible to maintain the gardens and the artificial lake with its little island in their former condition. The Middenhall itself didn't need maintaining. It was too gracelessly solid for that. All it seemed to require was sweeping and polishing and dusting, and this was done by the indoor staff.

But change, however imperceptible, did come, as Frederick Midden, the pathologist, pointed out with morbid glee. 'The process of extinction is marked by a number of fascinating bodily conditions. First we have the healthy person whose physiological state we call normal. Then we have the onset of disease, which may take many forms. From that we move on to the dying patient, who may linger for a considerable time. Parts of the body remain unaffected while vital organs degenerate, sometimes to the point where pre-mortal putrefaction begins to take place as in gas gangrene. Now, consequent upon this most interesting process the patient is said to die. In fact, paradoxically, he may become far more alive than at any time during his previous existence. Flies, maggots –'

'For God's sake, shut up,' Herbert shouted. 'Can't you see what you've done to Aunt Mildred?'

Frederick Midden turned his bleak eyes on his aunt and agreed that she didn't look at all well. 'Why isn't she eating her soup?' he enquired. 'It's very good soup and in her condition, and out of delicacy for her feelings, I won't give my opinion –'

'Don't,' Herbert ordered. 'Just shut up.'

But Frederick insisted on making his point. 'All I have been trying to tell you is that changes take place in a variety of unforeseen ways.'

He was proved right. None of the Middens had foreseen the coming of war in 1939 and the changes it brought about. The Middenhall was requisitioned by the Ministry of Defence for the duration. Herbert Midden was killed in an air raid on Tween and succeeded by Miss Midden's father, Bernard, as heir to the estate. Since he was only eighteen when he was captured at Singapore by the Japanese and spent the rest of the war as a POW, it was left to Lawrence, now in his eighties, to do what he could to see that the house was damaged as much as possible by the various units that occupied it. The unspoken prayer in everyone's minds was that the Germans would do their bit for the architectural heritage of England by dropping their largest bombs on the place. But it was not to be. The Middenhall remained inviolate. In the grounds Nissen huts proliferated and a rifle range was constructed in the walled garden while round the estate itself a barbed-wire fence was erected and the lodge at the top of the drive became a guard house. What went on inside the camp no one knew. It was said that agents and saboteurs were trained there before being dropped into

Occupied Europe; that much of the planning for the invasion on D-Day took place in the billiard room; that somewhere in the grounds a deep shelter had been built to house resistance fighters in the event of a successful German occupation of Britain. The only two certain facts were that the Canadians had used the house as a hospital and that at the end of the war German generals and senior officers were held there and interrogated in the hope that the mental disorientation produced by the architectural insanity of the Middenhall would persuade them to cooperate.

There were other consequences of the war. Black Midden's hidden funds were, according to the Trustees in Liechtenstein, badly hit by the fall of Hong Kong and, worse still, his investment in certain German industries had been wiped quite literally off the face of the earth by thousand-bomber raids by Lancasters. To cap this series of financial catastrophes a number of gold bars the old man had placed for safe keeping in a bank in Madrid had disappeared, along with the directors of the bank. The news, together with the suspicion that the Trustees were lying, confirmed Lawrence Midden in his loathing for anything foreign, and particularly foreign bankers. 'It could never happen in England,' he murmured on his deathbed two weeks later.

But change continued. As Britain withdrew from the Empire, Black Midden's fortune declined and with it the quarterly cheques. At the same time people from all over Africa and Asia who claimed to be Middens also claimed their right to accommodation and full board at the Middenhall. They brought with them their colonial prejudices and a demanding arrogance that was commensurate with their poverty.

The house became a cauldron of discontent and heated argument. On summer evenings the verandah echoed to shouts of 'Boy, bring me another pink gin,' or 'We used to get a damned sight better service from the kaffirs in Kampala. Nobody in this bloody country does a stroke of work.' Which, since the 'boy' in question happened to be a young woman from Twixt who was helping her mother in the kitchen where she was the cook, did nothing to enhance the quality of the lunches and dinners and may well have accounted for the discovery of a slug in the coq-au-vin one particularly vehement evening. Miss Midden's father, a mild man who had spent most of his life since the war working in an office in Stagstead nursing various digestive complaints caused by his stint on the Burma railway, found the situation intolerable. He was constantly having to placate the cook and the other staff or having to find replacements for them. At night he would lie awake and wonder if it wouldn't be better to up sticks with his family and disappear to somewhere peaceful like Belfast. Only his sense of duty restrained him. That and the thought that the damned colonials, as he called them, were bound to die before too long either naturally or, as seemed only too likely, as a result of mass poisoning by a justifiably demented cook. All the same he had moved into the old farmhouse and had tried to forget the Middenhall by being away for a few hours in the evening and at night, sitting by the old iron range in the kitchen and reading his beloved Pepys. But the house had worn him down and in the end, a broken man, his ill-health forced him to retire to a rented apartment overlooking the sea in Scarborough. Miss Midden remained behind to take over 'that hell-hole'.

She had done so readily enough. She was made of sterner stuff than her mild father and she resented the way he had been treated by the very people he had been supposed to be defending in the war. 'Those damned colonials,' those Middens who had scuttled from the Far East and India, from Kenya and Rhodesia as soon as their comfort was threatened and who had fought no wars, were going to learn to mend their manners. Or leave the Middenhall and make way for more deserving cases. Within months of becoming what they jokingly and disparagingly called 'The Mistress of the Middenhall' she had mastered them. Or broken their spirit. Not that they had much to break, these gin-sodden creatures who had lorded it over native peoples whom they called savages and whom they had done nothing to educate or civilize. She did it simply and with malice aforethought, a great deal of forethought, by choosing

Edgar Cunningham Midden, or E.C. as he liked to be called, as her target. He it was who, having spent a lifetime bullying and beating his way to the top of some obscure province of Portuguese East Africa where he had a vast commercial empire, had once threatened to bastinado a black student from Hull University who had made the mistake of taking a holiday job at the Middenhall and had spilt a bowl of soup on E.C.'s lap while serving at dinner. Miss Midden had not wasted words on the old brute. She had simply and deliberately broken the tap on the central heating radiator in his room during a very cold spell, had refused him the use of an electric fire and, to compound his discomfort, had used her knowledge of the intricate system of plumbing in the Middenhall to cut off the hot water in his bathroom. E.C.'s complaints had been met with the retort that he wasn't in Africa now. And when he demanded another room immediately – 'and don't waste time about it, have my stuff moved by the servants' – before stumping off downstairs to a late breakfast, Miss Midden had complied with his request.

Edgar Cunningham Midden came back from his morning constitutional to find he had been allocated a very small room above the kitchen which had previously been occupied by the man who in earlier years had attended to the central-heating boiler which needed stoking during the night. There was no bathroom and the view from the window was an unedifying one of the back yard and the dustbins. E.C. had exploded at the prospect not only from the window but of walking down a long corridor to a bathroom and had demanded his old room back. Miss Midden said she had allotted it to Mrs Devizes and that she was already moving in. 'She didn't like her room so I've given her yours,' she said. 'If you want it back you should ask her for it.'

It was the very last thing E.C. was going to do. Mrs Devizes, a Midden by marriage, was a woman he detested and whom he had openly referred to as 'that half-caste'. He had suggested instead moving into her old room only to be told that it was being redecorated. A week later, during which he had been kept awake by the noise coming from the kitchen directly below him – Major

MacPhee had been sent down to spend the nights there and to drop several large pots every quarter of an hour – the old bully left the Middenhall in a battered taxi. Miss Midden stood with folded arms on the verandah and saw him off. Then she had turned on the other guests and had asked if anyone else wanted to leave because, if they did, now was the time to do it. 'I have no intention of allowing the staff to be treated impolitely,' she said, slapping her breeches with the riding crop. There had been no misunderstanding her meaning. The guest Middens had behaved with great civility to the cook and the cleaning women after that and had confined their quarrels to themselves. There had been some further weeding out to be done but in the end Miss Midden was satisfied.

Now, driving back to the farm, she was in a dangerous mood. Her plans for the weekend had been thwarted by her own pathetic sentimentality. That was the way she saw it. She had taken pity on the wretched Major from the very first day she met him at the bus station in Tween where he had arrived in answer to an advertisement she had put in *The Lady* for a handyman. Standing there in his little polished shoes and regimental tie and with an old raincoat over one arm he was so obviously neither handy nor entirely a man that Miss Midden's first impulse was to tell him to forget it. Instead she picked up one of his old suitcases, hoisted it into the back of the Humber, and told him to get in. It was an impulse she had never been able to explain to herself. The Major had been rejected so often that his anticipation was almost palpable. In other circumstances Miss Midden would have followed her common sense but the bus station at Tween was too desolate a place for common sense. Besides, she liked surprising people and the Major needed a few pleasant surprises in his life. He was also easy to bully and Miss Midden had recognized his need for that too.

'You'll just have to do,' she thought to herself as they drove away that first afternoon, though what someone like the Major could do was an unknown quantity. Make a hash of everything he attempted, probably. And ruin a weekend for her five years later.

'One of these days, one of these days,' she said out loud to wake him up as they drove up to the back yard of the old farm. It was an expression of hope and increasingly of intention. One of these days she would seize some sudden opportunity and break out of the round of relatives and housekeeping and managing other people's lives and find . . . Not happiness. She wasn't fool enough to chase that will-o'-the-wisp, just as she'd never supposed for a moment that marriage and a family was an answer. She'd lived too long with family to think that. Families were where most murders took place. Besides, Miss Midden had few illusions about herself. She was not a beautiful woman. She was too stout and muscular to be called even attractive. Except to a certain type of man. One of the nastier thoughts that occasionally occurred to her when the miasma of Major MacPhee's sexual fantasies seeped into the atmosphere was that she might play some unspeakable role in them. No, her hope and intention was that one day she would regain the sense of adventure she had known as a child playing by herself among the fireweed and rusting machinery in the abandoned quarry on Folly Down Fell. She had known ecstatic moments of possibility there and the place held magic for her still. But now as she got out of the old Humber her feelings were anything but ecstatic.

'If you've got any sense at all, you'll keep out of my way in the morning,' she told the Major, and left him to hobble shoeless up the steps to the kitchen door. Five minutes later she was upstairs, asleep.

Chapter 12

Major MacPhee sat on the edge of his bed feeling sorry for himself. His head ached, the stitches over his eye hurt, so did his lips, and one of his teeth was loose. His hands were bandaged and worst of all he had lost an expensive pair of shoes. Not that they were both lost, but a pair of shoes had to be a pair and he'd lost one. He was proud of his shoes in a way he would never be proud of himself when he was sober. They were possibly the most important things he possessed to mask his wretchedness. Especially the brogues. He'd bought them at Trickers in Jermyn Street and had polished them assiduously every evening as he sat on the edge of the bed before, as he put it, turning in. And now he had lost them and Miss Midden was furious with him too. She'd been furious with him before but this time he knew her anger to be different. It was less coarsely abusive and far colder than he had ever known it to be.

The Major was a connoisseur of anger. People had been angry with him all his life, contemptuously angry and scoldingly angry, but nobody had ever hated him. There was nothing to him to hate. He was simply silly and weak and had never had the courage to do anything. Things were done to him and always had been. 'You bloody little wet,' his father had shouted at him time and time again, 'can't you stand on your own two feet?' And his mother hadn't been much better. Kinder, but perpetually scolding him and making him wash his face and hands or, more often, doing it for him. He had been brought up having things done to him and for him. He had tried to escape from his own dependence over and over again, but each time he had been defeated by fear and his own passivity. And with each defeat he had come to hate himself more. In the end he had run away to sea. He hadn't even done that properly. He had drifted away to sea as an assistant cook on an oiler

97

that made short runs between Rotterdam and small ports along the coast. The job hadn't lasted but it had taught him how to get work on ships and he had joined a cruise liner as a cabin steward. It was there that he had observed how the rich and elderly passengers behaved. It was on his third voyage that a retired army officer whose cabin he attended took a fancy to him. He was a Major, too, and had saved up for the cruise in the faint hope of finding a rich widow whom he wouldn't find too repulsive to marry. Instead he found the young Willy MacPhee and did things to him. It wasn't the first time. It had happened on ships and in ports. He was used to it, used to being beaten up and forced down onto his knees. But the Major was different. He was the genuine article, even if he was poor, and he knew how to dress. MacPhee could tell that by the labels sewn inside his jacket pockets and by the cloth. But most of all by his shoes. They too had come from Trickers and the leather gleamed with polish. He had five pairs, three brown ones, all brogues, and the one thing he wouldn't allow the steward MacPhee to do for him was polish them. 'I always do it first thing before turning in. Had to when I joined the army and I've made a habit of it ever since. So don't let me ever catch you touching them. Understand that, steward?'

'Yes sir,' MacPhee said in an attempt to adopt a military bearing himself. 'Understood, sir.'

In fact he did touch them and, when the real Major died of a heart attack in Barbados brought on by the unexpected vigour and unwonted sexual expertise of a very rich woman from Sunning-dale, he inherited them. Or stole them. He stole several suits, too, and hid them in his locker. It was at that moment MacPhee decided on his future career. He would join the army and have his own suits made for him and buy brogues at Trickers. When the ship docked in Southampton MacPhee went ashore for the last time and looked around for a recruiting office. The only one he found was for Royal Marines. The Sergeant had turned him down. 'You can go for a medical, lad, if you want it. But I shouldn't bother. You're not up to

98

standard. Not RM 1 anyway. Try the Army,' he had said with kindly contempt.

It was the first of many rejections. In the end he got a job as a manservant for a military family in Aldershot and spent three years studying the way officers talked and comported themselves. He picked up the lingo and heard stories he would be able to repeat as if they were his own. The need to become an officer, if only in his own mind, became an obsession with him. Outwardly subservient, he was inwardly rehearsing the confident manner and practising the assumptions of the military. On his evenings off he would go to the pubs and learn army lore from the NCOs and ordinary privates whose disrespect for most officers taught him even more. He learnt in particular to steer clear of the other ranks who would most likely see through his pretence and ask awkward questions. Officers didn't do that. They took you at face value and it was only necessary for a Captain or a 2nd Lieutenant to say sheepishly that he was in the Catering Corps for there to be no further questions asked. The Royal Army Service Corps was another useful foil. The danger lay among the better regiments, whose officers received deference. MacPhee had sufficient wiliness to know that he must never rank himself too highly, Major was quite sufficient, and that he must live among elderly people and gentlefolk who knew better than to be too inquisitive.

He observed all this in the Colonel's house, where occasionally some old Indian Army hand would call Mrs Longstead 'Memsahib' and junior officers were not encouraged to express their opinions too readily. And all the time the real Willy MacPhee seethed with envy and only very occasionally went on a bender, in every sense of the word, in London or Portsmouth. But that was a long time ago. Since then he had drifted about the country from one barracks town to another acquiring the patina of the man he would have liked to be. In the end he had found and been accepted by Miss Midden. The position suited him perfectly. The Middenhall was far from any large town and the Middens from overseas were too old or self-centred, and, like him, too dependent on Miss Midden to show more than superficial curiosity about the 'Major's' past. And until this weekend Miss Midden herself had accepted him without making her understanding of his pretence too obvious.

But now it was different and he was afraid. With painful care he undressed and put on his pyjamas and got into his narrow bed and wondered what to do to please her. He also wondered, though only slightly, where he had picked up the smell of dogshit. Presently he went to sleep. Eight inches below him the cause of the smell slept on. The Valium and the whisky still worked with the residual Toad to keep Timothy Bright unconscious. Only towards dawn did he stir slightly and briefly snore. To Major MacPhee, woken by the sound, those snores were an indication that he was far from well. It wasn't simply his bodily injuries that alarmed him. His hearing had evidently been affected too. He reassured himself by thinking he must have imagined what he had just heard, or even that his own snoring had woken him. He turned gingerly over and went back to sleep.

It was seven when he woke again, this time because his bladder was full. He got up and limped through to his little bathroom. When he came back and sat heavily down on the bed he thought for a moment there was something wrong with the mattress. It wasn't a very thick one but it had never had a hard lump in it before. The next second he was absolutely sure his brain had, as Miss Midden suggested, been damaged. There was a groan and the lump underneath him (it was Timothy Bright's shoulder) moved. Major MacPhee lay still, except for his racing heart, and listened in terror for another sound but all was quiet in the room. Unless . . . unless he could hear someone breathing. He could. There was someone under the bed, someone who had snored and groaned. Transfixed by fear he tried to think. He succeeded, though only in the most primitive form. Childish panic held him in its grip. For ten minutes he lay still listening to that dreadful breathing and tried to summon up the courage to get up and turn the light on and look under the bed. It was almost impossible but in the end he managed it. Very, very carefully he pulled the curtains – he wasn't going to turn the light on – then bent down and peered into the shadow under the bed.

The next moment he was upright and stumbling towards the door. The face he had just seen had fulfilled his worst fears. It was covered with blood and was ashen. There was a murdered man under his bed. Or one who hadn't yet been murdered but was dying. And the man was bollock-naked. The Major fled into the dining-room and was about to go through it to the hall and call Miss Midden when he was stopped in his tracks by the thought of her reaction. She'd told him to keep well clear of her in the morning and she had meant it. But he had a dying man in his room, or a naked man who'd been murdered. Major MacPhee's wits failed him. All his pretence dropped away from him and left him as childish and helpless as he had ever been in all his life. All he could see was that this was the ultimate in having things done to him. His own bruised and stitched face shrank in on itself, and he too was ashen. He had no resources to fall back on. Leaning against the wall he trembled uncontrollably. He trembled for twenty minutes before recovering sufficiently to sit down. Even then he couldn't think at all clearly. His sense of guilt swept up from its hiding-place in his mind, swept up and over him. He had never overcome it and now it flooded his whole being, intensifying his terror. Finally he got to his feet and went to the sideboard where there was a decanter of whisky. He had to have a drink. He had to. Major MacPhee sat at the dining-room table and drank.

He was still there when Miss Midden came down at nine o'clock. The decanter was empty, the Major had been sick on the floor, and now lay in a drunken stupor in his own vomit.

'You filthy bastard, you disgusting little phoney,' she shouted. The Major didn't hear her. 'Well, this is the bloody end for you. I'll have you out of the house before nightfall. By God, I will.' Then she turned and went through to the kitchen in a blazing temper and made a pot of very strong tea.

The Major didn't hear her. He was lost to a world that had too many horrors in it. But under the bed Timothy Bright heard those words and shivered. He was cold, his mouth tasted vile, his head hurt, and visions of a skinned pig flickered in his mind. In front of him a pair of bedroom slippers loomed menacingly and it took him some time to realize there were no feet in them and no legs above. Even so, there was something terribly threatening about them. They didn't belong to him. He didn't wear cheap felt bedroom slippers. His were leather and wool. Slowly moving his eyes away from the things he saw the legs of a wooden chair, the bottom of a door, a skirting-board, the lower quarter of a wardrobe with a mirror in it, pink floral wallpaper, and a brilliant shaft of sunlight that ran down it and a short way across the floor. None of these things made any sense to him. He had never seen them before and the angle at which he now saw them made them even more unrecognizable and meaningless. They intimated nothing to him. He did not know them or understand them. They were the adjunct to his sick horror, which was internal. But the words Miss Midden hurled at the supine MacPhee in the dining-room conveyed some meaning to him. He understood 'You filthy bastard, you disgusting little phoney' and 'This is the bloody end for you. I'll have you out of the house before nightfall. By God, I will.' Timothy Bright knew that very well. He lay under the bed and tried to come to terms with his condition.

It took him some time, another hour during which heavy footsteps in the passage and the slamming of a door echoed in his head. But finally, after some more muttered threats in the next room – Miss Midden had looked furiously down at the Major and had been tempted to kick him into wakefulness – he heard the front door slam and footsteps crunching on gravel.

Miss Midden, sick with disgust and revulsion that she should ever have taken the creature MacPhee under her wing, had left the house and, passing through the narrow gate in the garden wall, was striding across the open fell towards Carryclogs House. Sheep rose and scattered at her coming. Miss Midden hardly noticed them. She too was absorbed in a private world of anger and frustration. She was almost sorry the Major was still alive. She had seen him breathing. She was also totally unable to understand what had come over the dreadful little man. He'd behaved badly often enough on his so-called 'benders' in Glasgow, but in the house, her house, he had always remained sober and obsequiously well-mannered. And now this had happened. Her only conclusion was that he must be mad, mad and beyond help. Not that it was going to do him any good. She had enough problems with the people down at the Middenhall without adding his alcoholic mania to them. As soon as he was able to move she would have him out of the house, lock, stock and barrel, even if she had to do it at the point of her shotgun. Certainly he would be gone before nightfall.

As she came in sight of Carryclogs House, Miss Midden veered away. She had no intention of revealing her feelings or the state of affairs to Phoebe Turnbird. Her own sentimentality was burden enough and she wasn't going to allow Phoebe the pleasure of sympathizing with her. And gloating. At twelve o'clock Miss Midden sat down on an outcrop of rock overlooking the reservoir and ate the sandwiches she had brought with her. Then she lay back in the grass and looked up at the cloudless sky. At least it was clean and blue. Presently she dozed off, exhausted by her late night and her feelings.

Chapter 13

Sir Arnold Gonders hadn't had a pleasant day either. Or night. It had been nearly four by the time he left the Land Rover by the byre and walked up to the house where he was alarmed to see a light on in Auntie Bea's bedroom. 'That bloody woman,' he muttered bitterly and wondered what on earth, in addition to a massive dose of Valium in gin, was needed to keep her asleep at night. Avoiding the front door, he sneaked round to the study windows to let himself in. Sir Arnold crept upstairs and was presently fast asleep. He had done all that he could do. The rest was up to fate.

In fact it was in large measure up to Genscher. The Rottweiler had spent a ghastly night in the cellar desperately trying to deal with the insulating-tape muzzle. In his brutal attempt to prevent the dog from exercising any right to bark or, more dangerously, to bite when he was kicked in the scrotum, Sir Arnold, never a brave man, had made it almost impossible for Genscher to breathe as well, and the dog had spent hours trying to scratch the beastly tape off before evidently deciding that it was likely to lose its nose as well. Unable to whine or do anything at all constructive – backing away from its nose had done not the slightest good and had only resulted in its banging its bruised backside against the wall – it had dementedly climbed the steps to appeal for help by head-butting the cellar door. By seven o'clock the house was reverberating to the thud of one hundred and fifty pounds of maddened Rottweiler hurling itself against the door every few seconds. Even Mrs Thouless, usually a sound sleeper and one whose deafness prevented her from being included in the nastinesses of the household, was shaken to the conclusion that something very like an air raid was taking place in the vicinity. Since she had been brought up during the war in Little Kineburn under the very shadow of the great dam when it had been widely supposed the Germans would bomb the dam and loose the waters of the reservoir onto the tiny village, Mrs Thouless was particularly nervous about air raids. By 6.20 she was driven from her bed and went into the kitchen in her dressing-gown with a view to possibly taking refuge in the cellar. By then Genscher's efforts to attract attention had diminished slightly. All the same, the cellar door shuddered every time the dog launched itself at it. Mrs Thouless looked at the door. She wasn't at all sure about it. Then very cautiously she unlocked it and lifted the latch.

A moment later she knew with absolute certainty that there was no danger of being drowned or bombed in her bed. A far worse horror had bowled her over in the shape of a huge and demented Rottweiler with twenty metres of insulating tape wrapped in a grotesque black knot round its head. Mrs Thouless, never fond of dogs at the best of times and particularly wary of large German ones, found the experience and the apparition too much for her semi-deferential servility, and screamed. If anything more was required to send Genscher into an even greater state of panic, it was the sound of those screams. Nowhere indoors was safe. Only the outdoors would do. Without hesitation it hit the back door – and recoiled against Sir Arnold's golf clubs which clattered onto the tiled floor. A further crash, mingled with Mrs Thouless' Scottish screams, followed as the great beast, its head lolling under the weight of so much insulating tape, mistook the Welsh dresser for an easier door and hurtled into it. But Genscher's course was run. In the midst of cascading plates and saucers the Rottweiler, now notably short of oxygen and breathing stentoriously through its bloodied nostrils, slithered across Mrs Thouless' recumbent body and fell back into the darkness of the cellar.

Upstairs, the din in the kitchen had woken even the exhausted Chief Constable from a deep and welcome sleep. He sat up in bed to find Lady Vy in her dressing-gown, clutching his .38 Scott & Webley, marching towards the door with her black eyeshade pushed back menacingly on her forehead.

'What the fuck's going on?' he asked hoarsely.

'Another of your dumb tricks, no doubt,' said his wife, and pushed open the door with her foot. Downstairs Mrs Thouless' screams had redoubled and the crockery bouncing on the tiled floor suggested that someone was breaking up the entire kitchen.

It was this, far more than the housekeeper's screams for help, that enraged Lady Vy. 'Oh my pedestal plates,' she yelled and hurled herself down the stairs.

Behind her, hideous in a diaphanous nightie hastily tucked into a black leather skirt, Auntie Bea lurched out of her room in the mistaken belief that her beloved Vy was being battered by the revolting Sir Arnold. 'Let go of her,' she shouted as she entered the bedroom, girding her loins with the skirt she had so hastily put on. 'Let go, you vile creature. Haven't you done enough harm already with your foul ways?'

Sir Arnold, who was crouched over the side of the bed in the process of locating his slippers, was unable to make any suitable reply before finding himself enveloped in black leather as she hurled herself at him. For half a minute they wrestled on the bed before Auntie Bea pinned him down and, realizing her error, was wondering what to do next. What she could see of Sir Arnold, one eye squinting malevolently over the edge of the black skirt while the other was possibly savouring the delights that lay below it, did not make her anxious to relinquish the hold she had on him. To lend weight to this already weighty advantage there was the knowledge that she would never again be in a position to make him taste some of his own medicine. With a hideous relish she leered down at him and then with a swift hand thrust his entire head under the skirt.

It was an unwise indulgence. Sir Arnold, weakened as he was by the incomprehensible horrors of the weekend, was still sufficiently strong to resist the ghastly prospect of going down on his wife's lesbian lover, which was, he supposed, what she intended. In the folds of the black leather it was difficult to know, and the alternative – that she intended to smother him – was possibly even worse. The alternatives left the Chief Constable no choice. With all

106

the desperate strength of a man embedded in a heavy woman's crotch, Sir Arnold Gonders took an awful breath and thrust himself upwards. It was a hideous experience but for a moment he glimpsed daylight. His bald head broke through the waistband of the skirt, only to be plunged down into darkness as Auntie Bea, for the first time in her life experiencing the sort of pleasure a man, albeit a terrified and frantic one, could give, forced him back. For a few more minutes the mêlée went on as with each new surge by the panic-stricken Sir Arnold she felt the delights of dominance and Sir Arnold experienced the horrors.

When at last he subsided beneath her and it became obvious that he was beaten, she unwisely raised the skirt and smiled down at his flushed and sweating face. The Chief Constable, peering beyond her pudenda, saw that smile and, in one final assertion of his own diminished ego and just about everything else, jerked his head to one side and sank his teeth into her groin. That the teeth were not his own and that what he had hoped would be her groin wasn't hardly mattered to the Chief Constable. With a fearful yell Auntie Bea lifted from the bed, seemed to hover on a cushion of pain and then crashed back towards Sir Arnold. This time there was no mistaking her intent. She was going to murder the swine.

It was precisely at this moment that Lady Vy returned with the smoking revolver. She had come back to tell Sir Arnold that the bloody fellow in the cellar had somehow managed to escape after first winding yards of insulating tape around the family pet's head, and she was in no mood to find her husband quite evidently making very peculiar love to her Auntie Bea. More to the point her Auntie Bea, to judge from the look on her face, was finding the proceedings such a delicious agony of passion that her tongue was protruding from her mouth while she uttered grunts and cries of satisfaction. This sight was too much for Lady Vy following so closely on the discovery in the kitchen of Mrs Thouless lying full length on the floor by the cellar door with her dress strangely disarranged and moaning about some great beast. With a courage that came from years of conviction that she was morally superior to any servant and must of course demonstrate this in a crisis, particularly when she was armed with a loaded revolver, Lady Vy had stepped over Mrs Thouless and unhesitatingly fired into the cellar. This time Genscher had no doubt why it had been muzzled so horribly. While it hadn't actually read about the fate of the Tsar and his family, it did recognize that the cellar made an ideal killing-ground and that, having failed to hang him when they had the chance, the master and now the mistress were bent on shooting him. As the bullet ricocheted round the walls, Genscher whimpered silently and took refuge in one of the wine racks.

Lady Vy turned the light on and came slowly down the steps holding the revolver in front of her. 'Come out and face the music,' she shouted. 'I know you're down here. Come out or I'll fire.'

But the Rottweiler knew better than to move. It cringed at the very back of the stone wine rack and waited for death. Surprisingly it passed him by, and the next moment Lady Vy was hurrying up the steps again.

Now as she entered the bedroom she was too startled by what was taking place there to utter the message she had brought.

'Bea darling, how could you?' she asked piteously, and fanned her face with the muzzle of the revolver.

Auntie Bea turned an awful face towards her friend. 'I haven't finished yet,' she snarled, misinterpreting the past tense. 'But when I have –'

'You mustn't,' screamed Lady Vy. 'I won't let you demean yourself in this horrible way. And with him of all people.'

'What do you mean "with him"? I can't think of anyone else I want to –'

'I can't bear it, Bea. Don't say it. I won't listen.'

Sir Arnold, taking advantage of this interchange, managed to get an intake of air and squawked, 'Help, help me,' rather feebly.

Auntie Bea bore down on him. 'Die, you monster, die,' she shouted, and dragged the skirt tightly over his mottled face.

Lady Vy sank onto the floor beside the bed. 'Oh Bea darling, me darling, not him,' she sobbed.

Auntie Bea tried to understand this bizarre request. She knew Vy to be a submissive woman but she had never been asked to kill a loving friend before. The request struck her as being positively perverse and decidedly tasteless.

This was more than could be said for the Chief Constable. Fighting off death by suffocation in the folds of black leather, he would willingly have swapped places with his wife or anyone else who felt inclined to die in such a dreadful fashion. And as for being tasteless that was not what he'd have called it either. If anything quite the reverse, but that was not of much concern to him at the moment. Staring into the black hell that was Auntie Bea's idea of bas couture, he was appalled at the thought of his imminent obituary. It would read like something in one of the magazines God was always telling him not to borrow from the Porn Squad's store of confiscated material. He couldn't for the life of him imagine how the *Sun* and the *News of the World* editorial staff would find words sufficiently ambiguous to satisfy both the Press Complaints Commission and the salacious appetites of most of their readers. Not that he had more than a passing interest in his post-mortem reputation. He was dying a terrible death, if not at the hands at least at the legs of a woman he had particular reason to loathe. As he began to pass out he was vaguely aware of Vy's voice.

'But you swore to me you hated men, Bea,' she screamed in a fit of hysterical jealousy. 'You promised me you would never ever, ever, touch a man and now look what you're doing.'

'I'm trying to,' Auntie Bea screamed back, grappling with the skirt, 'but he isn't dead yet.'

'Isn't dead yet?' repeated Lady Vy in a voice so vacuous that even the Chief Constable wasn't sure he had heard right. What did the fucking woman think he was doing? Having a whale of a time?

Finally it dawned on Lady Vy that the situation was not as she supposed. 'Oh God, no, no, you mustn't, Bea darling,' she bawled. 'Don't you see what this will do to us?'

'I don't care what it does to us,' Auntie Bea shouted back, 'all I care right now is what it does to him. You should see what the monster's done to me.'

The invitation was too much for the distraught Lady Vy. 'Show me, oh show me, darling,' she said, and hurled herself onto what the Chief Constable had come to regard as his deathbed. As she scrabbled at Auntie Bea's curious skirt his face emerged, almost as black as the garment itself. Sir Arnold gulped relatively fresh air and stared through bloodshot, bulging eyes up into the face of his moronic wife. For the first time in twenty-two years it had some appeal for him. And what she was doing had even more. Lady Vy was dragging the skirt off Bea's legs. For a moment it seemed she was about to join him in the filthy thing but Aunt Bea's attention had switched. She was less interested in killing her assailant than in finding out if she was likely to bleed to death from his bite. She fell back onto the bed and the Chief Constable and Lady Vy were just seeing what he had done, when there was a sound from the bedroom doorway.

'I've come to give my notice,' Mrs Thouless announced in a loud voice. 'I'm not staying in a house where there are such strange goings-on. I mean, begging your pardon, ma'am, for interrupting but that thing downstairs has come out of the cellar again and it isn't a fit sight for a decent woman to see first thing in the morning.'

With an insouciance that came from years of dealing with embarrassing moments and awkward servants, Lady Vy flounced off the bed and advanced on the poor housekeeper. 'How dare you come in here without knocking?' she demanded.

To the Chief Constable, peering over Aunt Bea's knee with all the enthusiasm of a man temporarily reprieved from death and one who no longer cared with any real intensity what his public reputation might be, Mrs Thouless' intervention was a Godsend. On the other hand, if Lady Vy came all high and mighty, the damned housekeeper might walk out of the house straightaway. It was not a prospect to be borne. 'Dear Mrs Thouless,' he called out, 'you mustn't leave us.'

From the doorway the housekeeper became aware of the very

110

dubious nature of her employers' marital arrangements. She stared short-sightedly at Sir Arnold's head and then at Auntie Bea and finally up at Lady Vy. 'Ooh mum,' she said, all trace of a Scotch accent entirely gone. 'Ooh mum I don't know what . . .'

Lady Vy forestalled her. 'Now pull yourself together, Mrs T.,' she said. 'I know it's been a trying morning and you've had a long weekend but there is no need to overdramatize. Just go downstairs and make us all a nice pot of tea.'

'Yes, mum, if you say so, mum,' said Mrs Thouless with her jaw sagging, and went off down the landing utterly bemused.

Lady Vy turned her attention back to more urgent matters and picked up the revolver again. 'I must say,' she said with a renewed air of social confidence, 'it's come to a pretty pass when the staff march into bedrooms without knocking. I can't think what the country's coming to.'

On the bed Auntie Bea responded to the call of her upbringing. 'My dear,' she said, 'I have exactly the same trouble at Washam. It's almost impossible to get anyone to stay and they demand quite exorbitant wages and two nights off a week.' And with a final obscene flick of her skirt she signalled to the Chief Constable that he could go now.

Sir Arnold scrambled off the bed and hurried through to the bathroom and was presently busy with a toothbrush and some cold water. There was no hot. There had been no time to have the tank repaired. He was staring into the bathroom mirror and wondering what message God had intended to have put him through such an awful ordeal, when it dawned on him that Mrs Thouless had said something important. What was it? '. . . that thing has come out of the cellar again . . .' What thing? And why wasn't whatever it was a fit sight for a decent woman to see? For the first time that morning the Chief Constable suddenly saw things in a longer perspective of time than the previous five minutes. Someone had been down into the cellar and found the young bastard gone. Of course. That explained everything, and in particular Auntie Bloody Bea's murderous assault on him. She had found her accomplice had disappeared and had come upstairs to kill him in revenge. Or something. The Chief Constable's late night and fearful weekend had taken their toll of his capacity for rational thought. All he could be certain of was that he was in an isolated house with three women, one of whom he detested, another he despised, and a third who was presently making a pot of tea in the kitchen. Of the three only Mrs Thouless held even the faintest of charms for him and they were entirely of a practical order. He was about to hurry from the bathroom and get down to the relative safety of the kitchen when he remembered the shot. And Vy had taken the bloody gun downstairs with her. What the hell had she been firing at? Without thinking clearly Sir Arnold stumbled out of the bathroom to find his wife swabbing Auntie Bea's groin with eau-de-Cologne and discussing the advisability of a tetanus shot.

'Or rabies,' said Lady Vy, looking villainously at her husband.

Sir Arnold gave up all thought of questioning her. Instead he went down to the kitchen to see for himself what had been going on there. He found Mrs Thouless, quite recovered and restored to her own domestic role, unwinding the demoralized Rottweiler's insulated muzzle. Sir Arnold sipped his cup of tea and cursed the dog, his wife, his wife's murderous lover, and most of all the swine who had deposited a drugged lout in his bed.

Chapter 14

After a while Sir Arnold concentrated his thoughts on some method of getting his revenge. He could confront that bloody lesbian bitch upstairs and demand to know what the hell she had hoped to achieve by having the lout brought to the Old Boathouse. It didn't make sense. On the other hand she had just tried to murder him and had very nearly succeeded. Would have succeeded if Vy hadn't, for once, come in at the right moment. So fucking Bea had to be mad. Mad, insane, out of her tiny, way off her trolley and a homocidal maniac. (The Chief Constable hadn't got the word wrong: 'homocidal' was exact.) And in addition she had an accomplice. He had no doubt about that either. She couldn't possibly have left the Old Boathouse and driven somewhere to find the young lout and drug him, and then driven back and carried him upstairs on her own. That was out of the question. She had been drinking with Vy all evening. He'd asked Vy that and she'd told him the truth. He was sure of that. His wife had been just as astonished to find the bastard in bed with her as he'd been himself. So there was someone out there – and here the Chief Constable's mind, never far from paranoia, turned lurid with fury. And fear. A conspiracy had been hatched to destroy him. Hatched? Hatched wasn't strong enough, and besides it was too reminiscent of eggs and hens and things that were natural. There was absolutely nothing natural about drugging some young bastard to the eyeballs before stripping him naked and shoving him into a respectable Chief Constable's marital bed. It was an act of diabolical unnaturalness, of pure evil and malice aforethought. Hatched it wasn't. This vile act had been plotted, premeditated and planned to destroy his reputation. If this little lot had got out he'd have been ruined. If it got out now he'd still be ruined. In fact now that he came to think of it, he was in a far worse position than before because he had beaten the young bastard over the head and had kept him tied up in the cellar for twenty-four hours. He might even have killed the sod. For all he knew the bastard was dead and at this very moment under that narrow bed at the Midden rigor mortis might have set in.

A cold sweat broke out on the Chief Constable's face and he went through to his study to try to think. Sitting there at his desk feeling like death he searched his mind for a motive. Blackmail was the first and most obvious. But why, in God's name, should the beastly Bea want to blackmail him? There was no need. The woman had enough money of her own, or so he had always understood from Vy. Mind you, Vy had the brain of a mentally challenged peahen but she was good at smelling incomes. One of her upper-class virtues. No, Auntie Bea's motive had to be something else. Pure hatred for him? She had that all right. In spades. Not that the Chief Constable cared. A great many people hated him. He was used to being hated. He rather liked it, in fact. It gave him a sense of power and authority. In his mind hatred went with respect and fear. To be feared and respected gave him a sense of worth. It assured him that he meant something.

On the other hand, he was damned if he could see what anything else meant. There had to be some other more sinister motive. No one would go to all this trouble simply to ruin him. No, Auntie Bea was merely a willing accomplice, a subordinate who could open gates and keep Genscher quiet. In all likelihood she had been blackmailed, or at least persuaded, into acting as the insider. She wouldn't have needed much persuading either. Yes, that was much more like it. There was somebody out there — here the Chief Constable's horizons expanded to include every villain in Twixt and Tween — who had deliberately set out to destroy him. Or, and this seemed a more rational explanation, to hold him to ransom by threatening to expose him. That was much more likely. Well, that was going to take some doing now. Unless, of course, that young bloke was dead, in which case the fat would really be in the fire.

114

Again the cold sweat broke out on his pallid face. The Chief Constable gave up trying to think. He was too exhausted. Making sure that Vy and Bea were now in the kitchen having breakfast, he went upstairs and climbed into bed. He needed sleep.

He didn't get much. Half an hour later his wife stormed into the room and woke him. She was in a filthy mood. 'You disgust me,' she told him. 'Can't you leave anyone alone?'

'Leave anyone alone? I never went anywhere near the bitch. She was the one who attacked me.'

'You really expect me to believe that? Bea has an aversion to men. She finds them repulsive.'

'The feeling is mutual,' said the Chief Constable. 'And I don't care what she finds repulsive, she's got no right to go round attempting to murder people.'

'You must have provoked her in some way. She's a very lovely, peaceful person.'

Sir Arnold looked at her with bloodshot, unbelieving eyes. 'Peaceful?' he snarled. 'Peaceful? That woman? You've got a bloody odd idea what peace is like. There I was hunting for my slippers – that's all I was doing, trying to find my slippers under the bed – and without the slightest warning she hurled herself on me.'

'I don't believe it. But I haven't come here to argue with you. Bea and I are leaving now. We're going to Tween. You can come when you feel up to it.'

'Like never,' Sir Arnold thought, but he didn't say it.

'And while we're on the subject, I suppose you know that young man has escaped from the cellar. He wrapped insulating tape round Genscher's nose and got away.'

'Really?' said Sir Arnold, trying to think how he could use this new interpretation of events. 'The bloke escaped after wrapping tape round Genscher's nose? How very peculiar.'

'He got through the hatch,' said Lady Vy. 'You can't have tied him up very well. Thank goodness the whisky and the Valium didn't kill him.'

'How very remarkable,' said Sir Arnold. 'You don't think the people who brought him could have realized they'd made a mistake and moved him to the place they'd intended?'

'How the hell would I know what to think?' Lady Vy answered and looked at her husband suspiciously. 'And you look as if you hadn't had much sleep, come to that. You should take a look at yourself. You're not at all a picture of health.'

'I don't feel it,' said the Chief Constable, 'and you wouldn't either if you'd been half suffocated by that beastly Bea. And for Heaven's sake, don't mention anything about the fellow in the cellar to her.'

'You don't think she doesn't know already? Honestly, you are a fool. With all that noise going on? She hasn't said anything because she's too tactful. She just thought you'd been beating me up. Mrs Thouless saw the blood too.'

The Chief Constable sat wearily up in bed. This was the sort of news he least wanted. 'Has she told you that?' he stammered.

'Not in so many words, but she asked what to do with the rug in your study with the blood on it. And of course you had to leave a bloodstained bedside lamp by the desk.'

'Dear God,' said the Chief Constable. 'It's a wonder she hasn't sold the story to the *Sun* already.'

'Since she didn't see anything else she can't be certain what has been going on.'

'Not the only one round here,' said the Chief Constable and slipped miserably back under the bedclothes. He felt like death.

So did Timothy Bright. After lying under the bed listening for sounds of movement in the house and not hearing any, he crawled slowly and awkwardly out and tried to get to his feet. He almost succeeded. He got halfway up before falling over and banging his head against the edge of the chair on which the Major had folded his clothes. The chair toppled over and Timothy Bright's scalp wound began to bleed again, this time onto the Major's tweed jacket and his natty little waistcoat. Timothy Bright lay there for a bit trying to think where he was or how he came to be naked and cold and hungry and why his mouth tasted like . . . He didn't know what his mouth tasted like. He tried again to get up by clutching the bed, then slumped down on it and lay there. Thought was returning. To get warmer he pulled the duvet over him and felt slightly better. Only slightly. A terrible thirst drove him to try to stand up again. He succeeded and stood, wobbling a little, listening.

The house was silent. Nothing moved. The sun shone in the window and outside he could see a patch of vegetable garden with some broad beans and a row of twigs for peas. Beyond it a wooden shed and a copse of tall trees and a drystone wall with more trees behind it. There was no sign of life, apart from a thrush breaking a snail's shell on a concrete path. A cat appeared round the pea twigs and stopped, its eyes fixed on the thrush. Then it turned and slid round the broad beans and crept forward with the utmost stealth. For a moment Timothy Bright was almost transfixed by the drama, but the thrush flew off and the cat relaxed. Only then did he notice the blood on the pillow and the duvet. It was fresh blood. He was bleeding. Oh God, he had to do something about it.

The bathroom door was open and he went through to it and grabbed a towel and wiped his hair with it. There was a lot of blood on the towel and when he looked in the mirror over the washbasin he didn't recognize himself. His face was covered with dried blood, his hair was matted with it and his chest was scratched and horribly bruised. In an instant the vision of that skinned pig returned and he lurched back. The Major's bathroom was not a large one, was in fact merely a shower-room with a little shelf under the shaving-mirror on which he kept his bottle of Imperial Russian eau-de-Cologne (at least the bottle was genuine, he had pinched it from a rich friend, but he had long ago used up the contents and refilled it with 4711). Timothy lurched backwards into the shower curtain, a plastic one to which the Major had neatly sewn a rather pretty piece of Laura Ashley floral material, and as he tripped he clutched the shelf. The Imperial Russian Cologne bottle fell into the basin and broke. It was followed by the shaving-brush,

117

the Major's cut-throat razor which he used very carefully to trim his hair before dyeing it, his toothbrush and the scissors that were necessary for his moustache. But it was the cut-throat that threw Timothy Bright. It brought to mind a scene from a nightmare, the nightmare that had become central to his being, that of a man with black shiny hair in the back room of a bar who had sliced the end of his nose and talked about piggy-chops and what was going to happen to Timothy Bright if he didn't do something terrible. It brought to mind that terrifying photograph of the pig. Somewhere still deeper within him it may even have rekindled the forgotten horror of Old Og's ferret, Posy, with blood on its snout after killing the bought rabbit. In his panic reaction he fell back into the shower taking the curtain with him and sat with blood running down the curtain and the wall. There he sat crying, with tears and blood running down his face. He cried noiselessly. The house was silent again.

It remained so through the midday and into the afternoon. It was only then that Major MacPhee rose from his vomit and on all fours crawled out into the hall. The silence suited him too. It seemed to indicate that Miss Midden had gone down to the Middenhall and that he could use the upstairs bathroom and not go through his room past the body under the bed to clean himself up. Never, except by military convention, a very clean man, he felt the need to wash at least his face and neck before getting dressed . . . He had reached the bathroom and had turned the tap on before it dawned on him that his only clothes were in his bedroom and to get them he would have to go in there. He held the edge of the basin and sensibly didn't look at his face in the mirror but bowed his head over the warm water and dipped his face into it very gently several times. The stitches above his eye stung. He washed his hands and somehow his neck with soap. He emptied the basin and dipped his face into the water again and very carefully used a flannel to clean it.

All this took time and had to be done slowly and deliberately.

His physical state demanded it. He felt awful, more awful than he could ever remember feeling in his life, even after a particularly frightening experience with a sadistic sailor from Latvia in Rotterdam who had threatened to kill him with a knife and had cut him, very slowly, right across the chest. But it was his mental state that was worse. He had to get rid of the body before Miss Midden found it and called the police. He had to clear up the mess in the dining-room. And she might come back at any moment. He took a clean towel from the cupboard and dried himself and took it downstairs with him, holding onto the banisters as he went. But when he came to the bedroom door his terror returned and it was only the thought of Miss Midden and the police that compelled him to open it and peer in.

What he saw held him rigid. His clothes were on the floor beside the overturned chair and there was blood on them. There was more blood on the duvet and the pillow was bright with the stuff. The Major whimpered and looked frantically round the room. Finally he crept in and made his way to the chest of drawers for a shirt, all the time keeping his eye on the door of his little bathroom. The man was evidently in there. Somehow he got the shirt on and had opened his wardrobe for a clean pair of trousers and a jacket when he heard a noise in the bathroom. It was a strange and horrible sound, a sobbing moan and a groan. The Major grabbed the clothes he needed, took a pair of shoes from the rack, and hurried into the dining-room to finish dressing. The situation was almost worse now than it had been when he thought the young man was dead. He might just have got rid of a dead body, taken it out and hidden it somewhere before deciding what next to do. With a live man that was impossible. To take his thoughts off the subject for a moment he went out to the kitchen in his socks, fetched some water and a rag from the sink, cleared up the vomit on the floor, and put the empty decanter back into the sideboard. He could always fill it with whisky again. Miss Midden seldom drank the stuff and perhaps she wouldn't miss it for the time being. He had just finished and was back in the kitchen when he heard footsteps in the yard.

Miss Midden had returned.

Chapter 15

Miss Midden had woken from her snooze under the clear blue sky and had got to her feet with a refreshed determination. She wasn't going to go on living like this. She wasn't going to have her weekends spoilt by a wretched sponger like MacPhee, for that's what he was, no more than a sponger on her hospitality and good nature. She had had enough of him. But her feelings went deeper than that. She had had enough of looking after the Middenhall and the spongers down there, for that was really what they were too, arrogant, self-centred, spoilt spongers who had always had servants to do things for them and who, if she hadn't been the sort of person she was, would have driven her into the role of a servant too. MacPhee (she was no longer prepared to use his phoney rank – he was MacPhee and that was probably a false name too) had had his uses with them. He made up a foursome at bridge, he listened to their repeated stories about Africa and the good life they had enjoyed there and he was happy to sympathize with their views about the way things had deteriorated everywhere. Miss Midden wasn't. 'The good old days' – their good old days – had been other people's bad old days with long hours and miserable wages and the brutal assumption that the lower classes, black or white, were there to be despised and set apart. And they grumbled. Oh God, how those people grumbled. They grumbled about everything, particularly the National Health Service to which they had contributed not one penny during their spoilt, distant lives. Old Mr Lionel Midden had been furious when he had to wait to have a hip replacement and had come back from the Tween General Hospital complaining about the bad food and the fact that the nurses had refused to call him 'Sir'. And all he had ever been was a so-called recruiting officer for some mining company in Zambia, which he still insisted on calling Northern Rhodesia. Mrs Consuelo McKoy, who had lived for thirty-five years in California until her husband died and she found he had left her nothing at all in his will and had in fact spent his last few years gambling his fortune away, deliberately, she said, to spite her, was always saying how much better things were done in the United States. 'People are so hospitable and friendly there. Over here there is no friendliness at all.' Miss Midden particularly resented that 'over here'. It suggested that Mrs McKoy was an American herself, whereas she had been born in London where her father had had a grocer's shop in Hendon. She had married Corporal McKoy of the US Airforce during the War and had lorded it over the family on the occasional trip to Europe. Miss Midden could remember her driving up to the Midden in an absurdly large Lincoln Continental Bob McKoy had borrowed from a business associate (he had gone into electrical engineering at the end of the war) in London. Now she demanded to be driven in the old Humber staff car when she wanted to do a little shopping in Stagstead and insisted on sitting in the back while Miss Midden drove.

It was the same with all of them. Almost all. Mrs Laura Midden Rayter, who as long ago as 1956 had insisted on keeping her maiden name when she married, was different. She helped with the washing-up and vacuumed her own room and generally made herself useful about the place. Arthur Midden, who had been a dentist in Hastings and who suffered bouts of depression when he did bizarre charcoal drawings of gaping mouths as a form of therapy, actually paid for his room and board.

'I don't like to inflict myself on you, my dear,' he said when he first came to the Middenhall, 'but it's peaceful up here and I need company since Annie died. You don't make many friends in dentistry and Hastings has deteriorated with so many young people injecting themselves there. I never liked giving injections and the sight of hypodermics still unsettles me.' No, they weren't all spongers or complainers, but most of them were. Besides, Miss Midden had never liked the Middenhall even as a child. It was dauntingly ugly and she had shared her father's distaste for it. She had only agreed to take over to allow him to go into a retirement home. The house and its inmates had broken him. Miss Midden had given him a few years in which to sit and read in his own room in Scarborough and nurse his ailments. Even so she resented the treatment he had suffered at the hands of the so-called family.

Now, stepping out across the rough grass and avoiding the wet places where the sedge grass grew, she knew the time had come to get out herself. She would see her cousin, Lennox, who had taken over as the family solicitor from his father, Uncle Leonard, and tell him she was no longer prepared to take responsibility for the place. He would have to find someone else. She would keep the farmhouse, possibly letting out to summer visitors to earn some money, but she wouldn't live there. She would go away and find work of some sort. She had a small amount of money put away, not enough to live on but enough to allow her time to make a different life for herself. With this sense of resolution, the decision made, she walked into the yard and steeled herself to give MacPhee his marching orders. But as she entered the kitchen and saw him she knew that something far worse than a hangover afflicted him He stood staring at her with terrified eyes and he was trembling all over. For a moment she thought he might be dying. She had never seen such palpable terror in anyone before. The man had ceased to exist as a man or even an animal. He had become something amorphous, almost liquefied by fear. For a few seconds his state kept her silent. Then she said, 'What in God's name is the matter?'

MacPhee held on to the kitchen table and opened his mouth. His lips quivered, his mouth moved jerkily, he gibbered.

Miss Midden pulled a chair out and pushed him down onto it. 'I said what's the matter,' she said harshly. 'Answer me.'

The Major raised anguished eyes to her. 'It's in my room,' he gasped.

'What's in your room?' She was almost certain now that he had delirium tremens. 'Tell me what's in your room?'

'A man. He's been murdered. There's blood everywhere. On my bed, on the duvet, on my clothes.'

'Nonsense,' Miss Midden snapped. 'You've been having delusions, drinking all that whisky.'

The Major shook his head – or it shook uncontrollably. It was impossible to tell which. 'It's true, it's true. He was under my bed and his face was covered with blood. He was naked.'

'Bollocks. You've just poisoned yourself with alcohol. A naked man with blood all over his face under your bed? Poppycock.'

'I swear it's true. He was there.'

'But he's not there now? Of course he isn't. Because he never was.'

'I swear –'

But Miss Midden had had enough of his terror. 'Get up,' she ordered. 'Get up and show me.'

'No, I can't.'

'Get up, get off that chair. You're going to show me this man.'

The Major tried to rise and flopped back. Miss Midden seized him by the collar of his jacket and dragged him to his feet. But he just shook and whimpered.

'You sicken me,' she said and let go. He slumped down into the chair. 'All right, I'll go myself.'

She moved across the kitchen but the Major spoke. 'For God's sake be careful. I'm telling you the truth. He's in the bathroom. He could be dangerous.'

Miss Midden looked back at him with utter contempt and went out into the passage. She entered the dining-room and crossed to the door of the Major's bedroom and opened it. Then she stopped. Blood. There was blood on the bed, a lot of blood. And on the clothes by the fallen chair. Miss Midden felt her own fear and her own horror. But not for long. She stepped back across the dining-room and went into the little office where she kept her twelve-bore. Whatever had happened in the bedroom and whoever was in the bathroom, and for all she knew there was more than one person there, was going to have to face a loaded shotgun. She put two cartridges into the breech and closed the gun. Then she went back. As she entered the dining-room she saw the open window. Alert now to the reality of the break-in, she noticed the mud on the floor under the window. She crossed to the bedroom door and looked round carefully before stepping in, holding the shotgun pointed at the bathroom door. Two yards away she stopped. 'All right,' she said in a loud and surprisingly steady voice. 'Come out of there. Come out. I'm standing here with a twelve-bore so open that door and come out slowly.'

Nothing happened. Miss Midden hesitated and listened intently. She heard nothing. She moved back towards the dining-room and then hurried through to the kitchen. 'You come with me now,' she told MacPhee, and this time he stood up. Some of her courage had communicated itself to him and besides the sight of the shotgun was persuasive. He came across the room and she ushered him through into the bedroom.

'What do you want me to do?' he asked with a low quivering voice.

Miss Midden indicated the bathroom door. 'Open it. And then stand aside,' she ordered.

'But . . . but . . . suppose . . .' he began.

'Don't suppose anything. Just open that bloody door and stand aside,' she said. 'And if anyone is fool enough to try anything they are going to get two barrels.' She said this loudly. 'Now do it.'

Major MacPhee went forward and turned the door handle and shoved. The door flew open and he scuttled away into a corner of the bedroom and put his hands over his ears. Miss Midden had the gun up to her shoulder and was moving cautiously towards the bathroom. It was very small and now she saw the dirty feet protruding from the shower. She moved round to the side. Still keeping the shotgun to her shoulder she peered in. On the plastic tray of the shower, with the curtain crumpled beside him, was huddled a young man. His face was covered with dried blood, his chest was bloody too and water dripping from the shower had made a patch of clear skin with a runnel down past his navel. But he was alive. His eyes staring wildly at her from the mask of blood told her that. Alive and frightened, almost as frightened as the Major. All the men seemed to be frightened. But this one was wounded and his fear was understandable.

'Who are you?' she asked and lowered the gun. The question seemed to give the young man comfort. There might even have been hope in his eyes now. 'I said who are you? What's your name?'

'Timothy,' said Timothy Bright.

'Can you stand up? If you can't, just lie there and I'll call an ambulance.'

The fear returned to Timothy Bright's eyes but he got to his feet and stood naked in the shower.

'Now come through here,' she said. 'Come through here and sit on the bed.'

Timothy Bright stepped out of the shower and did as he was told. In the light of the room Miss Midden could see him more clearly. He was quite a young man and well-built. She leant the shotgun against the corner of the Major's bookcase. She had no fear of the man who called himself Timothy.

'How did you get yourself in this state?' she asked, and parted the matted hair to get a better look at the wound on his head.

'I don't know.'

'Someone beat you up? Must have done.' The scalp wound wasn't so bad after all, and scalp wounds always bled profusely.

'I don't know.'

'All right, lie down and let me have a look at your eyes.' She looked into each one, turning his head towards the window. 'And you don't know how this happened?'

'I don't remember anything.'

'Concussion. I'll call the ambulance. You need to be in hospital. And I'll call the police too.'

She pulled the duvet over him and was about to go through to the hall where the phone was when Timothy Bright stopped her. He had suddenly recalled what the piggy-chops man with the razor had said: 'One more thing you got to remember. You go anywhere near the police, even go past a cop shop or think of picking up the phone, like your mobile, you won't just get piggy-chops. You won't have a fucking cock to fuck with again first. No balls, no prick. And that's for starters. You'll have piggy-chops days later. Slowly. Very slowly. Get that in your dumb fucking head now.' And Timothy Bright had. Even now, when he had no idea what had happened to him or where he was or who this woman was who had forced him out of the little bathroom at the point of a double-barrelled shotgun and was saying he might have concussion and ought to be in hospital, that terrible threat was as vivid as it had been at the moment it was uttered. And the cut-throat razor had quivered where the man with slicked-back hair had thrown it so expertly.

'No, not the police, not the police or an ambulance,' he gasped, 'I'm all right. I really am. All right.'

Miss Midden turned back to the bed and looked at him. 'No ambulance? No police? And you say you're all right? That's one thing you're not. Are you on the run or something?' There was very little sympathy in her voice now. Timothy Bright shook his head.

From the corner the Major eyed him intently. He was a connoisseur of little sordid criminals and their fears. He couldn't make this one out at all. Snob. Upper crust. Not your standard lager lout. This one had background. Even in his naked and filthy extremis this one carried a degree of assurance the Major would never begin to achieve. Envy intensified his insight, the social insight that had been his chief weapon in the battle to keep his head above the raging maelstrom of his own self-contempt. This one wasn't all right, but what he was the Major couldn't tell. Not queer either. He'd have spotted that straightaway. But he wasn't all right.

Miss Midden stepped back into the room and picked up the gun she had left against the bookcase. Standing over the bed she asked, 'Just what has been going on? You'd better tell me or I am going to phone for the police. Spit it out, sonny. What have you been up to?'

Timothy Bright fought to find a plausible explanation. He didn't know what he had been up to. Perhaps he did have concussion. He couldn't remember anything coherently. Something to do with going to Spain. Something about Uncle Benderby. He'd been on his bike. 'I had a motorbike,' he said, and tried to remember.

'Go on. You had a motorbike. What happened to it?'

Timothy Bright had no idea.

'How did you get in here then?' Miss Midden demanded.

But again he had no answer for her.

'You may not know but I'm going to find out. Me or the police. It's up to you.'

Timothy Bright lay on the bed and whimpered.

'Men,' said Miss Midden. 'Pathetic.' She turned on her heel and walked out of the room. In the dining-room she looked at the mud on the floor and then at the open window. She went to the front door and out onto the gravel and looked at the flower-bed under the window. There were footmarks there, and some white petunias the Major had planted had been crushed by someone's feet.

Miss Midden went back into the house and tried the sitting-room on the other side of the hall. There was nothing there to indicate anyone had been into it. Nothing in the hall either. She mounted the stairs and looked into every room. There was not a sign of any disturbance. And there were no clothes to be found anywhere. Her office was just as it had always been. And the kitchen. Not a trace of clothes. She went out into the back yard and walked slowly round the house, even looking into the byre and the shed but there were no jeans or shoes or shirt. Everything was just as she had left it. Mystified, she went back into the house and was about to go into the dining-room when she heard voices. She stopped. The Major was asking questions.

Miss Midden slipped into the room to listen.

Chapter 16

This was a very different Major from the one she had left cowering in the corner. And what he was doing was most useful. He was talking sympathetically to the young man. MacPhee's feelings, as shallow as they were squalid, were soon calmed and now that the immediate danger was over he was looking for some advantage from the situation.

'You've been done over really badly so that's why you can't remember,' he said, 'but it'll come back to you. I have had the same experience myself. Only two days ago I was cycling along minding my own business when this tractor came out without looking. I had to have six stitches and I couldn't remember even having them. You probably came off your motorbike . . I hope you were wearing a crash helmet. You'd have been killed otherwise. Something must have gone through it. Ever so dangerous, motorbikes are. What sort is yours?'

'A Suzuki.'

'Is that a very fast one?'

'I've done a hundred and forty on her,' Timothy said.

'Oh, how could you? I mean that's twice the speed limit. You were lucky the cops didn't time you. Is that why you don't want the police?'

Timothy Bright jumped at the excuse. 'Yes. I don't want to lose my licence.'

'And what about your family? They'll want to know you're all right. Where do they live?'

'They've got a place . . . I don't know,' said Timothy Bright.

Miss Midden tiptoed away. The Major was earning his keep after all. Naked and injured young men were his cup of tea. She needed a real cup herself and time to think what to do. Her first impulse to call the emergency services had evaporated. The young man Timothy wasn't as badly hurt as he looked. He was talking quite clearly, was probably suffering from mild concussion and not the fractured skull she had first feared.

She had other reasons for not involving the authorities. She had never got on with the people in County Hall whose gainful employment consisted in finding reasons for being there. There had been a man and a woman from the Health Department who had calmly walked into the kitchen down at the Middenhall on the assumption the place was an old people's home and in the altercation that followed had accused her of not having a licence to run a nursing home and having no authorization to ... Miss Midden had chased them off the premises and had got her cousin Lennox, the solicitor, to issue a formal complaint to the County Council on the grounds of trespass. Not that that had deterred the officials. A man from the Fire Department had arrived shortly afterwards, this time with an official document declaring his right to inspect the 'Middenhall Guest House or Hotel' to ensure that it had the requisite fire escapes and internal fire doors. Miss Midden had disabused him of the notion that it was anything more than a private house and had abused him personally in the process. He had gone away with a good many fleas in his ear and Lennox Midden had had to write another letter. Another time the Twixt and Tween Water Board, claiming jurisdiction over all water in the county, in particular the stream that fed the artificial lake Black Midden had constructed, had sent inspectors to check that no noxious substances were flowing from it down to the reservoir. The only noxious substance they had encountered had been Miss Midden herself. Again Lennox had been forced to point out that the lake had been constructed in 1905 and that any noxious chemicals entering the reservoir were almost certainly coming from the slurry of a dairy farmer six miles away on the Lampeter Road.

Altogether Miss Midden had had interfering busybodies in official positions up to the eyeballs. And when it came to the police her feelings were incandescent. They had chased old Buffalo across the lawn and had held him in the cells at Stagstead overnight after roughing him up and accusing him of drunken driving. And that damned Chief Constable had tried to fence the common land known as Folly Moss for his own private use. She had fought him over the issue and won, just as she had won in court over Buffalo Midden. She'd won and humiliated the corrupt brute. He'd be only too delighted to have his men in the house asking questions and poking their noses into her private affairs. They'd want to know where the Major had got his injuries and . . . No, the last people she wanted to bring in were the police. And in any case the young man clearly didn't want them anywhere near him. He had been terrified by the prospect of her calling them. Presumably he was some sort of criminal, or a junkie. Miss Midden sat at the kitchen table and poured herself another cup of tea.

She was still sitting there an hour later when the Major reappeared with the news that Timothy Bright had cleaned himself up in the bathroom and said he was hungry and could he have something to drink. Miss Midden turned an angry eye on him and said, 'Water.' She got up and opened the Aga and got out some eggs to make an omelette. She was feeling hungry herself and the Major definitely needed food. He looked ghastly and he deserved to. And now it appeared he was upset because the young man had broken an eau-de-Cologne bottle in his washbasin and had torn the shower curtain. Pathetic. But he had managed to wheedle some more information out of the young man. 'He's some sort of financier in the City. He doesn't remember where exactly.'

'Financier? Financier, my foot!' said Miss Midden, whose ideas were distinctly old-fashioned and who imagined financiers to be middle-aged men in dark pin-striped suits.

'A yuppie sort,' the Major went on. 'They sit in front of computer screens and telephone people. You must have seen them on TV.'

It was a silly thing to say. Miss Midden didn't watch television, didn't have one in the house and wouldn't allow the Major to have one in his room. 'If you want to watch that stuff, you can go down to the hell-hole and watch it with them,' she had said each time he had asked to have a set in his room. 'The exercise will do you good.'

'Why's he so scared of the police?' she asked now. 'Did you find that out too?'

'He's terrified because someone has threatened to do something horrible to him if he goes anywhere near them.'

'Near the police?'

The Major nodded.

'So he's involved in something shady. Charming. Now I've got two of you in the house. What I want to know is how he got here in the first place.'

'He doesn't know himself. He has a motorbike. A very fast one. Perhaps he crashed it and –'

'And then takes all his clothes off and climbs in through the window and . . .' Miss Midden stopped. She had just remembered that she had put the chain on before leaving for the weekend and when she had gone out just now the door had been partly open but the chain was still on the hook. The young lout hadn't got into the house on his own. And why had he gone to sleep under the Major's bed? Somebody had brought him, and that someone had stepped on the flower-bed to open the window. Finally that person had known she had gone away for the weekend. Her thoughts, as she broke the eggs into the bowl and began to beat them, focused on the people down at the Middenhall. No one else knew she had gone away to the Solway Firth. Come to that, no one even at the Middenhall knew she had returned. Miss Midden beat the eggs with the whisk in a new frenzy.

Sir Arnold Gonders' thoughts followed a parallel course, and had rather more in common with the frenziedly whisked eggs. He woke from his sleep only partly refreshed. If anything his total exhaustion earlier had to some extent deadened his perception of the danger he was in. Now the full force of it hit him. He might well have murdered . . . surely manslaughter was a justified plea. No, it wasn't. Not in his case. He was the Chief Constable, the supreme keeper of law and order in Twixt and Tween and the media would have a field day tearing him to pieces. Oh yes, he had cultivated them in the past, some of them at any rate, the commercial TV people in particular, to get his own back on the *Panorama* shits at the BBC who'd given him and the lads a hard time over that murdering rapist who had done a tidy stretch of a life sentence before it was found his sperm didn't match that found in his victims. But the Chief Constable had been around long enough to know that there was no loyalty in the media and that the stab in the back was established practice. He thought of all the papers who'd go to town on him too, the *Guardian* and the *Independent*, God rot them, then the *Daily Telegraph* with that bloody tough editor. Even *The Times* would join in. As for the *Mirror* and the *Sun* . . . It didn't bear thinking about.

As he shaved, as he tried to eat breakfast, as he dragged Genscher, now in a state of total funk, to the Land Rover, as he drove down across the dam to Six Lanes End and along the motorway to Tween, the Chief Constable's thoughts raced. He'd have the tyres on the Land Rover changed to make certain that no one could trace any remnant of mud from Miss Midden's back yard to them. He might have left the imprint of the tyres on the old drove road. Christ, why hadn't he thought of all these things the night before? In the back the Rottweiler lurched and bounced and tried to keep away from the bloodstained sheets and the parcel tape in the corner. Sir Arnold got rid of them separately in two bins several miles apart, the tape in the first and the soiled sheets in the second.

After that he felt slightly better. He began to think more constructively. He'd wait until the next day to go into the office. He had a perfectly good excuse not to go in today. He had to keep out of the way of those media hounds who wanted to interview him about the DPP's decision. And he had a hangover to beat all hangovers. Harry Hodge, his deputy, would cover for him. In the meantime he'd start his own investigation to discover who had set him up by using that bloody Bea cow. It had occurred to him that the bastard had to be someone who knew his movements and had known he wasn't going to be at the Old Boathouse that night. That was an important discovery.

The Chief Constable considered it and came to no very clear conclusion except that his return must have screwed up the plan somehow just as Miss Midden's return hadn't done him any good either. It was as he was driving along the Parson's Road that another idea occurred to him. He pulled up at a roadside telephone and checked there was no one anywhere about. Then he dialled the Stagstead Police Station. When the duty officer answered, the Chief Constable muffled his voice with his hand and spoke in a high disguised voice. It was a short message, short and to the point, and he repeated it only once before putting the phone down and hurrying on. Miss Midden was going to get another nasty surprise.

In fact it was the Chief Constable who would have been very nastily surprised if he could have heard the conversation that had taken place in his house in Sweep's Place, Tween, between Auntie Bea and Lady Vy when they got back that morning shortly before lunch.

'My darling, if I'd only known,' said Bea, 'if I'd known what he was putting you through, I would never have allowed it.'

'I didn't know what to do,' said Vy tearfully, 'I felt so alone. He told me he'd see all the ghastly gutter papers got the story if I told anyone. I couldn't bear to think of the scandal. And there was a young man in the bed. I couldn't deny that.'

Bea looked at her narrowly. 'Oh he's a cunning devil, there's no doubt about that,' she said. 'I have to give him his cunning. But two can play that game and after all he wasn't very subtle.'

'Darling, you're talking way above my head. What are you saying?'

'Ask yourself this question,' said Bea. 'There was a young man in your bed, I don't doubt that. But where is he now?'

'I've no idea,' said Lady Vy. 'I went down to the cellar and he'd disappeared in the night.'

134

'Exactly. Arnold got you to help tie him up in the cellar so that you were even more of an accomplice. Isn't that the case?'

'I suppose it must be,' said Lady Vy. 'I hadn't thought of that.'

'And you say he was tied really tight? In two plastic bags?'

'Well, actually he couldn't get him into the garbage bags. He had to use the sheets off the bed. And lots of tape. You've no idea how much tape he tied round him.'

'And yet the young man disappears. Doesn't that strike you as peculiar?'

Lady Vy tried to stretch her tiny brain. It was reassuring to have Aunt Bea telling her things, but sometimes she couldn't understand what she was saying. 'The whole thing struck me as peculiar,' she said. 'I mean I've never found a young man in bed like that before. He was quite nice looking too if you didn't look at the blood.'

Auntie Bea controlled her temper with difficulty. 'No, dear, what I meant was . . . well, didn't it seem very strange that he should have escaped so quickly after you had helped tie him so securely?'

'Yes, I suppose it did,' said Lady Vy. 'And Arnold drugged him too to keep him quiet.'

'Oh sure. Arnold said he drugged him. Arnold said he did this and he did that but the only thing you really know is that you helped tie him up and then when you went to look for him the next day he had escaped. What a miraculous thing to happen, wasn't it? Or it would have been if Arnold hadn't untied him himself and helped him on his way.'

'But why should he have done that?' asked Vy, still stumbling about in her attempt to plumb the mystery.

'Because, dearest, because this was all an elaborate plan to make sure you didn't leave him and wouldn't make things awkward for dear Arnold at any time in the future.'

'But why should I . . .' Vy began before coming to her own conclusion. 'Oh, Bea dear, do you really think . . . ?'

It was a thoroughly unnecessary question. Aunt Bea was

thinking very hard indeed. She had already concocted a rational explanation for the succession of weird events that had taken place. They all pointed to the same conclusion: she must take Vy away from the malign influence of her husband. If there had been any doubt about the matter before the weekend, and there hadn't been, she now felt sure she was saving Vy from a man who was prepared to use any sort of crime for his own vile ends. Being bitten in the groin by Sir Arnold had not exactly inclined Bea to see him in an even faintly sympathetic light and now she had the evidence she needed to break him. And she would be protecting darling Vy at the same time. She got up and took Lady Vy by the hand. 'My darling, I want you to go upstairs and pack your things. Now you're not to argue with me. I am going to take care of everything. Just do what I tell you.'

'But, Bea darling, I can't just leave –'

'You're not leaving, dear. You are merely coming down to London with me today. No argument. We're going to see your father.'

And with this dubious reassurance – Sir Edward Gilmott-Gwyre was not someone she normally wanted to see – Lady Vy went up to the bedroom and began to pack. 'I must leave Arnold a note just the same,' she thought, and wrote a short one to the effect that she had had to go down to London to see Daddy because he hadn't been well and she'd be back in a few days.

'Now come along, Vy dear,' Auntie Bea called. Lady Vy went downstairs obediently and left the note on the table by the front door. Aunt Bea saw it there, opened the envelope, read the note and put it quietly into her handbag. Sir Arnold could worry himself sick. And Vy wasn't coming back, so there was no need to deceive him. On this nice moral note she went out to the Mercedes and presently they were on their way south. By the time the Chief Constable parked the Land Rover in the garage, they were halfway to London.

Chapter 17

That evening Miss Midden and the Major moved Timothy Bright, wearing only a towel, up to the old nursery. The term 'nursery' was a euphemism. The bars in the window were substantial and the door thick because one of Miss Midden's ancestors in the late eighteenth century, one Elias Midden, acting on the same extravagant impulse that had prompted Black Midden to build his domiciliary mausoleum, had bought a small bear from some gipsies at Twixt Fair. Elias, who had just won the wrestling match and been proclaimed Champion of the Fells, had drunk a great deal of beer to celebrate and had supposed that the bear was fully grown and also that it would be fun to match his strength against the beast of an evening. In fact the gipsies had been anxious to get rid of that bear. They had bought it from some sailors on the quay at Tween and the sailors had brought the bear back from a voyage to Canada where one of them had shot its mother. In short, the bear was a very young one and it grew into a very big one. Having paid a great deal of money for the animal Elias Midden was anxious to provide it with the best accommodation and to have it close to hand for evening bouts.

His wife did not share his enthusiasm. She disliked sharing the farmhouse with a young and growing bear, even if it was kept muzzled. She had threatened to leave Elias and his bear and take the children with her unless he kept it safely locked up. Reluctant to give the animal up, and conscious that he would be laughed at by every farmer between Stagstead and . . . well just about everywhere if he drove his wife out of the house on account of the bear – people would say coarse things about his relationship with it – Elias Midden had built a very strong room in which to keep it. It was just as well. As the weeks and months passed the bear grew. It grew to the point where even Elias, a proud man with a magnificent physique, had to admit defeat. That bear was not for wrestling. It was extremely strong and extremely nasty. And it became huge, so huge and so nasty that feeding it became a hazardous procedure. In building the bear room on the assumption that it was fully grown and amiable he had not made a hatch in the door through which to pass it its food and since the heavy door opened into the room rather than out of it (Mrs Midden had sensibly suggested that precaution – she had a horror of the bear bursting out of that room in the middle of the night and doing dreadful things to her and the children) Elias risked his life every time he opened it. The final straw, and the term was literal, came when he lost three fingers of his right hand between the door and the door jamb trying to push some litter through. 'It's all your fault,' he had bellowed at his wife. 'If you hadn't complained about the smell.'

Mrs Midden had retorted that he'd been fool enough to waste a great deal of money and had bought a pup or whatever young grizzlies were called into the bargain and she knew now how the family had got its name and she wasn't sharing her house with a bear that couldn't go outside to do its business and the smell was appalling and not the sort of thing a decent woman with a reputation for keeping a clean home to consider could put up with and he'd got to do something or else . . .

Elias Midden had said he intended to do something about the bloody bear. In fact he did nothing. He wasn't opening that door again for all the tea in China. The bear could lump it. The bear did. It had been living on a restricted diet before, but now it starved. Its last snack had been those three fingers. Day after day and night after night it battered that door and scratched at it. It tried the walls too and it bent the bars on the window. In the end it died and Elias put it about that he had killed it in a fair fight, losing his fingers in the encounter. He buried the emaciated corpse and double dug several barrowloads of bear's excreta into the kitchen garden, where it did more good than it had done in the house. Then, because his wife still refused to enter the bear's den, he scrubbed it out and repainted the walls. He didn't touch the door. It remained scratched and bitten and battered so that he could show visitors just how fierce the bear he had killed had been.

It was left to later and more refined Middens to alter the name of the room to 'the old nursery'. With its bent bars and battered door the name had a nicely macabre touch to it and the young Middens who slept in it suffered terrifying nightmares which in more enlightened times would have required the attentions of psycho-therapists, trauma relief specialists and stress counsellors. It was there in that bear room that Black Midden had first dreamt of a ferocious life in Africa where there were no bears. Now it was where Timothy Bright was confined.

'You can stay in there until you tell us who you are and how you came to break into my house,' Miss Midden told him after he'd eaten. 'If you don't want to stay, you have only to say the word and I shall call the police.'

Timothy Bright said he definitely didn't want the police but could he have his clothes please.

'When we find them,' Miss Midden said, and locked the door. Then she went downstairs and sat in the fading evening light wondering which of the arrogant and idiotic Middens down at the Hall was responsible for this crime. In other circumstances she would have suspected the Major, but he'd been with her and his state of terror on finding the young man had been genuine. On the other hand he would be able to tell her, if anyone could, which of the inmates at the hell-hole had sado-masochistic tendencies. Not that she wanted to talk to the silly little man. She was still furious with him and her contempt at his cowardice was immense. All the same, she had to ask him. She found him looking at his soiled bed. There was a nasty smell in the room too. 'Dogshit,' said Miss Midden. 'That's what that is.' But no one down at the hell-hole had a dog.

'It has to be someone who knew I was away,' she told the Major, 'and the only people who knew for certain are down there.'

'Do you want me to go down and find out what I can?' he asked, but Miss Midden shook her head. 'One look at you and whoever did this would sleep easy. You're the perfect suspect with your black eye and stitches.'

'But I can prove I got them in Glasgow in that pub.'

'Which pub?'

The Major tried to remember. He had been in so many pubs and had been so very drunk. 'There you are. You don't even know,' said Miss Midden. 'And what did you call yourself at the hospital? I bet you didn't call yourself MacPhee because you are no more a Scot than I am.'

'Jones,' the Major admitted.

'And that overworked doctor didn't like you in the least. So she isn't going to be at all helpful. And that's not all. We don't know when that young man got into the house and we don't know when whatever happened to him did happen. You could have been trying to establish some sort of alibi. Only a madman would get himself beaten up in a pub. Or a frightened and guilty person. You go down to the Hall and the police will get an anonymous call from a certain person down there who knows the man is in this house and may think he's dead. And what about your record?'

'Record?' said the Major beginning to tremble.

'Don't tell me you haven't been inside. With your nasty tendencies? Oh yes, you've been had up before now. Probably for peering through a hole in a public lavatory. Or worse. You don't fool me. The police would be only too happy to lay their hands on you. Well, you needn't worry. They're not going to if I have anything to do with it.'

'What are we going to do then?' he asked.

'What we aren't going to do is show ourselves. We are not here. We are going to sit tight and see who comes up to check on that young man and find out if he is still alive. That's what we are going to do. They came through the dining-room window. The next time they come I'll be waiting for them. And now I'm going to put the car out of sight in the barn. This could be fun.'

It wasn't Major MacPhee's idea of fun.

In London the man who had called himself Mr Brian Smith was looking distinctly peaky. He wasn't enjoying himself at all. 'The little shit has done a a flyer,' he told someone on the phone. 'With the fucking piggy-bank too. Yeah, I know how many megabytes it was. But . . . No, I never dreamt. I wouldn't have thought he had the fucking guts. He should have been on the boat and he wasn't . . . Yeah, I know it's not a fun matter. I'm the first to know that, aren't I? Of course he could have had an accident or gone over by a different route. I only had one bloke at Santander to check him out and he wasn't on any ferry. If he doesn't do the rest of the job on time we'll know. Yes, yes . . . yes . . . of course.'

He put the phone down gently and cursed Timothy Bright loud and long and with a ferocity that justified all that young man's fears.

Sir Arnold Gonders was on the phone too, in a public phone box talking to the sod who ran The Holy Temple of Divine Being and The Pearly Gates of Paradise. He could see the lights on in the room above the painted-over window of the sex shop and had already walked past it twice in a raincoat and with a flat cap pulled down over his face. He was also wearing gloves. On the second occasion he had stopped briefly to stuff a brown envelope through the letterbox. Now he was using a voice distorter. The Chief Constable was taking every precaution and no chances.

'I am interested in young people,' he said in tones that he hoped were mincingly authentic. 'Know what I mean?' The proprietor said he thought he did. 'Male or female, sir?' he enquired.

'Both,' said Sir Arnold.

'And young?'

Sir Arnold hesitated. 'Yes, young,' he said finally. 'Like tied up, know what I mean?'

The proprietor knew perfectly well what was meant.

'Pictures. Mags. And I need discretion. If you go down to your shop you'll find an envelope with my money in it. I want you to send the material in a box to me at the address I have supplied. Two hundred should cover the cost, shouldn't it?'

'I'm sure it will, sir.'

'So I've added another hundred for discretion. Right?'

'Right, sir. Very kind.'

'And there'll be an additional order if I like what I see. Name's MacPhee.' Again he hesitated before going on in a far more sinister tone of voice. 'And don't think of not sending me the stuff and keeping the cash. I got some connections.'

'Connections, sir?'

'Like with Freddie Monce, like The Torch. I wouldn't want to have to call them.'

The sod wouldn't want him to call them either. Having a firebombed sex shop wouldn't do him any good at all. The Chief Constable put the phone down and hurried away. The first part of his plan had begun. He went home and changed. It was time to begin his other investigation. It was ten o'clock when he left the house again in his own Jag and drove down the coast to Urnmouth. Maxie at the Hydro knew what was going on with just about everyone. He wanted a chat with Maxie.

Chapter 18

The Urnmouth Hydro is an imposing building. Built in the age of mid-Victorian splendour along impeccably classical lines, it stands in its own elegant grounds like a Grecian temple. Its white columns are made of cast iron from the Gundron cannon foundry while its walls are of brown ironstone. But it is inside that the classical ambience is most appropriate to its present use. The original owner had insisted the interior should reflect Roman taste as authentically as the exterior was to be a mirror of something in Athens. The architect and decorator had followed these instructions as exactly as his knowledge of Roman history and custom allowed. One elderly cleric, already stunned by the Darwinian controversy of the time, had been so overwhelmed by the scenes of debauchery depicted on the walls of the atrium that he had died of apoplexy in the arms of the butler. These murals even now struck all visitors forcibly. It was even claimed that several gentlemen had been known to experience *ejaculatio praecox* before they had rid themselves of their overcoats. And it was due to these friezes that, after a considerable period of neglect, the house had been turned into what was called a hydro by Maxie Schryburg, an entrepreneur from Miami.

Sir Arnold Gonders had taken an interest in Maxie Schryburg's enterprise from the beginning. The Hydro would, he felt sure, attract the sort of people the Chief Constable wanted to know all about. Besides Maxie himself was of interest to Sir Arnold. Maxie had always claimed he was 'outta da Big Apple' but the Chief Constable had information that he had in fact been a minor operator in Florida and had found it wise to move away on account of some Cuban competition there. Certainly Urnmouth was the last place anyone would look for a restaurateur of his recondite type.

The cold wind blowing in off the sea made the little town an inhospitable place for strangers. The Hydro offered its only entertainment apart from a straggle of pubs in the high street but membership, while open to all who could pay, was in fact restricted to those who could pay a great deal either in cash or in kind. Sir Arnold, who always used the nom de guerre of Mr Will Cope, belonged to the latter sort, but at the same time extracted a great deal of information from Maxie in return for his patronage.

Now, having entered by the private door at the back which led along a covered way to Maxie's bungalow, he climbed the stairs to his usual private dining-room in the happy knowledge that with Vy and the foul Bea away, presumably in Harrogate, he could afford to relax and combine pleasure with investigation. He accepted the menu from the obsequious Maxie in his role of maître.

'May I suggest that for the hors d'oeuvres you have Number Three?' he said. 'Very fresh and tender.'

'Really? Interesting. Ample proportions, eh?'

'I think you'll find them adequate, sir. Very, 'ow you say, "well hung".'

'Sounds all right to me,' said Sir Arnold. 'And for the main course? What's on tonight? Anything special?'

'The mixed grill will be ready about ten. Before that we are a bit short, I'm afraid. Times ain't what they used to be.'

'Same every place, Maxie, same every place,' said the Chief Constable, adapting to the argot. 'I think I'll wait for the mixed grill. Fresh, is it?'

Maxie combined a nod with a shrug by way of a disclaimer. 'Well, Mr Cope, what can I say? I provide fresh but what comes in I have to take pot luck. Pay top rates too.'

'Mixed grill it is,' said Sir Arnold, and sat back to watch the floor show. It was, to say the least, entirely appropriate for the setting. Two girls danced rather awkwardly on an oil-covered water-bed before wrestling with one another's panties and finally going in for a prolonged bout of peculiar kissing.

The Chief Constable finished his whisky and ordered another.

'Make it a Spanish, Maxie,' he said, 'and what's with this starter? It's a long time coming.'

'Hasn't arrived yet,' Maxie told him.

'So what do I do while I wait?'

'You could always have a bit of massage maybe.'

'I'm surprised at you, Maxie. You know me. I don't do none of that.'

Again Mr Schryburg nodded and shrugged. 'Me neither,' he said, 'me neither. You wouldn't believe it but I am a believer always in family values. Sure, you laugh but it is true. Like the Great Lady said, "What we need is family values like the Victorians." And she was right. You know, Mr Cope, she should have toughed it out. Some great lady. I drink to her. The Iron Maiden.'

The Chief Constable raised his glass and drank. He felt rather embarrassed whenever Mr Schryburg talked like that. Like someone farting in church. It was inappropriate and besides he wasn't at all sure about the Iron Maiden bit. While he waited he tapped the channel controller on the multiple TV screens. Nothing happening in Diner 1. In Diner 3 a thin and rather nervous individual was helping himself to neat Polish vodka. Sir Arnold shook his head disapprovingly. It was no help doing that. All the same he stayed with Diner 3. The fellow had taken his trousers off and had folded them neatly beside his shirt. The Chief Constable switched on the video recorder. He had recognized Fred Phylleps, the Tory party campaign manager for South Twixt and also an influential figure as the transport manager at Intergrowth Chemicals. In fact Sir Arnold had had it on good authority that F.F., as Fred Phylleps was known to his friends, had been the bagman in a pay-off to someone who knew a little too much about the financial affairs of a certain person's close relative. No names, no packdrill. It would be a good thing to add F.F. to his little collection of videoed notables, though frankly Sir Arnold wasn't impressed by his choice of dishes. Thirty-five-year-old-playing-teenybopper did nothing for him, and he had recently gone clean off leather. Still, F.F. might yet come in handy by way of protection.

Presently, when he had tried several other Diners, the Chief Constable turned back to his own needs. He hadn't come here for a meal. He needed information. 'You haven't got many customers for a Monday night,' he said when Maxie brought his third whisky.

'Comes and goes. Mondays. Sometimes there's a big rush on like when the wives are away or we get a convention. And of course the regulars come in the afternoon though we do have some in the morning. Come with their fishing rods mainly. Mornings is surprisingly good.'

'I suppose they must be,' said the Chief Constable. 'By the way, do you have many bondage merchants?'

'Try the Dungeon,' said Maxie and leant across to press a button marked D. Sir Arnold found himself staring at a room containing what looked like a surgical table with straps, a dentist's chair and, most sinisterly, a small gallows with a hangman's noose. On the walls were an assortment of instruments and whips.

'I like to think we got some good equipment,' said Maxie. 'Yeah, man, we can give them the works. We got one customer's a medical man and he reckons all we need is a resuscitation room and we could help out with the National Health operations. What he don't know is we've got a resuscitation room right through that door in the corner there. You wouldn't believe what some people like doing to themselves. We had this old guy in one time brought his own priest for confession like and I'm meaning a kosher priest. I swear to God the guy's got a real priest. Like he's a Roman Catholic or something. So one of the girls has got to be dressed in nothing but a hood and these pants and an open-teat bra, all black leather. And she's the hangman and two other girls they strap the old guy up real tight and the priest takes his confession and the last rites, you know, the works. And that's when I know the priest is for real because he doesn't like what he's into one bit. Keeps sweating and crossing himself. And Ruby, she's the hangman, puts this silk bag over the old guy's head and then the noose on this bungy

146

rubber and takes her time to give him his money's worth because this is costing, with that equipment and the overheads like the gallows and all. Then she steps back and pulls the lever and the old guy goes down on the bungy. You should have seen it. Thing is we've got the noise right on the audio player so we don't hear his real noise. Man, was I glad we had a top doctor in Diner 10 that night. Only time I've ever asked a customer to stop and come urgent. The old guy had had a seizure even before he did the drop scene. Then he's having this fucking fit and it's boomsadaisy and he's on the bungy having his neck stretched and it don't do him no good at all, jerking around and twitching like there's no tomorrow which just about happens to be true in his case. And that bungy don't help none either. He keeps coming up through the fucking trap again and the priest is so fucking thrown he's off into the last rites again. And as if that isn't bad enough, I call the ambulance fast and they rush in what's the first thing they see? Ruby in the leather and a naked fucking doctor with a condom on trying to get the old bastard down so's he can give him the kiss of life and he's hacking away at the bungy rope with some scissors won't cut and there's this priest on his knees moaning in Latin or something. Only time I've seen the last rites done twice in ten minutes the same guy. You think of the outlay for a caper like that. Shit. I have to buy the ambulance guys off and give that doctor three weeks free and that ain't all. I got to join the Catholic Church so I can confess for real and calm that fucking priest down he's so hysterical. Yeah, sure the old guy is paying. When he comes out of intensive care which was iffy at the time and he's in hospital seven whole weeks. After that I said we got to have our own resuscitation room. And was I lucky. We had an accident one time with the electric chair. Wasn't no accident either. The guy was a bad one. I mean a hurter, a real mean bastard. He wants to go all the way with torture like he's read they do in South Africa or El Salvador some place. Terminals and electric shocks and you know. The works. So he's got Lucille in there. She's the one does the S and M roles both. Big girl and not the sort you'd think was that way. Motherly, you know what I mean?'

The Chief Constable did. He had a video in his safe of Lucille working the Member for East Seirsley with the butt of a bull whip with genuine pleasure. She was enjoying her work, which was more than the MP appeared to. Afterwards, when he had the gag out, he'd said as much. It was an interesting tape.

'So this mean bastard has brought his own transformer,' Maxie went on. 'After him we screened the gear people bring but this was earlier. Gets Lucille in the chair with the straps on and the head terminal down on her and the mask he leaves off and he cranks his own machine. Both. You believe it? Lucille's expecting to imitate when he fires but she don't have to do no imitations. You should have seen the fucking burn marks he leaves on her. Real nice bastard. Even had the nerve to query the bill. Some guys you don't have back. And we search bags since.'

Sir Arnold added the Dungeon to his list of future viewings. He also came up with an important question. 'Got any bondage freaks use the Dungeon?' he asked.

Again Maxie Schryburg smirked. 'Mr Cope, have we got bondage . . . Man, we got every kind of kook you can name and some you never heard of. Had a publisher in the other day wants to shrink-wrap Pauline. ''Shrink-wrap her?'' I says to him. ''What you mean 'shrink-wrap'? You gonna suffocate her.'' You know what he says? Says he wants her shrink-wrapped because he wants to use her as a dump bin. There's some things in this business I don't understand and I been in it so many years and dump bin is something too much. Right? And I say so to Pauline. I say, ''You got a guy in there wants to have you shrink-wrapped in plastic for a dump bin.'' Jesus, that Pauline took off. She's a sassy girl too. Water sports, wind surfing, husband and wife, the two-way stretch with muffins, she's not fussy. So when she says dump bins is out, boy, they're definitely off the menu. You think that guy takes it easy? He gets real rude and mean. So, he's in the door, he's a member since he's here and I don't want no trouble because he's a big-time publisher from London. So I tell him he can't have Pauline, he'll have to take pot luck like out of house and I calls Mrs Ferrow and she says sure she'll do it just so the guy doesn't see her face. She don't want to be known, though everybody I know knows her. Fine with me. Who wants to look at Mrs Ferrow's face? Only one thing is I tell her, "This customer wants you down under." Fine with Mrs Ferrow. Wants to know what sort of fucking animal, like a koala bear or a kangafuckingroo. Must be pissed or something. So I go back to this big guy and say which way he wants the dump? He looks at me he doesn't understand what I'm asking. Miles of fucking cling-film he's undone already all over the fucking floor and he doesn't want the dump. You know what he says? He's never heard of it like that and I believe him. Practically throws up when I tell him. Dump bins in his world are things you stack books in not Mrs Ferrow assfacing him and —'

'Maxie, I don't want to hear,' said the Chief Constable, who knew Mrs Ferrow by sight and didn't like to think what was coming. 'All I want is all the names of your bondage freaks and men who drug young men. All, you understand, all the names.'

Maxie pulled a long face. 'Come on, Mr Cope, you know I don't —'

'I know you don't, Maxie,' Sir Arnold said in a conciliatory fashion, 'that's one of the things I like about you. And you know I never make any use of any information anyone can trace back to you. That's good insurance for us both. So you got any information about guys who like boys out of their skulls on LSD, I want it.'

Maxie Schryburg relaxed. 'You want that sort of thing I can supply it easy,' he said. 'You want it private is fine with me. You want to be the boy, eh? Nothing easier . . .' He stopped. The Chief Constable was turning a very nasty colour.

'You just want the names, sure,' Maxie said hurriedly, trying to make good his mistake. 'Sure, I'll get it now.' And before the Chief Constable could tell him what he thought of him, he was off.

For the rest of the evening Sir Arnold sat back and watched the mixed grill on the water-bed. But every now and then he would switch the button marked D and study the apparatus in the Dungeon with interest. He'd get Maxie to show him round it in person. Only trouble was he had never gone further than the video room he was in and he didn't intend to now. No one was ever going to catch him on tape.

At 11.30 he left cautiously by the covered way and drove back to Tween. He had a list of names in his pocket that might lead to the boy in his bed and he was feeling rather satisfied with himself. In fact he was thinking of having some relaxation and Glenda never went to bed before midnight. Unless he was there, of course. On the whole, he thought not. He'd had an exhausting weekend and he had to get to work in the morning.

Chapter 19

Far away to the south Auntie Bea was doing her best to persuade Lady Vy that she must take her case to her father. 'Darling, you must see that it is the only way you can save yourself. Arnold's trying to blackmail you with unfavourable publicity and getting your name in the tabloids. If you get your father to act now . . .'

'Oh but Bea, don't you see Daddy would be so shocked,' said Lady Vy, looking vaguely round the restaurant as if for support. Le Clit, decorated in a specious art deco and newly opened in a renovated garage in the Fulham Road, didn't seem the right atmosphere in which to talk about Daddy. Sir Edward Gilmott-Gwyre held strong views about women like that. 'And anyway,' she went on, 'even if I do tell him, what can poor Daddy do? He's almost eighty and he hasn't been at all well –'

'Tosh,' said Auntie Bea masterfully. 'Your father is a very fit old man and he loves nothing better than demonstrating his power of influence. If you tell him what Arnold has been doing –'

'Oh, but I couldn't,' said Vy. Auntie Bea's gloved hand closed firmly on her wrist and the fingers tightened on her painfully. She looked through half tears into Bea's eyes. 'You're asking too much of me.'

'Suppose I said I was going to be asking so much more of you later on,' Auntie Bea hissed softly. She moistened her lips with her tongue and Vy felt hopelessly weak. 'And I am. You will go to your father in the morning and tell him everything. Everything, do you hear?'

Lady Vy nodded. Her soft blue eyes had misted over. 'Everything? About us too?' she asked in a girlish whisper.

The gloved fingers bit deeper into her wrist. 'No, not about us,' snapped Bea fiercely. 'Of course not about us. About Arnold and the young man in your bed.'

'Oh no, Bea, I couldn't. Don't you see Daddy would believe I'd asked him to come to bed with me. He wouldn't believe I hadn't. He's never believed anything I've said. He thinks I'm –'

'Yes, dear,' said Auntie Bea hurriedly, and considered this new problem. Sir Edward Gilmott-Gwyre's stated views on the place of women in the kitchen, and silent women at that, were well known. It was even rumoured that he had stopped his eldest daughter from having an abortion on the grounds that if she must behave like an elephant in musth she had better learn to live with the consequences. The fact that only male elephants got in musth was of no influence on Sir Edward's opinion that all women were by nature driven by obscure and sinister sexual urges which had to be tamed or, better still, ignored. Lady Vy had particular reasons as well for fearing his anger.

'Now, listen, darling,' Bea went on, using her eyes to will Vy's obedience and still grasping her wrist, 'you must tell him straight away that Arnold put the boy there himself with the deliberate intention of involving you in his own crimes.'

'But Bea, I don't see how.'

'Doesn't it tell you anything about Arnold's proclivities that the boy was naked and tied up in bed linen and that Arnold kept drugging him with Valium?'

'Well, I suppose he could be a bit that way,' Vy admitted. 'He can get very violent and I'm sure he has a bit of fluff in Tween somewhere.'

'But is it just a bit of fluff? What about a pretty boy?'

'Oh I don't know. It's all so confusing,' said Lady Vy, pining for a change in the conversation. 'I was so looking forward to going shopping for that coat at Tamara's. Do you really think it will suit me?'

But Auntie Bea was not to be diverted by the siren calls of very expensive dressmakers in Davies Street. She was about to come up with the trump card. 'What you don't seem to realize is that the media are already onto Arnold,' she said. 'They've got the scent of a major scandal, much more serious than the last one, and you have to act before it breaks and you are dragged in along with Arnold and the others.'

'What new scandal? What's it about? You've got to tell me.'

'Only if you promise to go and see your father in the morning. Promise?'

For a moment Lady Vy hesitated, but the gin and the need to know were too much for her. 'Promise,' she said but Auntie Bea still refused to tell her.

'You must go and tell him everything you know about Arnold. You've got to do it to save yourself. Your father will know what to do.' Auntie Bea signalled for the bill.

They went back to Bea's flat by taxi. 'Now you're going to have to sleep on your own tonight,' Auntie Bea said. 'I want you to think carefully what you're going to say tomorrow and you're going to tell me in the morning.'

And with a light kiss she was gone. Lady Vy went to bed with a sigh. She didn't like to have to think about nasty things. And going to see Daddy was a very nasty thing indeed.

Things were hotting up all over the place. At twelve-thirty that night the telephone rang at Voleney House until Ernestine Bright got up and answered it in her dressing-gown. 'Do you know what time it is?' she demanded in her haughtiest tone of voice and was horrified when Fergus phoning from Drumstruthie said that as a matter of fact he did.

'Yes, I do know it's damned well after midnight,' he said, 'and I wouldn't be phoning now if it weren't important. Where is that boy of yours, Timothy?'

'I suppose he's in London. That's where he usually is.'

'I realize that, and I wouldn't be phoning you if I could find him there. I need to know very urgently where he is now.'

'You don't sound your usual self, Fergus,' Ernestine told him.

'A man of your age shouldn't drink spirits. It's bad for your blood pressure. Now, if you like to call in the morning –'

'We can refrain from the admonitory if you don't mind,' said Uncle Fergus. 'I want you to know that I have not been drinking. I also want you to know that I have Boskie here and –'

'Boskie there?' said Ernestine, genuinely shocked now. 'Aunt Boskie? But you told us she was at death's door last month. She can't be with you.'

'I assure you she is and she certainly isn't dying, are you Boskie?' From the sounds there was little doubt that Boskie, for all her ninety-one years, wasn't yet dead. 'Now then, Ernestine, she wants to talk to that son of yours.'

'But why? What does she want with Timothy?'

'My impression, if you really want to know, is that she wants to kill him,' said Fergus. 'If I were in her position, which thank God I am not, I would wish a really painful death, like boiling alive, for the little shit. Anyway here's Boskie and she can tell you for herself.'

There were various noises on the phone. Ernestine tried to get in first. 'Hullo Boskie,' she said, clutching her dressing-gown to her and wishing she'd put slippers on. It was really rather chilly.

But the coldness was nothing to the ice in Boskie's tone when they had finally accommodated her hearing-aid to the require-ments of the telephone. 'Is that you, Ernestine?' she demanded. 'I said "Is that you?" She's not saying anything. I said she's not saying anything, Fergus.'

'I am saying something,' Ernestine bawled down the phone and was rewarded by a squawk from Boskie who told Fergus there was no need to shout, she could hear quite well for her age. To Ernestine, holding the reverberating telephone away from her ear, the portents of this midnight call were not at all obvious. Evidently Timothy had done something to annoy old Boskie –

She was interrupted by old Boskie yelling that if her Guillermo were still alive he'd know what to do to that dirty little . . . Ernestine held the phone even further away, then tried to intervene

154

on her son's behalf. 'This is Ernestine, Boskie dear,' she screamed. In the kitchen the dogs had begun to bark. 'Boskie dear,' she repeated, 'this is –' Again the phone reverberated quite alarmingly as Boskie screamed at the other end.

'There's some vile creature on the line calling me "Boskie dear." Impertinent slut. Tell her to go away, Fergus, I want to talk to that fool Ernestine. If there is one thing I detest in a woman, it is foolishness. That Ernestine . . .' After what sounded like a scuffle in the hall at Drumstruthie the phone was dragged away from the old lady and Fergus came on the line.

'That was Boskie,' he said rather unnecessarily.

'I know that,' said Ernestine angrily, 'and you can tell the old woman from me that –'

'I don't think I'll tell her that at all,' Fergus interrupted. 'In fact, in your shoes I should bend over backwards to be nice to dear Boskie. You want to know why?'

'Why?' said Ernestine unwisely.

'Because your darling little Timothy has just sold all her shares, all one hundred and fifty-eight thousand poundsworth of her shares, and has disappeared –'

'But he can't have,' said Ernestine desperately. 'He's not allowed to sell someone else's shares.'

'No, Ernestine, that's quite right. I'm so glad you have taken that on board,' said Fergus. 'And now the dear boy has scarpered, vanished, done a runner, disappeared, you can call it what you like. I know what Boskie's calling it.'

Ernestine had a pretty shrewd idea too. A wailing noise in the background seemed to suggest that Boskie was having some sort of seizure. Ernestine tried to get a grip on the situation. 'She must be making a mistake. Timothy wouldn't do a thing like that, and besides how could he, even if he wanted to? The shares must have been in Boskie's name.'

'Oh, quite simply. He forged her signature on a power of attorney,' Fergus told her.

'I don't believe it,' said Ernestine. 'Tim would never do a thing like that. What did you say? Oh you do. Well, you'll just have to prove it. Boskie is obviously demented.'

'That's the first sensible thing you have said,' Fergus agreed. 'Unfortunately her dementia is not of the senile variety. She happens to be looking better than I've seen her for some time. I wouldn't say she's a picture of health but for a woman of ninety . . . well, let's just say she's not suffering from low blood pressure. Now, if you don't mind, I'd like to speak to Bletchley.'

'You can't. He's not here.'

'Oh, of course it's the weekend,' said Fergus. 'I suppose he's with . . . Is he golfing again?'

'I don't know what you mean,' said Ernestine, resuming her hauteur in an attempt to regain some confidence.

'No, all right, all right,' said Fergus, acknowledging there were some things better left unsaid. 'Well, if you can get through to him, get him to understand that I'm holding Boskie back from calling the Commissioner of Police at Scotland Yard personally, but I won't be able to contain the situation very much longer. Just tell Bletchley that that money has to be found and repaid. Repeat, has to be. I mean it, Ernestine. This is definitely not a joke. Boskie's sons are flying home from Detroit and Malaga to –'

Ernestine put the phone down and sat in a huddle on the chair. She was not aware of the cold any more. Presently she picked the phone up and dialled Timothy's number in London. The signal indicated there would be no answer. In the end she went through to her husband's study and found a number she had never used before. She dialled and a sleepy woman's voice replied.

'I want to speak to Mr Bletchley Bright,' said Ernestine firmly, 'and please don't waste time by saying he isn't there. This is an emergency.'

She waited while the message was passed and finally her husband came on the line. 'What in God's name are you doing?' he demanded angrily.

'You had better come home, dear,' said Ernestine coldly.

'Home? Now? Why? What's the matter? Has someone died?'

156

'In a way, yes, you could put it like that,' said Ernestine. 'If you want to know more, phone Fergus at Drumstruthie, but I think it would be better to do it here. I'll wait up for you.' She put the phone down and went through to the kitchen to make herself a nice . . . a cup of tea. Nice it wasn't.

By morning the search for Timothy Bright had begun.

In the old nursery at the Midden Timothy Bright lay in bed staring at the terrible scratch-marks on the thick wooden door and wondered where on earth he was. And all the time he tried to remember what had happened to him. He could recall being on the motorcycle going down to Uncle Victor's cottage, but that seemed a long time ago. Even the ride was isolated from the events that had led up to it and for a while he couldn't remember why he had gone down to Fowey. But gradually, as the effects of the drugs and his concussion wore off, he began to get glimmerings of that awful past. One sudden insight would suddenly lead to a much fuller recollection so that he jumped back to the casino and Mr Markinkus wanting to be paid in full in ten days. Then another jump, this time forward, to the man with the cut-throat razor in a wine bar and borrowing Aunt Boskie's shares. And selling them.

It was at this point that terror intervened to prevent him thinking at all and he lay back on the mattress almost green with fear. The knowledge that he had sold Aunt Boskie's shares filled him with greater panic than the threats by Mr Markinkus and Brian Smith. He could see now it had been the worst thing to do. He could always have evaded those cheap spivs by falling back behind the ranks of the family. Brights would always take care of their own if things got really awkward. They did it to protect the family name. But now it was different. He had sold Aunt Boskie's shares and couldn't give the money back and he would never be forgiven. His panic surged to such new levels he almost saw himself for what he was before the clouds of self-delusion and pity closed again and he was poor Timothy who had been hard done by. And what had happened to all that money he had taken from the bank? It had to be somewhere. Timothy Bright summoned up every scrap of memory he could to solve the mystery. He had put the money neatly into a big briefcase. He remembered that. And he had . . . No, he couldn't be sure he had taken the briefcase down to the bike. He had the impression that someone had phoned just then . . . No, something had happened. He tried the other end of the journey. Had he had the briefcase with him then? He had been so conscious of the parcel that looked like a shoe box which must have contained money too. In that case he must have taken the briefcase as well. And it must still be at Uncle Victor's. Oh God, he had to get down there and . . . He was interrupted by the arrival of Miss Midden.

'Have you got a surname yet?' she demanded.

'It's Bright. I'm Timothy Bright. Look here, can't you get me my clothes?'

'No,' said Miss Midden. 'You came here naked and you're going to stay that way until I find out why you came and who with and what exactly has been going on. You can use the towel to make yourself faintly decent.'

'But I can't stay here. I mean I don't know who you are or where this is and it's terribly important . . .' He stopped. He mustn't tell this woman anything more. He shouldn't have told her his name.

'What's so terribly important?' she asked.

'Nothing,' said Timothy Bright defiantly.

'Which is what you'll be having for breakfast,' said Miss Midden and went out and locked the door.

Timothy Bright got up off the mattress and looked through the bars at the open fell. There was no one in sight. Some sheep were grazing by the bank of an old track that ran away over a slight rise towards some distant blue hills. Far away the sunlight glinted on the water of the reservoir, but the sight did nothing to stir his memory. Instead another memory had surfaced. It had something to do with Uncle Benderby's yacht . . . Oh God, the brown paper parcel! He'd had to take it to Spain. As the memories, all of them quite dreadful, bubbled up, Timothy Bright became almost immobilized. At least where he was, in this room, he was safe for

158

the time being. He didn't want to think any more. He lay down under the bloodstained duvet and tried to sleep.

In his office at Police Headquarters the Chief Constable pushed the report on the weekend's activities away from him and wondered how he could possibly broach the subject of the anonymous phone call about the Midden Farm without arousing suspicion that he had made it himself. There was obviously no way unless . . . He sent for the Head of the Serious Crime Squad.

'Ah, Rascombe,' he said. 'A splendid bash on Saturday night. My congratulations. Thoroughly enjoyed it. Did you have any more trouble from the media?'

'The Saphegic brothers took their minds off our affairs, sir.'

'The Saphegie brothers? Are they back in business? I thought they had decided to buy their time,' said the Chief Constable.

'Oh, they've paid up all right, sir. Keep to the timetable nicely. But knowing the way the press works, I thought I'd give them the Puddley murder to get their teeth into. Take their mind off our little business.'

'But the Saphegie boys had nothing to do with the Puddley job,' said the Chief Constable, groping towards some sort of understanding.

'That's the point, sir,' Rascombe told him. 'It's no skin off their nose to have the press thinking they do. Enhances their reputation. In the circles they move in it counts, being linked in with a really nasty murder like that. I had a word with them first. Got them to agree, like.'

'Very obliging, I must say,' said the Chief Constable.

Rascombe grinned. 'Like they say, sir, there's no such thing as bad publicity.'

Sir Arnold Gonders said nothing. The absurdity of the maxim had never struck him with quite such force as it did at this moment. However, if the Saphegie brothers, who specialized in debt collection to the point where it spilled over into a protection racket, wanted to be connected in the public mind with the battery-acid murder of an entire family, that was their business. Sir Arnold's interest was quite the reverse. Somehow he had to pin the blame for the intruder on Miss Midden.

'Nothing else I ought to know about?' he asked, and gave the Inspector a very keen look. 'Nothing out of the ordinary anywhere?'

It was the sort of question and look Inspector Rascombe recognized, and in the usual way he would have known how to respond. This time he was at a total loss. 'Any particular area, sir?' he enquired.

Sir Arnold considered for a moment. Rascombe was a good copper, the sort of copper he himself had been, and anyhow he had enough on him to ensure that the Detective Inspector stayed loyal. Even so, the Chief Constable hesitated. It was best to keep certain things under his hat. On the other hand that damned Bea knew and in all likelihood had been party to whoever had dumped the bugger. The Chief Constable still couldn't get his mind round that problem at all sanely, and then there was Mrs Thouless. By this time she had probably been down to get the bread and milk at Solwell, in which case half the neighbourhood almost certainly knew by now. There was nothing for it. It was time to strike back and at least muddy the waters a bit. 'Ever had anyone try to fit you up, Rascombe?' he asked.

The Inspector smiled. 'It's been known,' he said, and understood the Chief's reluctance. He had heard something about Edgar Hoover too, now that he came to think of it. It was difficult to imagine Sir Arnold Fucking Gonders in drag all the same. Horrid.

'When you were first in the CID, I suppose,' said the Chief Constable encouragingly.

Rascombe wasn't fooled. 'No, they don't give up easy, sir,' he said. 'They like to think that being on the Force and all that and seeing so many villains make a bit, you know what I mean, weakens a man's resolve. So they come on again and I suppose sometimes they score. Course, other times they get their mittens in a fucking rat-trap. That's what my little lot did. Still wondering

160

what the fuck hit them, as a matter of fact, down Parkhurst. Fourteen and ten they got. I sometimes think of them at night sitting in front of the telly.' Detective Inspector Rascombe smiled reminiscently.

'Fourteen and ten?' said the Chief Constable. 'You don't mean Bugsy Malone and the Sundance Kid tried to fit you up?' The Inspector nodded. 'And you landed them with two kilos of coke for their pains? Oh dear, oh dear, Rascombe, and I always thought they'd done it too. Still, it does you credit. It does indeed. Fancy hanging that lot on them. That is a lovely one. Mind you, they deserved it for trying to bend a copper. By my book there's nothing dirtier than trying to turn one of us. Well, I daresay we can see they don't get any parole too. As I always say, a job done properly is a job worth doing.' And the Chief Constable made a note in his diary to have a word with a man he knew who was on the parole board for the Isle of Wight. 'Now, where were we?'

Detective Inspector Rascombe decided on a tactful approach. 'About suspicions that someone's on the move?' he suggested

The Chief Constable approved. 'Something like that,' he said and came to a decision. 'Just a word that came my way. Nothing certain, and of course there may be nothing to it.'

'Course. Most often isn't,' said the Inspector encouragingly. 'Still, it's often these little words that put a major thing our way, I always say. Anyone I know?'

Sir Arnold fell back on discretion. 'No one I know either. That's the bother.' He paused. 'Does the term "Child-minder" mean anything to you?'

'Only the obvious, like,' said Rascombe. 'You wouldn't be thinking of . . .'

'Could be, Rascombe, could very well be,' said the Chief Constable, 'and if it is, we've got to stamp it out before it becomes another fucking Orkney. And I do mean stamp. I'm not having Twixt and Tween go down in history as another place the paedophiles had a ball. That stuff is horrible.'

'Vile, sir, loathsomely vile,' said Rascombe, having to veer away from the idea that somebody had been trying to fit the Chief Constable up with a crime. There could be no doubting Sir Arnold's horror at the thought of a paedophile's ball. 'Have you got any idea where to look, sir?'

The Chief Constable stared out the window at the city. 'One place you can forget is the Social Services Child Abuse unit,' he said. 'Breathe a word of this there and it'll be right across the county in no time at all.'

'Agreed, sir, those do-gooders foul things up something terrible.'

'You can say that again,' Sir Arnold agreed, with the private thought that just about anybody could foul things up for him, never mind do-gooders. On the other hand the idea of paedophiles was an excellent one: the very mention of child molesters had an emotional appeal that blinded people to obvious facts. Muddy waters wasn't in it. And there was something else. A really nice goodie. Tailor-made for trouble. 'What I want you to look for is any report, anything that suggests something's wrong. Doesn't matter how insignificant it looks, check it out . . . And if I'm right in my hunch, and mind, that's all it is, if I'm right and what I heard has any significance at all . . .'

He paused and looked at Rascombe for a moment as though deciding that the Inspector was indeed the man to handle the issue. 'The words were ''up behind Stagstead.'' He's an old army chap and he's got this very convenient place for taking the photos of them. That's one source and it was purely accidental with a crossed line on the phone. In the normal way I wouldn't have taken any notice of it except that the bloke speaking had one of those voices you can't put a face to but I could swear that somewhere along the line I'd met him before with a bit of the old nasty stuff, you follow. I might have put the phone down but I didn't and then the other fellow said something that did strike me, ''Do you think it ought to go in Gide Bleu?'' What do you make of that?'

'Guide Bleu, isn't it, sir? Not Gide, surely.'

'Well, of course in the normal way I'd have said he'd been

162

mispronouncing too, except he sounded too toffee-nosed to make that sort of mistake. But the key thing was the other slimy-tongued bloke repeated it, ''I think they want to keep off any list like the Gide Bleu. Got to be careful.'' I lost them after that.'

'That Gide Bleu sounds a bit off, sir,' said the Inspector.

'More off than you'd imagine,' said Sir Arnold, silently thanking Auntie Bea for putting him in the way of this literary disinformation. She'd been encouraging Vy to brush up her French with *La Porte étroite* and the Chief Constable had been stung into admitting that he didn't know who Gide was. 'You are such a philistine,' Vy had said as they went to bed that night. Well, the old bag had handed him a good tip now.

'You see, Inspector,' the Chief Constable continued, 'I went back and looked this bloke Gide up and what did I find, a really horrible old faggot with a penchant for Arab boys. Wrote books about them. One of them is called *The Narrow Door* and it don't take two guesses to know why. Filthy sod. So you see the Gide Bleu is something else again.'

Inspector Rascombe was looking impressed. 'This could be something really big, sir,' he said. 'I mean after all the bad publicity we've been given lately with the SCS and all that, we could win ourselves a bit of popular support putting a lot of sex perverts behind bars.'

'My thoughts exactly,' said the Chief Constable.

'Another thing that occurs to me, sir,' the Inspector went on, encouraged by Sir Arnold's attitude, 'is that if I am thinking about the right area up behind Stagstead, there are some wealthy people up there with big houses and estates and so on . . .' He faltered and looked at the Chief Constable with a feeling that he was walking on very thin ice. After all, the old bugger had a place up there too. But Sir Arnold was quite relaxed, though he did look more than a bit weary.

'I know what you're going to say, Inspector, and I appreciate your tact and fine feelings, but you mustn't think of me,' the Chief Constable said. 'You have your duty to do and you must ignore my position in the community. Now you understand why I have entrusted you with this particular job. It is vital I take a wholly unbiased attitude and you're the man I can safely leave the whole matter with. All you've got to do is check out any known sex offenders on the computer and see if there's been anything unusual in that area.'

And with the certain knowledge that Major MacPhee's name would come up on the computer, and that any detailed enquiry at Stagstead would bring to light the anonymous phone call about the Midden and boys being buggered, the Chief Constable dismissed Detective Inspector Rascombe and went back to work on a sermon he had promised to give to the Church of the Holy Monument the following Sunday. He intended to stress the mysterious way in which God worked to achieve His ends. As usual, the Chief Constable had no doubt whose ends those were. He didn't have any doubt whatsoever that the ways themselves were filled with mystery.

He had got halfway through the sermon, and was stressing the need for punishment of offenders as a foretaste of things to come in the afterlife, when he began to have a nagging feeling that he was missing something important on the more practical side of his own life. There was something he ought to be doing if he was not to spend the rest of his life in fear of blackmail. He had to find out who really had been responsible for trying to fit him up with that young bastard. He would see if he could trap Auntie Bea, but first there were genuine areas of enquiry to look into. That wasn't all, either. Sir Arnold shook his head fitfully and got up to make himself a cup of strong black coffee. He really must start thinking clearly.

Chapter 20

By lunchtime Timothy Bright's memory was considerably improved. And by supper he had remembered everything with remarkable clarity. The process had been accelerated by hunger and the smells reaching him, he supposed, from the kitchen. They were, first of all, the smell of bacon being fried with eggs. Later came the scent of roast lamb with rosemary and finally, around six, he could have sworn they were cooking a leg of pork.

In fact it was merely a chop but with some crackling added to give it the desired effect. And the smell, the delicious smell, did not emanate from the kitchen. In her stockinged feet Miss Midden had climbed the stairs to the old nursery with trays and had allowed the draught to waft the smells under the door for ten minutes. Then she had crept downstairs again, put on her shoes and had come clattering up to enquire if he wanted any lunch. Timothy Bright did. He was ravenous. But he still refused to tell her exactly who he was or why he had broken into her house and hidden himself under the Major's bed. He tried bluster.

'You've got no right to keep me locked up like this,' he'd said after the roast lamb treatment.

Miss Midden had denied keeping him locked up. 'You are free to leave the house this very minute. Nobody is stopping you.'

'But you won't give me my clothes. I can't just go out with nothing on.'

'I can't give you your clothes because I haven't got them. I've looked for them all over the house. And the garden. They aren't to be found. If you choose to break into other people's houses stark naked, that's your business. I'm not here to provide burglars with trousers and jackets.'

'Yes, I can see that,' said Timothy Bright, 'but you are starving me.'

'I'm doing nothing of the sort,' said Miss Midden. 'I don't clothe intruders and I don't feed people who break in and then refuse to tell me who exactly they are or what they are doing here.'

Timothy Bright said he didn't know what he was doing in her house either.

'Then you had better think about it very carefully because until you tell me the truth and nothing but the truth you are going to remain a very hungry young man.' She turned towards the door and then stopped. 'Of course, if you want me to call the police, I shall be only too happy to oblige you.'

But Timothy Bright's face was ashen. 'No, please don't do that,' he said. If she called the police, he'd be in even deeper trouble. The man with the razor, piggy-chops and the money he had stolen from Aunt Boskie . . . No, she mustn't call the police.

It was the smell of roast pork that broke him. Particularly the crackling. The skinned pig came to mind, and the fact that it wouldn't have any crackling even if it was roasted. And the Major had visited him twice to ask how he was doing and to say that Miss Midden was a decent person and not at all hard-hearted. 'You can trust her,' he said. 'She's ever so nice really but she's a Midden and one of the old sort. Do anything for people, she will, if they treat her properly. She just won't put up with being lied to and messed about.'

'She doesn't seem very kind-hearted to me,' Timothy Bright retorted.

'That's because you won't tell her the truth,' said the Major. 'She hates people lying to her or making excuses. You tell her the truth and you'll be all right. And another thing. She doesn't like the police so she won't hand you over provided you tell her everything.'

Timothy Bright wanted to know why she didn't like the police.

'Because she says they're corrupt and beat people up in the cells. She's got it in for the Chief Constable too. He's a horrible man.

166

You must have read about the way they've framed people round here. It was on *Panorama* and in the papers. The Serious Crime Squad are as bent as a nine-pound note. Talk about brutal.'

On this cheerful note the Major had gone back to the kitchen to report. 'One more meal and he'll spill the beans,' he said. 'It's just that he doesn't trust you.'

'I don't trust myself,' said Miss Midden enigmatically, and busied herself with the piece of pork.

At six that night Timothy Bright broke down and wept. He said he'd tell them everything if only they'd promise not to tell anyone else.

Miss Midden wasn't giving any promises. 'If you've done something really horrible, anything violent like rape or murder,' she began, but Timothy Bright swore he hadn't done anything like that. It had to do with money and getting into debt and couldn't he have something to eat?

'That depends on what you tell me,' Miss Midden replied. 'If you so much as tell one lie, I'll spot it. Ask him.' She indicated the Major standing in the doorway behind her.

The Major nodded. Miss Midden had an uncanny nose for a lie, he said.

'And just because I have a personal quarrel with the Chief Constable, don't think I won't hand you over,' Miss Midden went on. 'If you lie to me, that is.'

Timothy Bright swore on his honour he wouldn't lie to her. Miss Midden had her doubts about that but she kept them to herself. 'All right, you can come down to the kitchen and tell us the story,' she said. 'In that towel. You're not getting any clothes until I know who and what I've got on my hands.'

At the kitchen table, with the smell of roast pork filling the room, Timothy Bright told his story. At the end Miss Midden was satisfied. She got out the pork and the crackling and the roast potatoes and the broad beans and carrots and the apple sauce and watched him eat while she considered what to do. At least he had good table manners, and what she had heard had the ring of truth about it. He was just the sort of conceited young fool who would get himself into trouble with drug dealers and gamblers. She had been particularly impressed by his admission that he had stolen Aunt Boskie's shares.

'Where does this aunt of yours live?' she asked.

'She's got a house in Knightsbridge but she's usually in a nursing home. I mean she's ninety-one or two.'

Miss Midden asked for her exact address. Timothy Bright looked alarmed. 'Why do you want to know that?' he asked. He was into the apple pie now. 'You're not going to get in touch with her, are you? I mean she'd kill me if she knew. She's a really fierce old woman.'

'I merely want to know if she exists, this aunt of yours,' Miss Midden said, and forced him to give her the address as well as that of his Uncle Fergus and his parents. Timothy Bright didn't understand, and he panicked when she went to the phone in the hall.

'Oh for goodness' sake, use what few brains you seem to possess,' she told him when he followed her into the hall clutching the towel round his waist. 'I'm only going to call Directory Enquiries. Go back and finish your supper.' But he stood there while she dialled and got confirmation that there was a Miss Bright who lived at the address he had given. And a Mr Fergus Bright at Drumstruthie.

'That seems satisfactory,' she said when she put the phone down. 'Now you can have some coffee.'

Half an hour later Timothy Bright went to the old nursery with a book Major MacPhee had lent him. It was by Alan Scholefied and was appropriately called *Thief Taker*.

Downstairs Miss Midden sat on over her own supper thinking hard. She had very little sympathy with Master Bright but at least he had had the good sense to tell her the truth. She would have to do something about it.

In his apartment overlooking Hyde Park Sir Edward Gilmott-Gwyre put the telephone down with a deep, ruminative sigh. It was not often he heard from his daughter and he was grateful for this infrequency. But now the damned woman had phoned to say she was coming round and had something terribly urgent to tell him. 'Why can't you tell me over the phone, my dear?' he had asked almost plaintively.

'Oh no, it's far too important for that, Daddy,' she had bleated. 'And anyway you wouldn't like it.'

Sir Edward shifted his bulk in the small chair and didn't suppose he would. He had never liked anything about his daughter. For one thing she reminded him too clearly of his wife and besides she was the only girl he had ever known who had progressed (sic) from the puppy-fat of adolescence to the several spare tyres of middle-age without a modicum of lissom grace in between. As for her mind, if it could be called that, it too had remained as vacuous as several expensive co-educational establishments and a Swiss finishing school could make it. To her undoting father, Vy Carteret Purbrett Gilmott-Gwyre at twenty three had had all the physical and mental attractions of a lead-polluted black pudding. He had been absolutely delighted when Arnold Gonders, then a mere Superintendent, asked for her hand in marriage. As had been said at the time, her father had not so much given her away at the wedding as thrown her. And now, to judge by the inane whimpering over the phone, she might well have got herself into really serious trouble. Sir Edward had no desire to get her out of it.

To prepare himself for her visit he had two very large brandies and hid the gin bottle. He was damned if he was going to top her up. Lack of alcohol would make her leave all the sooner. He had Elisha Beconn coming to dinner and he intended to have his daughter out of the flat long before that learned professor arrived. In the event he was shocked to find her completely sober and obviously genuinely disturbed.

'Now what's the matter?' he said with the total lack of sympathy that characterized all his emotional contacts with the women in his family.

Lady Valence, his wife, had once remarked that life with Sir Edward could only be compared with being smoked as a ham. 'Not that I mind his smoking,' she said, 'it is the remorseless misogyny of the brute that has turned me into the wizened creature you see before you.' It was an unfair comparison. The unutterable boredom his wife's conversation engendered and the crassness of his daughter had left Sir Edward a dedicated believer in the Women's Movement as a means of securing his own privacy.

'It is the great advantage of the liberated and educated woman that she wants to have nothing to do with me,' he had said, and had become an advocate of universal lesbianism to the point of female conscription into the army for the same reason.

Now, faced with his distraught and sober daughter, he could only sigh and wish that the next half hour should pass quickly.

'I don't know how to tell you, Daddy,' Vy said, sinking into the baby talk she misguidedly thought he enjoyed.

'Need you bother yourself?' her father asked. 'If you don't feel –'

'You see it's Arnold, Daddy,' she went on. 'He's become impossible.'

'Become?' said Sir Edward, who had always found his son-in-law quite unbearable.

'He's begun to plot against me, Daddy, he really has.'

'Plot? What the hell for?'

'He wants to silence me.'

'Really? Enterprising chap, your husband. I tried for years with your mother and it didn't do any bloody good at all.'

Lady Vy's face sagged still further. 'Why are you always so horrid to me, Daddy?' she whimpered.

'Because you come to see me, dear, that's why,' said Sir Edward. 'Now if you stayed away I couldn't be, could I?'

'But you don't even hear what I have to say,' she went on.

'I try not to, but some of it sticks. What part were you thinking of?'

'About Arnold plotting against me. You see, he wants to stop me talking to the newspapers.'

Sir Edward peered over his cheeks at her. 'Very sensible of him, I'd have thought,' he said. 'I agree with him. You shouldn't go anywhere near the newspapers. What are you complaining about, dear?'

Lady Vy looked wildly round the book-lined room and fastened on the heavy velvet curtains. 'He put a naked man into my bed the other day and then nearly beat him to death,' she almost screamed in her panic. 'Then he made me help him take him downstairs into the cellar and he tied him up in two sheets with yards of tape round him and he got a basting syringe from the kitchen and . . .'

'Wait a moment, wait a moment. I'm lost. Arnold got a basting syringe from the kitchen? What in God's name did he do that for?'

'He used it to give the boy the Valium with whisky. It was awful, Daddy.'

'I should rather think it was. Absolutely revolting and rather dangerous. You should tell him that. After all, he is your husband, though God alone knows what made you marry the shit. Still, it's your bed and you've got to lie in it.'

'But not with a naked man friend or whatever of Arnold's, Daddy. You can't expect me to do that.'

'Really? Don't see why not. I should think anyone would be better than Arnold. Ghastly fellow. Always thought he was.'

'But don't you understand what I'm saying, Daddy dear?' Lady Vy appealed pathetically.

'I'm trying not to, my dear,' said Sir Edward, rinsing his mouth out with brandy for emphasis and spitting into the fire. 'It all sounds too utterly filthy. Still, if you will bring these things to my attention . . .'

Lady Vy made a final attempt. 'Daddy, you've got to do something. Arnold mustn't be allowed to get away with it. He must be stopped.'

171

Sir Edward shrugged massive shoulders and remained silent. He often found that the best thing to do was to stretch his daughter's attention span past its limit so that she forgot what she had been saying. This time it didn't work.

'He's going to kill me when he finds out I've told you,' she went on.

Sir Edward looked at her appreciatively.

'There is that, of course,' he said presently.

But for once his daughter had been driven past the point of the baby talk she thought he enjoyed. 'He's going to blacken your name too. He said he'd have the whole family in the gutter press like Fergie's father and Prince Charles and he can, you know. He's been doing some terrible things and he's going to be arrested and he's trying to save his skin by using us. You don't understand. And I've left him for good. And he's out for blood.'

All the words Auntie Bea had dinned into her poured out and for the first time in his life Sir Edward took some notice of her. He was particularly horrified by the mention of Major Ferguson and he certainly didn't like talk about blood. In fact he was genuinely alarmed.

He had never had any time for Sir Arnold, but he had to admit that the man could not be not as cretinous as he looked. In his opinion it was a disgrace that such a creature should have been appointed a Chief Constable, and he had regarded the appointment as another example of administrative decadence and the failure of the men in Whitehall to think at all clearly on social issues. That decadence had spread all the way to the top now in the exposure of those private peccadilloes that had always been there but had never been made public knowledge to hoi polloi for perfectly sound reasons of state. All that had been changed, and even the Royal Family was not invulnerable to the smears of exposure and the destruction of the mystique that was essential to political stability. Sir Edward Gilmott-Gwyre knew his Burke, but he also had no illusions about the loyalty of all his friends once he had been pilloried. The pack would turn and rend him almost without any

172

hesitation. He put the tendency down to the need to get rid of the contagion of contempt as fast as possible. It was as necessary as the swift scavenging of hyenas to keep dead meat from rotting in the sun.

On the other hand he had no intention of becoming that dead meat and, for once, he had morality on his side. He was, if Vy was to be believed, being threatened by a man who was as brazenly corrupt as any police officer promoted and protected by Mrs Thatcher. It was necessary to redress the balance by bringing the past forward to purge the present. In such ringing and largely meaningless phrases Sir Edward had gulled the voters in the past. He saw no reason why he should not put his gifts for eloquence to more personal use.

'Now then, my dear,' he said to his daughter. 'I want you to put in writing, that is to write down, what you have just told me.' For a moment he hesitated. He was putting an unbearable burden on the poor woman to ask her to write anything vaguely coherent, indeed to write at all. 'Have you anyone who can help you write it down? Where are you staying?'

'With Auntie Bea, Daddy,' said Vy, much happier now that the storm seemed to have passed.

Again Sir Edward hesitated. 'Auntie Bea?' he said, and was conscious once more of a frisson of horror. He had once in the mid-seventies, while on a Parliamentary fact-finding mission to Outer Mongolia, been forced to share a tent with the so-called Auntie Bea and had found her fascination with thongs and the sexual attributes of leather at first exhilarating and then terrifying. He had never played the role of a woman in an encounter with a woman before. Eton had been bad enough: Ulan Bator was frankly appalling. That his daughter should now be the plaything of a woman like Auntie Bea struck him as being exceedingly bizarre and ironic.

All the same, there could be no doubting Auntie Bea's intellect when she chose to apply it. He could cheerfully leave Sir Arnold Gonders' baleful curriculum vitae in her hands. And, of course, Vy. Sir Edward cheered up. He had a purpose in life once more and his daughter had finally found a woman who could make use of her. When he finally got rid of Lady Vy he made several phone calls and then changed for dinner. He would sound old Elisha Beconn out about police corruption and ways of combating it and get another ball of influence rolling. It was worth decanting a really good claret. Besides, he had a theory to explain why Lady Thatcher was such a passionate advocate of arming the Bosnian Muslims. Her son was an arms dealer and by backing the Muslims so openly she was bound to help dear little Markie's standing in Saudi Arabia. It was in the discovery of real motivation in politics that Sir Edward Gilmott-Gwyre found his greatest pleasure.

Chapter 21

'Of course I don't know where he is,' Victor Gould said irritably. He disliked being phoned late at night and he particularly disliked being phoned late at night by Bletchley Bright with questions about his wretched son, Timothy. As a result, and because he had something of a bad conscience, he was less than forthcoming. 'It's true that he did come here some time ago . . .'

'What the devil did he do that for?' demanded Bletchley with his usual tact.

'Perhaps he wanted somewhere to stay,' said Victor, just managing to keep his temper. 'Why don't you ask him yourself?'

'Ask him? How the hell can I? I'm trying to find out where he has got to. The damned boy has disappeared.'

'I'm sorry to hear that,' said Victor. 'I can assure you that I haven't got him.'

'Didn't suppose for a moment you had,' said Bletchley. 'Can't see why he should come to you in any case. Still, if he does, be so good as to let us know.'

'Of course,' said Victor and put the phone down with a new and furious resolve not to have anything whatsoever to do with the damned Bright family in future. They were all impossibly rude and arrogant and Bletchley, who was usually one of the more polite ones, was showing his true Bright colours. Victor Gould turned out the light and lay in the darkness wondering what had happened to the ghastly Timothy. Perhaps he had been killed on that motorbike and his body hadn't been found. Victor didn't like the possibility but it had to be faced. Above all, he didn't like the thought of all that money sitting under the stairs. And finally and most decisively, there was Henry's future to be taken into account. No matter what had happened on that fateful night, Victor Gould was determined to keep his nephew's involvement out of it. After all, Timothy Bright had invited himself down to Pud End and had helped himself to – had stolen in fact – the tobacco with the Toad in it. Whatever had happened to him was of his own doing and no one else was to blame. Having come to this conclusion Victor Gould turned on his side and went to sleep.

Within the Bright family assembled at Drumstruthie there was no such peace to be had. The realization that his son was a thief came particularly hard to Bletchley Bright but while he was anxious to do something he was certainly not prepared to repay Aunt Boskie her one hundred and fifty-eight thousand pounds out of his own pocket.

'With interest of course,' Fergus told him.

Bletchley looked at the old man as if he had said something obscene. 'With interest be damned,' he retorted. 'Even if Boskie is correct, and I am by no means convinced that the full facts have been placed before us –'

'Balls,' Fergus interrupted. 'Don't talk like a Prime Minister at Question Time. No fudge, sir. Your son has stolen Boskie's savings and there's no getting away from it. If you want to keep him out of the courts, you will see that Boskie is fully repaid and with interest at a bank deposit rate. What's more, if those shares have moved up since that damned boy sold them, you'll make good that loss too.'

Bletchley looked desperately round at the other family members who had gathered at Drumstruthie, and found not a single sympathetic eye.

'It will almost certainly mean selling Voleney,' he said. 'And you know what that means. The old house has been in the family since 1720 and –'

'And it will remain in the family, Bletchley,' rumbled Judge Benderby Bright, who was still furious at having to fly back at such short notice from his holiday on his yacht in Llafranc. 'If you are forced to meet your boy's debts by selling the house, you will offer

176

Voleney to the family to buy at a properly adjusted price. Should you try to do otherwise, the Serious Fraud Squad will immediately be informed of your son's crimes. I hope I have made myself clear.'

There could be no doubting it. Even Boskie's empty chair was implacably censorious.

'If you say so,' said Bletchley. 'I suppose it will have to be like that.'

'It doesn't have to be, provided you find your boy and get Boskie's money from him,' said Fergus.

'But how am I going to do that without bringing terrible publicity down on us all?' Bletchley complained. 'I'm sure you wouldn't want that.'

No one said anything but all the eyes round the table watched him carefully. Bletchley sensed this shift of initiative in his favour. 'All right then, I'll take out advertisements in all the newspapers and put his photo in. That will surely bring results.'

It was a vain attempt. Still no one stirred, but their eyes indicated the veto. A true Bright would never have made such a terrible threat. Bletchley Bright came to the family heel.

'Oh, all right,' he said. 'All the same it's jolly hard to know how to go about finding Timothy if he doesn't want to be found. He's just vanished off the face of the earth.'

'Very wise of him,' muttered the Judge. 'In his shoes I'd stay there. Have you enquired of the French Foreign Legion?'

'Or the police,' said Vernon. 'You may have some luck with them. I always did think allowing him to have a motorbike was a most dangerous thing to do.'

'I never did encourage him,' Bletchley replied, 'besides he's twenty-eight. I'd hardly call him a boy.'

'Never mind what you'd call him. What I am trying to say is that he may well have come off the thing and even possibly . . . Do you happen to know if he's insured?'

'He's bound to be,' said Bletchley, taking hope from this prospect.

'I don't suppose he's sufficiently covered to repay Boskie,' said Fergus. 'And in any case it is too much to hope for.'

Bletchley Bright left the gathering a drained and drawn man. The realities he had spent a lifetime avoiding had finally caught up with him in the shape of a dissolute and criminal offspring.

When he arrived back at Volcney it was to be greeted by a distraught Ernestine. 'Oh God,' she said. 'It's too awful. Do you know that Boskie has escaped?'

'Escaped? What on earth are you talking about? She can't have. She's not being imprisoned anywhere.'

'That's what Fergus has just phoned to say,' his wife told him. 'He said I was to tell you that she has escaped from the clinic and gone to London to see the Home Secretary.'

'But she can't have. She's seriously ill and –'

'Fergus said that if she dies, the family will hold you responsible for her death.'

Bletchley stared at his wife through bloodshot eyes. It had been a long drive from Drumstruthie and he had had time to try to think. 'Never mind the old bitch dying. Why has she gone to see the Home Secretary? What on earth for?'

'To tell him about Timothy, of course. Apparently she knows the Minister personally. Fergus seemed to think she had an affair with him . . . In fact he's certain she did.'

As she broke down and began to cry, Bletchley took the decanter in his hands and poured himself a stiff whisky. 'If you're seriously telling me that Aunt Boskie who is ninety had an affair with a man who at best reckoning can't be more than forty-three, you must be mad. She'd have been in her sixties when he hit puberty. It's a positively filthy thought. She'd be older than you are now, for Christ's sake. Don't be silly.'

The taunt was too much for his wife. 'I'm only telling you what Fergus said. And why is it so silly? You think it's silly for a woman my age to want to be made love to by a young healthy man with real feelings and the body to express them with? You're the one who's mad. Mad, mad, mad, mad . . .'

As she dashed from the room and her words reached him distantly from the corridor, Bletchley Bright looked sorrowfully round the great room and let his mind, such as it was, roam back through the centuries to the time the first Bright, old Bidecombe Bright who was known as 'Brandy', had stood there and had been proud of the achievements that had culminated in the building of Voleney House. And now, thanks to the criminal lunacy of his damned son, he, Bletchley Bright, directly descended from old Brandy, was going to have to sell the house he had been born and brought up and had led such a wonderfully idle life in. It was an unbearable prospect. He poured himself another Scotch and went into the gun room.

Chapter 22

Miss Midden was entirely a different person when she arrived in Fowey. She had had to change trains to get to Plymouth and had had very little sleep. Looking at her face in the mirror of the station lavatory, she thought it was suitably careworn for the role she had chosen for herself. She went out and bought a round hat and a blue coat at a charity shop and put them on. She also bought a large canvas hold-all. Then she went to a car rental office, hired an Escort for the day, and drove to Pud End. She intended to arrive at lunchtime when Mr Gould would be too busy or hungry to want to bother asking too many awkward questions.

He hardly asked any at all. He didn't want to know about bloody Timothy Bright. He was still seething over Bletchley's rudeness on the phone.

'I'm from the hospital,' she told him. 'I've come for Timothy Bright's things. He's ever so much better now he's off the drip and he's asked for them.'

Victor Gould said he was glad to hear it, though whether he was glad Timothy Bright was off the drip or in hospital or simply because he didn't want the bloody lout's things in his house it was impossible to say. He went to fetch them and Miss Midden bustled along behind him chattering about how busy she was and how she had to go over to Bodmin because old Mr Reavis needed his insulin and . . .

Victor Gould watched her drive off before realizing he hadn't asked which hospital his damned nephew was in. Not that he cared. He was expecting Mrs Gould back next day and wasn't looking forward to her return. He decided to say nothing about Timothy or his things. Silence, where the Bright family was concerned, was golden, and anyway he was going to have enough of her forgiveness without getting further into guilt.

By two o'clock Miss Midden was back on the train. She had phoned the Major and told him to pick her up at eleven that night.

By that time Inspector Rascombe's investigation into any unusual activities in the Stagstead area had unearthed the anonymous phone call.

'Came in on Monday morning at 11.12 a.m.,' the WPC on duty told him. 'Man's voice. Wouldn't leave his name or address. Using a public phone booth. It's written down here.'

The Detective Inspector looked at the message. ' "Boys being buggered Middenhall,'' repeated twice. Interesting, very interesting. That's where that awful woman lives, isn't it?' he said. 'Gave us a lot of trouble some years back.'

The WPC didn't share his dislike. 'Miss Midden. Very respectable lady by all accounts. Middens have been up there for yonks.'

'That's all very well, but who are the people at the Middenhall?' said Rascombe, and went on to check out two car thefts at Pyal and a break-in at Ratfen and finally some sheep stealing over on Loft Fell Moss. Nothing added up to a definite lead to paedophilia.

He had more luck on the computer file of sex offenders and was particularly struck by the name MacPhee who had done time in 1972 for 'cottaging' and whose address in 1984 had been the Ruffles Hotel, Stagstead. MacPhee had also been arrested and charged on four charges of being drunk and disorderly over the years. 'You'd better check that fucker out,' said the Inspector. 'Yes, I'd like to know a bit more about this Major MacPhee.'

But in fact the Major came fairly far down the Inspector's list of interesting sex offenders and the area had a sufficient number to keep him busy for some time. It was only when he came back to his office and found that the same Major MacPhee's present address was The Midden Farm that he took notice of him again. 'We get a call from a hoaxer about some boy being buggered at the

Middenhall and we find this bloke living up there with a record for D and D and cottaging. This smells dirty to me, don't it just. What else do we have up there, Sergeant? I want to know.'

'There, or down the road at the Middenhall as well?' the Sergeant asked.

'The Middenhall? What's that?'

'Don't know how to describe it,' said the Sergeant. 'It's not exactly a guest house or a nursing home. At least I don't think it is. It's some sort of community place people come and stay in.'

'Really? A community place? What sort of people?' said Rascombe, whose nose for dreadful dirt was now firmly fixed on the Middenhall.

'Well, I don't know exactly. I heard someone say Miss Midden – she's the old biddy who owns the place – Miss Midden had told this person that they were all family and entitled to live there for free.'

'Really? Family? What sort of family? Got kids, have they?' said the Inspector. 'I want to know about this family.'

'I'll get the names from the council offices, the names for poll-tax purposes. Could get a lead that way.'

'Follow that up, Sergeant. I want to know everything there is to know about this Middenhall place and the people up there. Send someone over to the Council. Oh yes, and make sure the enquiry is discreet. This could be a very important case indeed.'

As a result of this instruction a plainclothes man visited the Community Charge offices with such awesome discretion that the news that the police were interested in Miss Midden and the goings-on at the Middenhall was guaranteed to spread rapidly through Shire Hall and thence to the general public in Stagstead.

That afternoon the Inspector brought in some of his men from Tween and set up a special unit to watch the Middenhall. 'I've called you here,' he told them, 'because this could be a big one and if it's as big a one as I think it is we've got to play dead cagey. We get this one right we're going to give our public image the car-wash it needs. What we are about to uncover is something the media's going to love us for. And considering the shit they've flung fanwise at us, this time they're going to lick arse and love it.' He paused to let the point sink it before going on. 'Only thing is we're up against people with a lot of influence and political pull. That's why I've called you in. You're not locals and you aren't known in the district. We can't afford any slip-ups. Right? Right. Any questions?'

A detective sergeant in the front row put up his hand.

'Yes, Bruton, what is it?'

'I'm local,' he said

'Yeah, well, we need you because you know the area. That's why you're here.'

'Could we know the area where all this is taking place, sir?'

'In due course, yes, of course you can. I'm just trying to set the scene in your heads so we don't blow the case. And the way we can do that is by being too nosy. In fact the moment these people get a whiff of copper in the air they're going to go to ground so fast we won't know they was ever there. So it's long-range surveillance all the way, which of course doesn't make it any easier for us. Right? Right.' And having answered his own question the Inspector asked if there were any from the floor.

And again the Sergeant in the front row put up his hand. 'When you say long-range surveillance, sir, what exactly had you got in mind?'

Rascombe looked at Bruton doubtfully. He was beginning to wonder if it was wise to have such a troublemaker on the team. In the Inspector's mind questions equalled trouble. The fewer anyone asked the better he liked it. And them. He was beginning to dislike the Sergeant.

'By long-range surveillance, Sergeant,' he said, going into official patter, 'we mean the avoidance of any line-of-sight contact with the suspect or, as in this case, suspects; the use of audio-visual auxiliary equipment in a non-observable context for the maintenance of continuous monitoring of said suspects' modus vivendis and operandis, the assessment of the material so obtained by trained officers with a view to building up a comprehensive and in-depth psychological profile of the suspect's psychology. I hope I've made myself clear, Sergeant.'

For a brief moment Sergeant Bruton looked as though he were going to give a truthful answer. But discretion prevailed. 'Sure, sir. I just wanted to know,' he said. 'Very clear, I'm sure.'

Inspector Rascombe checked the corridor outside, then shut the door with a furtive caution before turning back to the team. 'When I tell you the area of our investigation I think you will all appreciate the need for absolute discretion,' he said in a hushed tone, and unfolded a large-scale map of the fell district to the north. There was a sudden look of interest on the detectives' faces. They all knew who had a place up there.

Inspector Rascombe's pointer moved over to the Middenhall. 'As you can see from this map the particular target is not one that can be easily approached. That's almost certainly the reason it was chosen for these horrible activities. And it makes surveillance bloody difficult. Over here we have open fell country stretching away for several miles until you get to the Parson's Road and Six Lanes End here. No cover on that side except for one or two drystone walls and a number of sheep which as you can see is not a lot of help. Up here is the Midden Farm which is to be under surveillance at all times. Right, then over here down the road is the place called Middenhall. That is a major target, *the* major target in fact. And again as you can see there is a lake to the south and round the back here through these here woods is the quarry garden. Beyond them there's the river Idd with good cover along the banks and the water meadows in the valley here. That is as far as I can tell the only feasible route for the surveillance teams to take and that being the case we aren't going to take it. Anyone here tell me why?'

'I don't suppose it could have anything to do with the fact that Miss Midden might expect us to use it?' said Sergeant Bruton in the front row.

The Inspector looked at him with fresh interest. 'That's very

184

smart of you, Bruton,' he said, 'working that out for yourself. And may we know how come you know who I've been talking about all this time?'

Sergeant Bruton looked down at his knees and then up again. 'Well, sir, you said the Middenhall was to be kept under surveillance at all times and Miss Midden owns the Middenhall and the Midden Farm so I just reckoned she might be involved or something.'

'Very good. Glad to see you're taking an interest. Anyone else got any comments?'

'If we're not going to use the cover along the river to go in, where are we going to go?' asked a detective in the third row.

Inspector Rascombe smiled. 'Here,' he said and pointed to the open fell to the west. 'By coming up this way we will avoid doing the obvious which is what they'll be looking for. The last place they'll expect us to come is over the fell. So that's the way we'll take.'

'But I thought ... nothing, sir,' said Sergeant Bruton and refrained from pointing out that, if what Inspector Rascombe had said just now was correct and the suspects at the Middenhall would go to ground the moment they got a whiff of copper, they would already be well away and wouldn't be seen for dust because everyone in Stagstead knew Miss Midden was being investigated. It seemed safer not to say anything. In any case he had been involved with Miss Midden on several charity money-raising committees and he couldn't see her being involved in a paedophile ring. Still, if the idiot Inspector wanted to go ahead there was no way he could be stopped. Best to keep his own nose clean.

The Inspector was drawing up the various units and giving them their duties. 'Unit A is assigned to traffic identification,' he said. 'Symes, Rathers, Blighten and Saxton. Round-the-clock observation of all vehicles moving along this road here.' The pointer moved along the line of the road to the Middenhall and the farm. 'I want every vehicle number and, if there is anything unusual, you will call in to base here where Unit B will do the tracing and in the event of an outgoing vehicle needing trailing or intercepting they will do it.'

As the orders went out it became clear just how comprehensive the operation was. 'There will be no radio communication unless there is an absolute emergency,' Rascombe went on. 'Communication between Units A and B will be by direct telephone line. I have made arrangements with the telephone authorities for a line to be available as soon as possible. In the meantime Unit A will use the phone box at Iddbridge to report to Unit B. On the other side of the same surveillance coin this road at the back across the Idd valley will be watched by Unit C with men here on one side of the river and here on the other and a mean time of travel between the two watches will be established. Any vehicle which fails to emerge within the mean time and which may therefore have dropped off or alternatively picked up someone from the surveillance object will be noted with particular interest and if need be intercepted here.' He pointed to the crossroads three miles to the north.

'What if they're coming the other way, sir?' a detective asked, and was rewarded with a scowl which the Inspector turned into a smile.

'Very good point, very good point, glad you raised it,' he said in an almost staccato parade-ground voice. 'Vehicles proceeding in a north–south direction will be intercepted . . .' the pointer waved vaguely around in search of a suitable crossroads and finally settled on Iddbridge five miles away, 'Here. Or alternatively, here.' This was a cattle track some two and a half miles down the Iddbridge road. But before there could be any discussion of the various problems this might entail Inspector Rascombe had turned to another issue. 'I myself intend to direct Units D and S, which will be surveillance units covering the farm, the house and the estate. I intend to establish a mobile base in the approximate area here at Six Lanes End. We will move at night and hopefully be able to interpolate the estate grounds under cover of darkness and work in twenty-four-hour shifts depending on the circumstances obtaining at the time . . .'

186

For another three-quarters of an hour the Inspector droned on and it was only when Sergeant Bruton had scribbled 'Must look up "interpolate" in dictionary' for the fifteenth time to keep himself awake that Rascombe got back to the nature of the crimes they were supposed to be investigating.

'We have,' he said, 'to be on the particular look-out for any child or children plural being taken into the Middenhall area and hopefully taken out again . . . Yes, Sergeant?'

'You can't be suggesting that Miss Midden can have anything to do with child abuse, can you, sir?' asked Sergeant Bruton almost in spite of himself. 'I mean she's, well . . . I mean . . .' He gave up.

'When you've been in the Force as long as I have, Sergeant,' said the Inspector, who had in fact been in a shorter time than Bruton, 'you will learn that the outward appearance of some of the nastiest villains is in direct contradistinction to their horribleness. Remember that, Sergeant, and you won't be taken in. And of course vice versa.'

By the following night, the various units were in position around the Middenhall. Operation Kiddlywink, the codename Rascombe had chosen, had begun.

Chapter 23

By the time Miss Midden got home that night it was well past midnight and she was exhausted. And elated.

'I think a nightcap is called for,' she said, and took a bottle of sloe gin she had made before Christmas and poured herself a glass. Then she looked doubtfully at the Major. The poor man was looking so wistfully at the bottle, and he had behaved himself with Timothy Bright.

'All right,' she said. 'You too. Get yourself a glass. We've cause for celebration. I don't know how much money is in that hold-all but at a rough guess I'd say getting on for half a million pounds. There's a parcel in there which must contain money as well. He was to take it to Spain and deliver it to someone there. So, cheers. And don't look so stunned. It's only money.'

The Major was stunned, so stunned that he hadn't touched his sloe gin. 'Half a million? Half a million?' he stammered. And she said it was only money. Major MacPhee had never been in the presence of so much money in his entire life. And he had never been in the presence of a woman who could treat such an enormous sum with such disdain. He couldn't find words to express his shock.

'It may be less and it may be more,' Miss Midden went on. 'What does it matter? It's a great deal of money. That's all.'

'What are you going to do with it?' he managed to ask.

Miss Midden sat down at the kitchen table and grinned. It was an exultant grin with a hint of malice. The Major was a weak man and he needed to know that he wasn't going to lay his hands on any of the cash. 'I am going to sleep with the shotgun beside the bed. That's the first thing I'm going to do,' she said. 'And after that we shall see.'

She finished her sloe gin, picked up the hold-all, and went through to her office to fetch the gun and a mole-trap. Mole-traps were useful for catching things other than moles. Like hands.

Once in her bedroom she emptied the hold-all and put the money in a cardboard box on top of her old mahogany wardrobe. After that she stuffed the bag with empty shoe boxes and some old clothes. Finally she put the mole-trap, now set and open, in the middle with a piece of paper over it. She also locked the door and wedged a chair under the doorknob. Then she went to bed.

Outside, the weather had begun to change. A night wind blew across the open fell and with it there came rain, gusts of rain which blew against the window. Miss Midden slept soundly. She had begun to accomplish what she had set herself to do. It had very little to do with money.

It was still raining in the morning when a motorcycle turned up and a man with a brown paper parcel came to the back door. Miss Midden opened the door reluctantly. 'Package for Major Mac-Phee,' he said and handed it over with a receipt for Miss Midden to sign. She put the parcel on the kitchen table and watched him ride off. Then she went up to the old nursery with Timothy Bright's breakfast.

'I'll get you some clothes,' she said. 'The Major isn't your size. He's too small, but I think there are some things of my grandfather's that will fit you.'

Timothy Bright thanked her and started on his porridge and bacon and eggs. At least the food, wherever he might be, was good. He hadn't eaten so well for ages. And even his terror had left him. He was beginning to feel safe.

Miss Midden returned with a pair of blue dungarees, an old shirt without a collar, and a sweater that had holes in the elbows. There was also a pair of boots that looked as though they had been used in the garden and had rusty studs on the soles. The boots were several sizes too big for him and had no laces.

'But don't think about leaving the house,' she told him, 'or showing yourself at the windows. I want only one other person to know you are here.'

'What other person?' Timothy Bright asked in alarm.

'The one who brought you here,' said Miss Midden, and went downstairs to find the Major standing at the kitchen table looking at the brown paper parcel.

'Well, don't just stand there. Open it and look at the goodies inside,' she said.

'But I don't know what it is. I haven't sent away for anything. I can't think who sent it to me.'

Miss Midden started doing the washing-up. 'One of your admirers down at the hell-hole,' she suggested. 'Some old flame. Mrs Consuelo McKoy, probably. She thinks you're a real Major. That comes from living in California too long. Fantasyland.'

Behind her the Major got some scissors and cut through the parcel tape. For a moment he was silent and then she heard him gasp. She turned and looked at the things lying on the table. They were not goodies. They were anything but goodies. They were revolting. Miss Midden had never seen anything like them in her life. And she certainly never wanted to see anything like them again as long as she lived. She looked up at the Major with utter disgust.

'You filthy animal!' she snarled. 'You utterly revolting . . . you bloody pervert. Into children. Little children. You are the lowest form of animal life . . . not animal. Animals don't go in for torturing little children. Bah!'

But Major MacPhee was shaking his head and had gone a horrid patchy colour. 'I never sent off for these,' he stammered, 'I swear I didn't. I really didn't. I don't know where they come from. I don't like this sort of thing. I never . . .'

Miss Midden said nothing. She was thinking hard. For once she was inclined to believe the Major. If he had sent off for them, he wouldn't have been fool enough to open the parcel in her presence. She was sure of that. He'd have taken it off to his room and gloated

190

over these revolting photographs and magazines in private. On the other hand . . . Hand!

'Don't touch them,' she said. 'I'll get a box and a piece of cloth. Just don't handle them.'

In fact she used a pair of gloves and put the filthy stuff, the product of sick and profit-conscious minds and a product for sick and evil minds, into a cardboard box very carefully.

The bewildered Major watched her and kept shaking his head sorrowfully. 'Not me, not me,' he repeated, almost on the point of tears.

'More to the point, why you?' said Miss Midden. 'Ask yourself that question. First him under your bed, naked and knocked about. And now this obscenity.' She stopped. This was getting really dangerous. Someone was setting the Major up. And she'd be with him. She was damned if she would. And with all that money in the house it was even more dangerous. She would have to move quickly.

'We've come back early,' she announced. 'Weather changed or something. Anyway we are back. Put that filth in the back of the car and cover it with a . . . No, put the box in a dustbin bag.' And leaving the Major wondering what was going on in her mind, she dashed upstairs and hurled the contents of the hold-all out onto the bed where the mole-trap went off. Then she packed the money back into the bag and went downstairs. She put her old hat on, and a raincoat, and went across to the barn.

Five minutes later she was down at the Middenhall. There was no one about. They were late risers and she was able to sneak past the front door and round to the back of the house without being seen. In the walled garden, during the war, there had been a deep air-raid shelter with concrete steps going down into the darkness. The entrance was covered with brambles and a self-sown buddleia, and grass grew over the mound. As far as she knew nobody had ever found the entrance but she had known it was there since she was small. It had terrified her then when she once went down it with her cousin Lennox. There had been water lying six inches deep in the passages and the cold and dark and Lennox's claim that it had been used for torturing prisoners had given her the horrors.

But now she needed that deep and hidden shelter. She clambered through the undergrowth, cleared away the earth over the iron door, and finally opened it. Then she fetched a torch from the car and the hold-all and went down into the darkness. The water was still there – perhaps the same water she had waded through thirty-two years before. This time Miss Midden was unafraid. She was determined. Someone had thrown down a challenge to her. There was nothing better for her. She loved the fight.

At the very end of the passage, past rooms with rusted iron bunks on either side, the torch picked out what she had been looking for. It was a long narrow slot halfway up the concrete wall. Lennox had said it was for putting the dead bodies of men who had been shot down there. What use it had really had she had no idea. But it was out of sight of the door and anyone peering in would never spot it unless they came right into the room. She slid her hand along it and found it was dry. It would do. Then she pushed the hold-all in and went back for the box of obscene magazines and photographs and brought them down too, first removing the box from the plastic dustbin bag and putting in the hold-all containing the money to keep it dry in the sodden atmosphere of the old shelter. When that was done she splashed back and climbed the steps to the entrance and very carefully stared through the shrubs to make sure no one was about. After that the earth and grass went back over the iron door and by the time she returned to the old car there was hardly a sign that anything had been disturbed. Miss Midden went back to the house. It hadn't even been necessary to tell anyone at the Middenhall that she was home from her holiday. She had seen no one.

For the rest of the day she worked in the house and planned her next move. Outside the sheets of rain came down and the wind blew so that even the sheep seemed to huddle under the bank and the thorn trees along the old drove road. By nightfall the rain had grown even heavier and the wind continued to howl through the copse behind the Midden and across the chimney tops.

For the officers engaged in Operation Kiddlywink it was not a night to be out in. But Inspector Rascombe was adamant. A dark, wet and windy night was just the sort the paedophiles at the Middenhall would choose to stay indoors and watch pornographic videos. They certainly would not be on the look-out for teams of policemen dressed in arctic camouflage suits borrowed from the Royal Marines and intended to make them look like sheep safely grazing across Scabside Fell. He had assembled his men on the Parson's Road. From there they had to cross two miles of rough country to the Middenhall, and the night was very dark, wet and windy indeed.

'Now, when the advance party has established itself in the park opposite the house and the auxiliaries are ready to move forward to the farm, I want you to move with the utmost care. Rutherford, you and Mark will go forward round the lake here . . .'

At this point a constable opened the door of the British Telecom van the Inspector had borrowed as his Headquarters and the wind blew the Ordnance Survey map up the wall. The Inspector and Sergeant Bruton managed to get it straight again and Rascombe continued his briefing.

'As I was saying, you will rendezvous with Markin and Spender here at the bottom of the drive and attempt to make a visual survey of the house both back and front. Are there any questions?'

Sergeant Bruton had a great many, but he knew better than to ask them. Instead, a detective constable wanted to know what he ought to do in the event that he was stopped and asked by one of the suspects what he was doing.

'In the first place I very much hope that the exercises we have practised will prevent any such eventuality, and in the second I look to you all to act on your own initiative. The only thing I would not say is you are police officers. That is imperative if we are not to cause the suspects to go to ground in a big way. You can be hikers who've lost your way or anything that seems reasonable at the time. Just don't say you're ice-cream salesmen.'

On this hilarious note the Inspector wished his men good luck and the surveillance teams set out across the fell. It was 11.30. Four miles away on the road behind the Middenhall Unit C reported that no cars had travelled through their observation points since 9.30 and could they please pack up. Since they were having to use the public phone box in Iddbridge the call only got through to Rascombe when a detective from Stagstead drove up to the Mobile HQ at 01.41.

'Of course they can't go home now,' said Rascombe irritably. 'They have replacement officers to take over at the end of each stint.'

'Yes, sir, I know that,' said the detective, 'but the road is up for repair by the river and no one can use it anyway. There's no real need to watch it at all.'

But Inspector Rascombe was not to be persuaded. 'All the more reason for keeping our eyes on it,' he said. 'If anyone comes down it when it's closed, it must mean they are using it for some very sinister purpose. Stands to reason.'

'But nobody is using it. How can they?'

'Never mind how,' said the Inspector. 'Just tell them to keep an extra eye open from now.'

'Cyclops-style, sir?' said the detective and hurried out into the night before the Inspector could work the remark out and tell him not to be fucking impertinent.

In his room the Major played with his old radio. He was puzzled. He was picking up the strangest messages, none of which made sense to him. Inspector Rascombe's admonitions about radio silence were being ignored. The Major was astonished to learn, with quite surprising clarity and a flow of obscenities, that someone called Rittson had just fallen in a 'fucking stinking stream or something'. In fact it turned out to be a sheep-dipping bath and the Major was beginning to wonder what extraordinary event he had just been privy to when the person called Rittson was told furiously to maintain radio silence.

'Must be the Marines over on Meltsea Marshes,' the Major thought, and turned off his radio and went to sleep.

Out on the fell the ten constables moved forward in a strange series of small rushes as Inspector Rascombe had ordered. First two men would stumble forward and halt in a semi-crouching position while another four moved up and past them to be followed by the rest. In this curious and supposedly sheeplike fashion they moved forward against the driving rain and the searing wind. Around them genuine sheep scurried away into the darkness, only to stop and stare back at their weird imitators. And so the small group crossed the open ground, scrambled over drystone walls and, in the case of Detective Constable Rittson, fell into the sheep-dip.

By 2 a.m. they had reached their first objective, the wood on the far side of the lake, and were peering across the water at the Middenhall. The building was almost entirely in darkness and only one light burned in the house itself. But on the outside floodlights shone out onto the lake and were reflected there among the waterlilies. 'Bloody difficult to see anything with those fucking lights,' said the detective called Mark, 'and they can spot us dead easy.' They crawled back into the wood and tried the other side. The lights were still quite bright.

'He said we had to go up to the farmhouse,' said Larkin. 'So I reckon we'd better.' He and Spender set off round the lake and over the little bridge by the sluice gate and made their way up the drive towards the Midden. Behind them Rutherford had decided there was a patch of dark shadow at the corner of the Middenhall where the dustbins were and, leaving Mark to try the other side where there were a number of azalea bushes, he scurried across the lawn and had got to within ten yards of the house when something moved in front of him.

Unable to see what exactly it was, he obeyed orders and went into sheep mode, crouching down on all fours and at the same time trying to keep his eyes watching his front. In fact he had disturbed a family of badgers. There was a clang as a dustbin lid fell, a grunt and a slight noise of scrabbling. Detective Constable Rutherford turned and trundled himself away across the lawn and back over the wooden bridge. 'No bloody good,' he told the others. 'They've got someone round the back on the look-out. I reckon we'd best be off.'

The first phase of Operation Kiddlywink had been a complete failure.

Chapter 24

By Friday even Inspector Rascombe was becoming discouraged. Three of his squad were off sick, one with a nasty condition of the skin caused by the sheep-dip, one with a twisted ankle. The third had gone down with pleurisy. As he reported to the Chief Constable, 'That place is so out of the way and awkward to cover we're having real difficulty.'

The Chief Constable imagined they were. His own private investigations weren't getting anywhere either, and he was beginning to think Auntie Bloody Bea had thought the whole caper up on her own to take Lady Vy away from him. This opinion was reinforced by an acrimonious telephone call from his father-in-law in the course of which Sir Edward had told him in certain terms exactly what he thought of him and had let drop the information that for once his daughter was showing good sense by setting up house with a raving lesbian. There had been other intimations of trouble ahead in Sir Edward's outburst. He was lunching shortly at Number 10 and he intended to raise the matter of the Chief Constable's deplorable tendencies with the PM. It had been a most unpleasant monologue, punctuated by denials that he put drugged youths in his wife's bed and that he was 'into' garbage bags, parcel tape and used bed sheets.

'Are you seriously expecting me to believe you didn't insert a basting syringe into the bugger's mouth and dose him with a mixture of Valium and whisky?' Sir Edward shouted.

The Chief Constable was. Most emphatically. He'd never heard such a dreadful accusation.

'Well, I do believe it,' his father-in-law stormed, 'because that idiot daughter of mine hasn't the brain of a head-louse and she couldn't have invented that story in a month of Sundays. You drugged the bugger and you tied him up in tape. And I know you did. And if you think . . .'

Sir Arnold did. He spent hours at night compiling the names, addresses and sums of money involved that seemed his only protection now. All the same, he did nothing to discourage Inspector Rascombe. The idiot couldn't do any harm and he just might dig up something in his investigations in the Stagstead area.

Even Miss Midden had other things on her mind by that time. Every year in early August the Porterhouse Mission to the East End sent a number of children to the Middenhall. It had been a practice that dated back to the period shortly after the War when the Dean had brought reading parties up to the fell country and had stayed over at Carryclogs Hall with Brigadier General Turnbird, himself an old Porterhouse man and a very muscular Christian. The youngsters had originally been housed in bell-tents in the grounds of Carryclogs where, apart from some desultory hymn-singing and the occasional Bible-reading by the General's daughter Phoebe, they had had the run of the estate and the river Idd, which was quite shallow at that point.

'It is good for our townies to have a glimpse of Arcady,' the General had once explained to a deputation of neighbouring farmers who had come to complain that sheep had been stampeded over walls, cows had been subjected to vicious attacks with catapults, and a number of stooks of hay had been set alight by boys smoking while playing hide and seek. The farmers hadn't caught the reference to Arcady and wouldn't have given a damn if they had.

In the end their opinions and the rents they paid prevailed. Even before the General died the Mission had moved over to the Middenhall, which was sufficiently isolated to spare the farmers their previous depredations. There within the confines of the estate wall the multi-sexed and many-coloured group, some of whom came from Muslim families and consequently did not benefit from Miss Phoebe's readings, spent a fortnight exploring the woods and one another's bodies before going back to their homes in the now largely middle-class area on the Isle of Dogs where the Porterhouse Mission still operated. In fact, if it hadn't been for Miss Midden's insistence, which fitted in with the Dean's own inclinations, that the contingent of Porterhouse undergraduates who accompanied each year's batch be doubled in size to deal with the children, it is doubtful if the yearly visit could have continued. At least a dozen times in the past two summers elderly residents had returned to their rooms after dinner to find their belongings had been ransacked and items stolen, and on one awful occasion Mrs Louisa Midden had been approached by a fourteen-year-old with a very unnatural offer. Mr Joseph Midden, her husband and himself a retired gynaecologist of some repute, had been so appalled – as much by his wife's moment of hesitation before refusing as by the actual offer – that Dr Mortimer had had to be summoned to deal with his arrhythmia.

Now, as the coach carrying the children came down the drive, Miss Midden felt a strange sense of unease. The presence of so many inquisitive young minds in the grounds was a danger she should have foreseen. She would have to do something about the air-raid shelter in the walled garden. She had been so preoccupied with Timothy Bright's affairs that she had entirely forgotten the Mission. As the tents were erected on the far side of the lake Miss Midden put padlocks on all the doors in the walls of the kitchen garden and decided to make her next journey. She had a long talk with Timothy Bright in the privacy of the sitting-room, and made a phone call. Then she drove to the bus station and travelled south again.

The time had come to act.

The same thought was in Inspector Rascombe's mind. The arrival of a coach containing thirty children indicated such an enormous orgy of paedophilia that he could hardly believe the report that came in to him from the surveillance team on the Middenhall road.

'Thirty? Thirty children and some young men and women? In a coach? Christ, this looks like . . . I don't know what it looks like. But it's definitely the biggest one, this, has to be. I think we've got them this time, lads.'

As a result of this information the Inspector, reporting directly to the Chief Constable, asked if he could make the investigation Top Priority.

Sir Arnold hardly heard him. He was reading a letter from a firm of solicitors informing him that his wife intended to begin proceedings for divorce on grounds that would end his career. His Top Priority now was to stop the bitch. But he agreed, and Inspector Rascombe summoned a meeting of the Serious Crime Squad to outline the second phase of Operation Kiddlywink.

As usual, Sergeant Bruton raised awkward questions. He had been studying the details of the people living at the Middenhall. They were all in their seventies or older. 'That place is full of geriatrics,' he said.

Inspector Rascombe was unimpressed. 'So what?' he said. 'It's old men like that fancy little children. The only way they can get it up, the filthy bastards. We may be on the verge of uncovering the first Senior Citizens Sex Scandal.'

'But half of them are married or widows. There are three unmarried old biddies up there,' the Sergeant objected. 'They can't all be into child abuse.'

The Inspector considered this for a moment and found an answer. 'Maybe not, but it could be they've been threatened and are too frightened to talk. Hard-core perverts with a sadistic streak would frighten the lights out of old ladies.'

Plans for surveillance penetration of the Middenhall went ahead. 'It's a clear night on the weather forecast. So we'll close in around 01.00. I want the two-man surveillance teams in on the ground where they can video the action and install listening equipment which will relay information when to hit the place. One unit will be here in the wood and the other will be behind the house.

200

You've got rations for forty-eight hours and we should have the case wrapped up by then.'

That was Friday.

On Saturday Miss Midden struck. At 8 a.m. she left her boarding house in Clapham and presented herself at Judge Benderby Bright's town house in Brooke Street. The door was opened by a manservant, an ex-Metropolitan policeman who doubled as a bodyguard. Judge Bright's life had been threatened too often to let him feel safe except on the high seas. Even a Force Ten gale was mild compared to the feelings he had aroused among the members of families whose relatives had been sentenced to the maximum terms he could impose. He was not a popular man.

The bodyguard studied Miss Midden critically. 'What do you want?' he asked.

'I have come to see Judge Bright. It is important. And no, I have no appointment.'

'Well, you've come at the wrong time. Judge Bright is still in bed. He rises late on Saturdays but if you will leave your name and address –'

Miss Midden interrupted him. 'Go and wake him and say to him, "Auntie Boskie's shares." I shall wait here on the doorstep and he will see me,' she said. ' "Auntie Boskie's shares".' She turned her back and the man shut the door.

Inside he hesitated. Miss Midden didn't look like a nutter, but one never knew. On the other hand she had an air of authority about her and an impressive confidence. He picked up the house phone and woke the Judge, and, having apologized profusely, repeated Miss Midden's message and the fact that she wanted to see the Judge. The effect was hardly what he had expected.

'Don't let her get away,' Judge Bright shouted. 'Bring her in the house at once. I'll be down instantly.'

The manservant went back to the door and opened it. 'You're to come in,' he said and prepared to grab her if she tried to run for it.

'I know,' said Miss Midden and stepped past him. She was carrying the hold-all.

'I'm afraid I have to search that, ma'am,' he said.

'You may open it and look inside and you can feel the outside,' said Miss Midden. 'You will take nothing out.'

The man looked inside and understood precisely what she meant. He hadn't seen so many banknotes since an attempted raid on a bank in Putney. He showed Miss Midden into the sitting-room and before he could leave Judge Bright arrived in a dressing-gown. He was, as usual, in a filthy temper and he didn't like being woken with enigmatic messages about Boskie's shares. It had been bad enough late the previous night to be phoned by a demented Ernestine with the news that Bletchley had bungled his suicide attempt and had merely blown most of his teeth away with a very large starting pistol. 'The damned fool must be mad,' he had told her. 'Why didn't he use a shotgun and do the thing properly?'

'I think he tried, but he couldn't get his big toe onto the trigger. It's really too awful. He doesn't look at all well. I don't know what to do.'

'Go and get him a proper revolver,' said the Judge. 'A forty-five should do the trick, even with a skull as thick as his is.'

Now he turned an eye, the same terrible eye that had struck terror into several thousand of the nastiest villains in England, on Miss Midden. He judged her to be a very ordinary woman. He was wrong.

'Do sit down,' said Miss Midden.

'What?' demanded the Judge. It was less a question than an explosion. Outside the door the ex-policeman trembled and wondered whether to rush in or not.

Miss Midden struck again. 'I said "Do sit down",' she said. 'And stop staring at me like that. You'll do yourself a mischief.'

The Judge sat down. In a long and frequently forceful life he had never been told to sit down by an unknown woman in his own house. And she was right about doing himself a mischief. His heart was doing something eccentric, like racing and missing beats.

'Now then,' she went on when he had made himself slightly less uncomfortable, 'I have a question to ask you.'

She stopped. Judge Benderby Bright was making the most peculiar noises. It sounded as if he was choking. His colour wasn't any too good either.

'I want to know whether you want to see your nephew Timothy again.'

The Judge goggled at her. Want to see that infernal little shit again? The woman must be mad. He'd kill the bastard. That's what he'd do if he ever laid eyes on the damnable swine who had stolen all Boskie's shares. See him again?

'I can see that you don't,' said Miss Midden. 'That's as plain as the nose on your face.'

The nose on the Judge's face was not plain, not in his opinion at any rate. It was thin and distinguished. It was also white and taut with fury. 'Who the hell are you?' he yelled. 'You come into my house with some infernal nonsense about my sister's shares and –'

'Oh, do stop behaving like a fool,' Miss Midden shouted back. 'Just look in that hold-all.'

For a moment, an awful and extended moment, the Judge thought about hitting her. He had never hit a woman before, but there was a time and a place for everything, and the drawing-room at nine o'clock on a Saturday morning, before he'd even had a cup of tea, seemed a suitable time to him. With admirable restraint he controlled himself.

'Go on,' said Miss Midden. 'Don't just sit there looking like a totem pole on heat. Take a dekko.'

Judge Benderby Bright wasn't hearing straight. He couldn't be. Nobody, and he meant nobody, in his entire life had treated him in this appalling manner before. He had been subject to the most disgusting abuse from men and women in the dock. He could deal with that – he rather enjoyed sending them down for contempt. But this was a completely new and dreadful experience for him. He did what he was told and peered lividly into the bag. He peered for a long time and then he looked up.

'Where . . . where the bloody hell did you get . . .' he began but Miss Midden was on her feet. She had a look on her face he hadn't seen since his mother found him feeling the parlourmaid up in the pantry one late afternoon. It had unnerved him then, and Miss Midden's look unnerved him now.

'Don't you speak to me like that. I'm not some poor wretch in the dock or one of the barristers you can berate,' she said. 'Now, does the name Llafranc mean anything to you? You berth your yacht the *Lex Britannicus* in the marina there.'

It was hardly a question but the Judge nodded obediently all the same.

'Very fortunately for you, Timothy has saved you from becoming an unwitting drug-runner. You will find all the details in this envelope. I have made him write them all down. You can check on their veracity. I'm sure you are capable of that. And the money in that bag is what your nephew stole from his aunt. You will see that she gets it back. And now I must be going.'

And before the Judge could ask who she was or how she came to be involved with his beastly nephew, Miss Midden had passed out of the house. Behind her she left a bewildered old man who could only remember that she had faced him down in his own drawing-room. She'd been wearing what looked like an old tweed skirt with a stain on it. And a scruffy anorak. It was weird.

Chapter 25

Sir Arnold Gonders wandered the house in Sweep's Place and pondered his fate. That it was a fate he had no doubt. A fate that had crept up on him silently and with an awful purpose. It had to have some meaning. Everything had a meaning for the Chief Constable. He turned inevitably to God. He fell on his knees in his study and he prayed as he had never prayed before. He prayed for divine help, for inspiration, for some sign that would show him what to do in this, the greatest crisis of his life. Or, if God wouldn't meet that request, would he please tell him what he had done wrong to bring down on himself this terrible fate. The Chief Constable didn't actually compare himself to the Pharaoh who got it in the neck from God with plagues of locusts and years of dearth and so on, because clearly that Gyppo had been a right bastard and deserved everything the Good Lord chose to hand out. But he thought about him occasionally and hoped and prayed he wasn't going to have years of this sort of thing. He thought far more about Job. And he did compare himself with Job. After all, Job had been a thoroughly respectable bloke, pillar of society no doubt and with plenty of readies and so on, and yet look what he'd had inflicted on him.

The Chief Constable checked up on the misfortunes God had heaped on Job and was appalled. It had been a wipe-out for the poor bugger. Oxen and asses gone – the Sabeans fell on them and took them away after slaughtering the servants; then God sent fire and consumed the sheep and more servants; three bands of Chaldeans lifted the camels and bumped off even more servants (at this point Sir Arnold thanked God he hadn't been employed by Job and wondered how he had ever got anyone to work for him again); and, as if that wasn't enough, the sons and daughters had copped it in some sort of hurricane. Must have had a hell of a big funeral, though why Job should have shaved his head for the occasion was quite beyond the Chief Constable. And still God hadn't stopped. It was only natural that Job's health had suffered. In Sir Arnold's opinion it was amazing the bloke hadn't gone off his head. Instead he got boils just about everywhere 'from the sole of his foot to his crown'. And of course they didn't have antibiotics in those days. Sir Arnold had once had a boil on the back of his neck and he knew how bloody painful that had been. He couldn't begin to think what it was like to have them on the soles of the feet. And as if that wasn't enough his three so-called friends had called on him and kept him awake for seven days and seven nights and hadn't even said 'Cheer up' or anything useful. The Chief Constable had seen what keeping someone awake for a week did to a bloke. Mind you, they had taken it in turns to shout questions at the sod but then again that had given the villain something to think about. Sir Arnold would much prefer to be shouted at every now and again to having three bloody friends sitting there looking at him and saying nothing. Enough to drive a chap clean off his trolley. And all Job had done was open his mouth and curse the day. What the hell had the day got to do with it?

The Chief Constable couldn't go on. It was too dreadful to contemplate and, if memory served him correctly, Mrs Job hadn't been exactly helpful either, the rotten cow. Said Job had bad breath or something. Hardly surprising. With all those boils he'd probably stunk all over. Certainly no sane woman would want to go near him.

Sir Arnold skipped to the end of the Book of Job and was amazed and delighted to see that Job did pretty well after all he'd been through. Fourteen thousand sheep and six thousand camels and a thousand oxen and the same number of asses. And his wife had been ready and willing. Would be after all those months of doing without it. Seven sons and seven daughters and the girls really nice lookers. And to cap it all, Job lived for a hundred and forty years, which was amazing after all he'd been through. Must have been on ginseng or something. On the whole the Chief

Constable found the Book of Job almost comforting. Like doing three years bird and coming out to a few million quid. Just so long as God didn't tell Satan to give him the boil treatment. Boils on the bottom of one's feet weren't funny.

Nor was the message he received from London summoning him to Whitehall. It was pointedly brief and coincided with another letter from Vy's solicitors containing a full and sworn statement by the bitch asserting that he had repeatedly raped her, had insisted on sodomizing her on their honeymoon and had encouraged her to have sex with the wives of his friends . . . 'Bloody lying cow,' the Chief Constable roared – and saw the hand of Auntie Fucking Bea behind it all. She was screwing him just as she was almost certainly screwing his wife. Or something. The letter ended with the suggestion that Sir Arnold agree to allow his wife to divorce him on the grounds of adultery and pay all her costs to quote avoid unnecessary and most unfavourable publicity unquote.

What Sir Arnold said wasn't quotable. The costs of Lapline & Goodenough, Solicitors, were already exorbitant. He'd have to sell the Old Boathouse to meet the bill. Only then did he realize, and regret most vehemently, that he had made the purchase in Vy's name to avoid the accusation that he was taking advantage of his friendship with Ralph Pulborough, the new Director of the Twixt and Tween Waterworks Company. In short, Sir Arnold was in no position or state of mind to attend to police business. He was otherwise engaged.

Inspector Rascombe, on the other hand, was having a thoroughly engaging time. He had been particularly delighted to learn from the surveillance detective in the wood that an old bugger as naked as the day was long had emerged at half past seven from the Middenhall and had walked slowly across the lawn in the altogether before plunging into the lake and swimming on his back, repeat on his back, displaying his dooda for all the world, and in particular thirty children in the tents, to see.

'His what?' the Inspector had demanded over the mobile.

'His whatnot,' the detective constable told him. 'His dong, for Christ's sake. He's just come out of the water now and is drying himself.'

'What, in front of all those little kiddies? The bastard! Get it on film.'

'We've done that already,' said the surveillance man. 'Got the whole performance, but I wouldn't call them little kiddies exactly. I mean some of them are hulking great louts.'

'Those shits like them all sizes, the swine,' said the Inspector. 'What's he doing now, the old sod?'

'Going into the house bollock naked waving his hand . . . Hang on, he's blowing fucking kisses –'

'What?' bellowed the Inspector so loudly that a neighbouring rabbit went thumping away through the wood. 'Blowing kisses at the kiddies? He's going to do years for this.'

'Not at the . . . well, if you want to call them kiddies,' said the detective, 'you can, but they don't strike me as being –'

'Never mind what they strike you as. Get it on the camera. Him blowing kisses to the kiddies.'

'I'm doing that. But he isn't blowing kisses at the kiddies. He's blowing them at someone in the house. Up at some window. Hang on. There's not a soul at any window. I don't know what he's doing.'

'I bloody do,' shouted the Inspector, 'and I know what he's going to do. A long stretch of very nasty bird, the beast.'

But it was at 8.45 that Inspector Rascombe's most virulent hopes were finally satisfied, when Phoebe Turnbird arrived in her car with the Dean of Porterhouse. He was wearing a black cloak over his cassock and had on his head a shovel-hat. It was not his normal garb, but the late Brigadier General Turnbird had always insisted that the cloak, and particularly the shovel-hat, helped to impress the townies from the East End with the importance attached to religious ceremonies and, in memory of his old friend, the Dean kept to the custom. Phoebe by contrast had on the summeriest of summer dresses, a shimmering white frock that she thought gave her a strikingly youthful air. To complete this ensemble she had crowned her crowning glory with an extraordinary picture hat and, rather shortsightedly, had put on a particularly vivid lipstick.

'There are those wonderful undergraduates down there sleeping under canvas,' she had told the mirror in her room, and in any case it was lovely to have a man about the house, even if it was only the old Dean. Being given to fits of poetry she murmured, 'My youth, my beauty and my charm Can surely do nobody harm. It is such a lovely day I must look gay.'

It certainly looked that way to the surveillance unit, though they left out the youth and beauty bit. Charm was out of the question. Phoebe Turnbird, even in the saddle at half a mile, was sufficiently and distractingly uncharming to have saved the lives of a good many foxes who had found a second or even a third and fourth wind in their desperate flight from death. And she tended to rush her fences.

'Fuck me, this has got to be the drag queen of all time,' the detective muttered as he filmed the Dean and Phoebe moving to the jetty and getting into the little rowing-boat. Phoebe rowed with a vigour that was definitely out of keeping with her outfit. The Dean sat nervously in the stern and looked sinister. He was carrying a large brass cross and the late Brigadier General's family Bible, both of which were part of the tradition that went with the Mission's stay.

'What did you say?' demanded Inspector Rascombe in the Communications Centre.

The surveillance detective found it difficult to put into words. He had never much liked Rascombe but this time the swine had hit the nail on the head. 'I think they're going to have a Black bloody Mass,' he said. 'There's this priest bloke with a fucking great cross and a hell of a big old book being rowed across the lake by Mr Universe in a white frock. Got arms on him like an all-in wrestler. You've never seen anything like it. I haven't, anyway.'

'And you're getting it all on film?'

'I'm trying to. They're still some way off. Drove up in an old Daimler. Got any leads on that? Looks like a fucking hearse.'

'Jesus,' said the Inspector, simultaneously appalled and delighted at what was apparently happening, 'that's probably what it is too. They're going to do a human bloody sacrifice with one of the kiddies. Don't lose them.'

'Lose them? You've got to be joking. You couldn't lose that drag merchant on a pitch-black night. Not in that white frock and hat.'

'I didn't mean that. I mean keep filming, and for God's sake don't let them see you. This is going to hit prime-time TV on all channels. I'll get the Child Care do-gooders up and ready and I don't care if it is Sunday.'

'Best if you got the Armed Quick Response brigade in, and fast,' said the detective. 'They're getting out of the boat and some of the other blokes have arranged an altar thing in front of the tents. Gawd, this is horrible. I've got kids of my own.'

For a moment the Inspector hesitated. He didn't want to take the blame for allowing a kiddy to be murdered naked on that altar. 'Listen,' he said, 'the moment they have the poor little bugger up there stripped and naked and the priest sod's had his say, you are to up and hit them. Do you hear what I said?'

'I heard,' said the detective, 'I heard. But if you think I'm going to tangle with that monster in the frock and come out alive, you don't know what I'm looking at.'

There was a pause, then a gasp. Inspector Rascombe was too busy to hear that gasp. He was now fully occupied in trying to order up a platoon of battle-hardened Child Abuse Trauma Specialists through Police Headquarters in Twixt and getting nowhere fast because, he was told, it was Sunday and the strain of being called fucking shits by enraged and innocent parents all week and the CATS by colleagues in Social Services took its toll by the weekend and they liked to lie in . . .

'I know what they like and I know about their lying. I've heard them in court so don't give me that. This is a Top Priority Order.

You tell Social Services Emergency – and they can fucking get out of bed too – that we've got a Witchcraft Black Mass going on up here and the priest is doing the Communion bit at this very moment ... Yes, I know the cross has got to be upside-down. What the hell's that got to do with the price of eggs? It's the little kiddy lying naked on the altar I'm worried about. No, they're not going to bugger him, not yet at any rate, They're going to slit the poor little sod's throat first and drink his blood out of the chalice. Get that into your thick head. Over and out.'

At Police Headquarters the operator had got it only too well. He was over and out. Over the apparatus in front of him and out for the count.

Inspector Rascombe turned back to the Surveillance Unit. The gasping had stopped. 'What now?' he demanded. 'Have they got the kiddy naked on the altar yet?'

'Kiddy? No, not as far as I can see. They're waiting for a woman who is jogging round the lake and, blimey, is she worth waiting for. I mean this one is the real thing. A right smasher in a silver cat suit Got boobs on her like '

The Inspector didn't want to hear what her boobs were like. For all he cared she could be Dolly Parton with knobs on.

He wasn't far wrong. Consuelo McKoy could by no stretch of the imagination be called the real thing. She had used her years, and there were a great many of them, and vast sums of her husband's money to enrich some of the most proficient plastic surgeons from Santa Barbara to LA. At several hundred yards she looked a million dollars and she had spent far more to achieve that illusion. She had the gloriously lissom figure of a girl of eighteen, which, considering she was eighty-two rising eighty-three, was no mean achievement, particularly on the part of the late Mr McKoy. What liposuction hadn't done for her thighs and silicone implants for her breasts – her latest nipples were extraordinarily effective – the silver cat suit did. It constrained her and preserved the illusion that her navel was where it always had been instead of appearing, rather peculiarly, in her cleavage. Even in Santa Barbara she had

211

been something else. At the Middenhall she was something else again, a vision of such unutterable beauty that at two hundred yards in the morning sunlight it took the surveillance detective's breath away. He kept the camera running.

It was an action he would live to regret. It was only when she came round the lake and he was able to zoom in on her face that he began to realize something was terribly wrong. It didn't seem to gel with her body. In fact, it didn't gel at all. Even the finest cosmetic surgeons, using portions of skin stretched to the utmost from her throat and neck and even unravelled from her chest, had failed to make good the ravages of time and marital bitterness. Not that Consuelo McKoy, *née* Midden, had ever had a beautiful face. At eighteen her mind, never far from the cash register in her father's shop, had bred a mean and hungry look which should have warned Corporal McKoy what he was letting himself in for. Being an incredibly innocent and full-blooded man with a romantic passion for things English, he failed to look too closely into her eyes. He chose instead to think of them as the windows of the soul. To some extent they were. In Consuelo's case they would have been if she had a soul that needed windows. She didn't. She had about as much soul as a scorpion disturbed by the entry of a bare foot into an empty desert boot. Her eyes were dark and small, lasers of such malignancy that her mother, a placid woman not given to much imaginative fluency, had once said they made her think of the bit on the end of a dentist's drill, they were that spiteful.

To Detective Constable Markin, zooming in on that taut suntanned leathery mask, those eyes were proof that hell existed and that what was about to be done on the makeshift altar by the old bastard in the weird black hat was authentically diabolical. The hair on his neck seemed to have caught prickly cold. As the Dean began reading from the Turnbird family Bible the constable babbled into the mobile. 'For fucksake hurry,' he bleated, 'they've started. Shit, this is awful. I don't want to watch. Oh God.'

But Rascombe and the Quick Response Team were already converging on the Middenhall. Their cars and vans raced along the narrow roads, killed a sheepdog and two cats outside Charlie Harrison's farm and sped on without stopping.

It was just as well. At that very moment Mr Armitage Midden, or 'Buffalo' Midden as he preferred to be called, who had spent sixty years decimating herds of elephants, rhinos, lions, wildebeest and, of course, buffaloes across the length and breadth of Africa and who claimed to have spoored more animals than any other white hunter north of the Zambesi, was moving with deadly stealth across the leads of the Middenhall roof with an unlicensed Lee Enfield .303 rifle. From his bedroom window he had seen Unit B stir in the undergrowth behind the kitchen garden and take up a position in a small corrugated structure that had once served as a privy for the under-gardeners. Unfortunately he couldn't see what weapons, if any, they were carrying but men in camouflage jackets who slithered through the grass and then dashed for the outhouse were clearly bent on some dreadful and murderous course of action. Buffalo Midden had spent the previous evening reading an article on the IRA and terrorists in general that had chilled his blood. The Red Menace of Bolshevism might be dead – though he doubted it, it was merely lying in wait for the Civilized World like a wounded buffalo under a lone thorn tree where one would least expect it – but a World Conspiracy, comprising Zionists in alliance with Ayatollahs, Irishmen and of course Blacks and every other demon, still existed in his imagination. And now on this beautiful summer morning it was exercising its deadly skills against the Middenhall.

Buffalo Midden had already worked out why. The Middenhall was the perfect place. Isolated, cut off from the world and equipped with military huts and shelters, it had all the necessary requirements for a terrorist base. Alone on the roof of the awful house he lay in the shadow of a towering chimney and took the most precise aim on that privy and the murderous swine inside it. With all his old expertise he gently eased the trigger back. It was a hair trigger, one he had adjusted to his own specifications, and he knew it well. So, a fraction of a second later, did the two policemen in that corrugated-iron privy. Of course they didn't know precisely what was happening but they had a pretty good idea what was going to happen if they stayed there. They were going to die. The bullet had hardly slammed through the door of the privy and out through the back before they were out of there and running like hell for cover.

Buffalo Midden fired again. And again. And again. He was enjoying himself. The policemen weren't. Pinned down behind a concrete pig-pen which, fortunately for the pig, was unoccupied, they listened to the bullets ricocheting round the interior of the sty and radioed frantically for help. One of them had been hit in the shoulder and the other had had a bullet through his leg. At eighty-five, Buffalo Midden's eyesight was no longer 20/20 but it was sufficiently acute to hit a pig-pen at a hundred and fifty yards and the old Lee Enfield he had always maintained was all he needed to bring down a charging bull elephant so that it slumped at his feet fired a sufficiently powerful .303 bullet to make life behind the pig-pen a decidedly unpleasant affair.

On the far side of the lake the sound of that rifle raised some degree of apprehension. It was not equipped with a silencer. Buffalo liked to boast that when he fired the beast he fired at wouldn't hear anything again this side of the end of eternity and that the shot would so startle the herd of whatever he was killing that his next target would be moving like the clappers, which was much the most sporting way of shooting things. As the firing died away (Buffalo was moving to a position that would give him a better chance of hitting the swine cowering behind the pig-pen) the Dean and his peculiar congregation turned and looked at the Middenhall.

So did Detective Constable Markin. He was a firearms expert himself and he knew a heavy-calibre rifle when he heard one. For a moment he imagined that that moron Rascombe had thrown the whole weight of the Armed Quick Response Team against the house where it wasn't needed. It was needed on his side of the lake where the Black Mass was taking place. He was just wondering

214

what to do when the firing resumed. This time it was accompanied by screams.

Buffalo had found his mark once again and this time he was satisfied. He had heard that sort of scream before many times and it portended death, a terrible and agonizing death. He stood up exultantly and hurried from the roof. There was a Union Flag in his room and he intended to run it up the flagpole Black Midden had erected to celebrate the Coronation of George V.

Chapter 26

Looking back on the events of that Sunday, Miss Midden was wont to say that the Armed Quick Response Team, or whatever those buffoons were called, had arrived in the nick of time. It is not clear what nick of time, or possibly which nick of time, she was referring to, just as it wasn't clear to anyone taking part in whatever it was that was taking place around them whatever it was they were taking part in. Not even Detective Constable Markin, who had witnessed just about everything (he couldn't see what was happening or had happened round the other side of the ghastly house but he had a shrewd idea – that fucking hearse was going to come in handy after all) that seemed to have occurred since first light began, but even he, when it came to the inquests, and there were several, couldn't under oath, or cross-examination of the most persistent and thoroughly unpleasant kind, actually put his hand on his heart and swear to present a faintly lucid account of what he had seen. He had to admit that he had lain under a pile of leaves with a video camera and a mobile (they called it a walkie-talkie in court and the videos he had made were shown over and over and over again) and he was a trained and intelligent and observant police officer but it still didn't add up to a row of sane beans or perhaps he ought to say a sane row of beans. Anyway it hadn't, didn't and never would make any sense to him. All he knew was that an old bloke in the altogether had come out for a swim and . . . How the hell was he to know the thing under that hat and in that frock was a woman? (Fortunately Phoebe Turnbird was not in court at that particular moment. She was otherwise engaged. Literally though briefly.) And if small, fat, waddling clergymen went around wearing cloaks and weird flat shovel-hats, and he hadn't known what they were called at the time, carrying whacking great leather-bound bibles and bloody great brass crosses and got into boats and were rowed across lakes to a whole lot of children whom he had been officially informed by a superior officer were about to be buggered and abused, which was why he was there in the first place, how the hell was he to know they were genuine clergymen and the Dean of Porterhouse College, Cambridge, an ancient and important educational establishment etc? Asked if he needed trauma relief counselling or had had any, he said he didn't. The only relief he needed was to get the hell out of the Twixt and Tween Constabulary into another job where he wouldn't be required to try to assess situations he didn't and still couldn't make head or tail of even if that particular situation had had a head or a tail. The detective's was a garbled account but an accurate one, and it was infinitely more perceptive than that of Inspector Rascombe who had precipitated the whole appalling disaster and was responsible for its outcome.

At the head of the column of Armed Quick Response Teams (AQRTs) hurtling towards the Middenhall that morning, Inspector Rascombe was not exactly himself. Sleepless nights in the Communications Centre, and the sounds of rifle fire ahead of him, and the urgency of his mission to save the little kiddies from having their throats cut on an altar by the queen of the night in drag, or whatever it was in the frock, had awakened in the Inspector's mind a new vision of himself. He saw himself not as a mere police inspector of the Serious Crime Squad but (and this may have had something to do with a book he had been reading by Alan Clark about the war in Russia, called *Barbarossa*) as Standartenführer Sigismund Rascombe of the Waffen SS Sturmgruppe AQRT acting under orders from the Oberkommando der Wehrmacht to storm the Middenhall or die in the attempt. It was a most unfortunate delusion to possess or be possessed by. Inspector Rascombe did not lack the fanatical fervour of a Standartenführer — if anything he had about as much of it as would have made him a thoroughly obedient SS mass murderer in Russia, though at the lowest possible level of command. None at all would have been better. He'd have made a bad cook or baggage-handler. He lacked any degree of intelligence or capacity for organizing anything other than a major catastrophe.

He not only didn't have the faintest clue what he was leading his men into, he hardly knew where the Middenhall was. He had never seen it, it was no more than a mark on the Ordnance Survey map in his borrowed British Telecom van (here he muddled up Standartenführers with General Montgomery who worked from a sort of caravan) and his Surveillance Units hadn't bothered to try to describe it to him. It was in any case beyond description. (Even Sir John Betjeman hadn't attempted that awesome task and had retired to his hotel room in Stagstead for two days to recover after only looking at it for ten minutes from the bottom of the drive.) When finally the Inspector did see the great building it was not what he had expected.

The Armed Quick Response Team leaping from their vehicles with rifles weren't what Buffalo Midden had expected either. He had just managed to get his Union Jack to the top of the flagpole when they arrived, and he drew the worst possible conclusion. He thought he had fought off the attack of the Muslim–Zionist–Black–IRA terrorists, but he had been over-optimistic. The sods had come back in force. Buffalo hastily withdrew from the rooftop and hurried to his room to collect his shotgun, a revolver and a fresh supply of cartridges for the Lee Enfield. Then, to distract the bastards below and mislead them as to his eventual firing position, he put a bullet through the front tyre of each of the vehicles, holed the radiator of the lead one and retreated to the second floor where he could command the back and front of the Middenhall by scurrying to the turrets so conveniently equipped with arrow slits on the four corners of the building. Nobody in his, her or its right mind, not even Black Midden at his most megalomanic, had ever supposed those slits had any military purpose. They were mere ornamentation on the hideous building. Buffalo Midden knew better. From his warped point of view they were perfect for picking off the enemy. As the Armed Quick Response marksmen ran for cover he shot three of them, each in a different part of the garden and the anatomy, and then turned his attention on the relief party that was trying to reach the remaining and groaning Surveillance man still alive behind the pig-pen. By the time he had finished there were three wounded policemen behind that pen and he had pinned another eight down behind the rockery. It was time to change tactics.

He hurried down the curved staircase to the ground floor to deal with any terrorist trying to infiltrate the kitchen. There was no need. The cook and the entire domestic staff had already taken shelter in the cellar and the other guests, with the exception of Consuelo, were milling about in the corridors and hall asking each other what was happening. Buffalo Midden added to the confusion by shouting that they were being attacked by IRA terrorists and must fight to the death. Mrs Devizes already had died, though whether she had been fighting or merely peering shortsightedly out of the window when she was shot by a police marksman was a matter of some debate at the inquest. The police marksman was not there to give evidence. His moment of satisfaction had been short-lived. Buffalo, firing from behind the library sofa, took him out through the open window and then scuttled through to the breakfast-room to put paid to another dark-overalled figure who was sneaking round to the back door. Mr Joseph Midden, the retired gynaecologist, had been killed trying to enquire from a wounded policeman what he was doing lying on the drive. His wife's attempts to save him from falling out of the window had been in all likelihood misinterpreted.

As bodies began to accumulate, Inspector Rascombe's military fantasies evaporated. So had most of the Armed Quick Response Team. Those who had survived Buffalo's murderous fire had taken refuge in various secluded parts of the garden waiting to get the bastards in that fucking house, and the Inspector was cowering behind the leading vehicle unable to coordinate the next phase of Operation Kiddlywink because his walkie-talkie was lying out in the open and he had sufficient sense not to try to reach it. It was Constable Markin, on the far side of the lake, who made the call for help. 'There's a bloody massacre going on here,' he yelled into his mobile. 'Blokes are dropping like flies. For fucksake do something.'

It was a mistake to have shouted. The Dean had just decided it would be prudent to get the Mission children and Miss Turnbird away to a place of greater safety – he didn't give a damn what happened to that foul woman in the cat suit, if that's what she was – when Phoebe heard Detective Constable Markin's plea for assistance and drew her own conclusions about men in camouflage jackets lying under piles of leaves. They were as wrong as his conclusions about her sex (actually gender was, for once, a better word for Phoebe Turnbird's state of nature – sex she hadn't) but, in the circumstances, understandable. Being the brave woman she was, and one who had never in a lifetime of hunting allowed the horse she was riding to refuse a fence or a drystone wall with a ditch on the other side (one or two had tried and had learnt better), Phoebe Turnbird brought all her unrequited passion for men to bear on Detective Constable Markin. Sexual frustration lent weight to her fury.

It was an unequal battle. A policeman under a pile of leaves who is suffering from a perfectly natural bout of homophobia is not at his best when attacked by powerful women descended from a line of Turnbirds that could prove its ancestry back to Saxon times. A Turnbird had fought at the Battle of Hastings with Harold, and that same ancestral spirit inspired Phoebe now. She would die to get her man. In fact it was Detective Constable Markin who damn near died. It is not pleasant to be kicked in the head by a fifteen-stone woman of thirty-five who talks to mirrors and writes poetry before going out to make life hell for foxes and other vermin. That the thing under the pile of leaves was vermin Phoebe Turnbird had not the slightest doubt and, if anything was needed to prove how verminous it was, its supine lack of resistance provided that proof. That it kept moaning about not being buggered please I don't want

Aids didn't exactly increase her respect or liking for the creature. To stifle this flow of filth Phoebe Turnbird knelt on the constable and ground his blackened face into the soggy earth. Around them the kiddies shouted encouragement, and one of the older ones was taken into the bushes by Consuelo McKoy to be shown something he hadn't seen before.

But it was on the drive down to the Middenhall under the avenue of chestnut trees that new and more fearful developments were taking place. The Child Abuse Trauma Specialists were arriving in surprising numbers. They came from all over Britain and had been attending a conference in Tween devoted to 'The Sphincter: Its Diagnostic Role in Parental Rape Inspections'. There were witchcraft experts from Scotland, sodomy specialists from South Wales, oral-sex-in-infancy counsellors, mutual masturbation advisers for adolescents, a number of clitoris stimulation experts, four vasectomists (female), and finally fifteen whores who had come to tell the conference what men really wanted. If they were anything to go by, what men wanted was anything, but anything, with two legs, a short skirt and a mouthful of rotten teeth. And one that whined about being socially deprived. 'Disadvantaged' was the word of the conference. Sphincters were disadvantaged, sodomists were disadvantaged – there had been a prolonged debate on the subject of which were the more disadvantaged and on the whole the sodomists got the greater support largely because, in the experience of the delegates, sodomists didn't pose any threat to women under the age of sixty-five. Consuelo McKoy could have told them differently.

What she was getting under a dense thicket on the edge of the estate was not what she had expected or was enjoying. The kiddy from the Isle of Dogs might not have been able to distinguish with absolute assurance between a vagina and a sphincter, though that was to be doubted, but he knew which he preferred in Consuelo's case. Her screams, muted by distance and by her inability to open her mouth too wide if she were to avoid scalping herself, went unheard.

In any case even if they had heard those screams the Child Abuse experts would have ignored them. Granny Abuse came under another department. They milled about looking for the children they had come to counsel and their faces were alive with desperate care. Or, to be precise, dead with desperate care. They were concerned. They had come to deal with misery and helplessness and to dole out their own misery and helplessness in even greater measure. A miasma of mixed emotions and bitter hatred of anything faintly fond or normal seemed to hang over them. Cruelty and sadism were their specialities and they were infected with them. Suffused with guilt about massacres and droughts in faraway places, they appeased their worthless consciences by doing worthless things. And blamed society for everything. Or God. Or men and parents who loved and disciplined their children to be polite and civil and to work at school. Above all they blamed sex but never ceased to slobber on their own proclivities.

Now, dragged by duty from one another's beds in the most expensive conference hotel in Tween, few of them had had time to wash. Not that they would have washed if there'd been all the time in the world. They liked their own smells. They reminded them of their calling, those smells of stinking fish did, and they revelled in their rejection of the hygienic. The coven from Aberdeen was particularly noisome, and some of the oral sex counsellors still had pubic hair on their chins. As their cars piled up behind one another down the drive and blocked the lodge gates the women debated what to do. They held a conference, and one or two of the more determined ones actually looked around for some children to counsel and expend their care and concern on.

There were none to be seen. With a prescience that did him credit, the Dean and the undergraduates had driven them past Miss Turnbird far into the wood and had forced them to hide by the boundary wall out of harm's way. Only some of the prostitutes did anything useful, one of them giving a peculiar form of last rite to a dying marksman. He'd never been shot before and he'd never been

222

into fellatio. But the whore didn't know that. She was following her calling. So were the creatures under the chestnut trees. They had brought the atmosphere of a failed hospice to the Middenhall. They couldn't have brought it to a better place.

Chapter 27

To Miss Midden the sound of gunfire from the Middenhall was not altogether surprising. That old fool Buffalo had frequently boasted he was going to teach those youngsters from the slums about spooring and killing things like rhinos on the hoof at a thousand yards and generally being manly. Doubtless that's what he was doing. She turned over and went back to sleep. She had got home from London late, well after midnight, and she wanted to lie in. Whatever old Buffalo was doing wasn't any of her business.

On the other hand the roar of SS Standartenführer Sigismund Rascombe's Storm Group's vans as they pelted past the farm did seem to suggest that something bloody odd was going on. Miss Midden put on a dressing-gown and went downstairs to the kitchen to find the Major looking fearfully out of the back window at the Union Jack which could be seen fluttering from the flagpole above the rim of trees. 'Buffalo,' said Miss Midden, and put the kettle on. 'Bound to be that old idiot being a geriatric boy scout. Thinks he's Baden-Powell, I daresay.'

The Major wasn't so sure. His experience of military life might be largely imaginary and second-hand but he knew enough to realize that the direction of the gunfire and its intensity suggested that Buffalo Midden, far from showing the Mission children what a Lee Enfield could do to a charging rhino or something of that sort, was engaged in shooting at them. And while this was understandable – the Major had once been surprised by a number of the little brutes while practising self-abuse overlooking their tents and he didn't like them any more than those guests whose rooms had been burgled – but shooting at the little bastards was carrying things too far. He'd been particularly alarmed by the sight of Rascombe's armed column. It hadn't consisted of the armoured half-tracks of the Inspector's imagination, but there had been an urgency about its passing that gave it an altogether different authenticity. Major MacPhee recognized police vans when he saw them. He'd been in enough of them in his time. And he had been particularly alarmed by the presence of a singularly large van with 'Police Dog Section' painted on the side.

The notion that whatever was going on down at the Middenhall required the attention of quite so many dogs as that damned great van seemed to suggest was not a reassuring one. Major MacPhee was afraid of dogs. He had once been bitten on the ankle by a Jack Russell and that had been bad enough. To be savaged by an entire squad of police dogs filled him with the most appalling apprehension. The prospect never entered Miss Midden's mind, and it wouldn't have bothered her if it had. Rather more disturbing was the sound of agonized screams that wafted up from the Middenhall on the occasional breeze. Miss Midden opened the back door and listened. The firing had started again. And the screaming. She shut the door and thought very carefully.

'Oh, what are we going to do, dear?' asked Major MacPhee 'Something terrible is happening. It's too, too dreadful. People shooting and the police –'

'You are going to make some very strong tea,' Miss Midden ordered, 'and pull yourself together. I am going to make a phone call.'

'But the police are already here . . .' the Major began but Miss Midden was already at the phone and dialling her cousin, Lennox, the family solicitor.

'I don't give a damn if you were about to go for a round of golf, Lennox,' she told him when he complained that he couldn't possibly come out now, it was the Annual Competition at Urmmouth, 'and tomorrow won't do . . . No, I can't tell you what is happening but a police convoy has gone down there with dogs and there is a great deal of firing going on . . . Yes, I did say "firing" and yes, I did mean gunfire. I'll open the front door and you can hear it for yourself.' She held the phone to the open door and looked out in time to see the first of the Child Abuse Trauma Specialists' minibuses pass. The grimly caring faces of the women inside it shook her to the core. 'Fuck me,' she said.

'What?' said the deeply shocked Lennox. 'What did you say? No, don't repeat it. I heard that very distinctly.'

'And the gunfire, the screams?'

Lennox Midden said he had heard them pretty distinctly too. He'd be over as soon as he could. Miss Midden put the phone down and thought again. She had to do something about Timothy Bright – get him out of the house, for one thing, before an investigation by the CID into whatever was going on at the Middenhall began in earnest. She picked up the phone and this time called Carryclogs House.

'I'd like to speak to Miss Phoebe,' she told the serving wench, as old Turnbird had insisted on calling the housekeeper, Dora.

'Miss Phoebe's gone to Church,' the wench told her. 'She should be back any time now.'

Miss Midden thanked her and went upstairs to persuade Timothy Bright that he must go at once to Carryclogs. He didn't need any persuading. What he had heard and then seen from his window in the old nursery had convinced him that the people with razors had arrived to give him piggy-chops. He couldn't think what else could be happening. And the Major was happy to take him over. He hadn't liked the look of those women in the minibuses, and now the stream of cars backing up at the bottom of the farm track, any more than Miss Midden had.

'But I'll never get the car out onto the road,' he pointed out.

Miss Midden had to agree. 'Then you'll just have to walk. The exercise will do you both good,' she said. 'I'll stay and hold the fort here.'

The metaphor was apt. As the Major and Timothy Bright set out across the fell, the sounds of battle increased. Buffalo Midden had drawn fire from a bedroom window and had then retreated to the other end of the building where he might get that bastard hiding behind the lead truck. Failing that, he meant to hit that walkie-talkie thing lying on the ground in front of it. From the arrow slit in the east turret he took aim and fired. The walkie-talkie exploded. Bits of it hit Inspector Cecil Rascombe and smashed his glasses. Out of touch with the rest of the AQRT and with reality, the erstwhile Standartenführer SS played dead. It was just as well. Something even more catastrophic was about to occur.

It was a little thing but its consequences were to be immense. Only the cook, cowering with the rest of the indoor staff in the cool safety of the cellar, was aware that in her flight she had left two very large frying-pans containing a great many slices of bacon on the gas stove. As it was a Sunday, when some of the residents insisted on bacon and eggs at least once a week with fried bread and mushrooms and damn the cholesterol, she had been getting breakfast ready for them when Buffalo started shooting. But even she, a perceptive cook if not a very good one, had no idea what two pounds of fatty bacon (the late Leonard Midden, now lying with the late Mrs Midden over the window-sill of their bedroom, had always maintained on the most dubious medical grounds that fatty bacon was good for the uterus and had insisted on the most fatty bacon for his wife) would do when heated beyond endurance on a propane gas stove in the way of smoke. And flame. It was singularly delinquent of the girl who had come in from Stagstead to help to have put the kettle containing the potato chip oil next to the frying pans. As bacon smoke filled the kitchen the oil joined in. There was an explosion of flame and the first roar of what was to become known as the Middenhall holocaust.

Even then the situation might have been saved. That it wasn't was due to the well-meaning intervention of Mrs Laura Midden Rayter, who fought her way through the smoke with extraordinary fortitude but no understanding of what a bucket of water thrown into a chip-oil fire would do. She soon found out. This time there was no misunderstanding the roar as two gallons of flaming cooking oil went into orbit. The great scrubbed deal kitchen table joined the conflagration, within a minute the cupboards and shelves were blazing, and Mrs Laura Midden Rayter, having left the door into the hall open in her attempt to escape, had a brief glimpse of the arras Black Midden had used to decorate the panelled walls of the dining-room beginning to burn with all the rapidity its motif deserved. Upstairs various panic-stricken colonial Middens pinned down by the shots of the police marksmen, some of whom had managed to escape from behind the rockery to reach the safety of the trees on either side of the great house, tried to get to the huge oak staircase before it went up in smoke. And flames. They failed. The staircarpet was already ablaze and the heat in the hall was too intense. The great oil painting of Black Midden by Sargent over the marble fireplace presented a foretaste of hell. Never a lovely or even vaguely handsome man, even after Sargent had exercised all his cosmetic artistry, the portrait now had a truly infernal look about it. Not that any of the guests stayed around long enough to examine it at all carefully. There was an urgency about their desire to escape the Middenhall that even exceeded the insistence they had shown in getting rooms there when they had arrived. Nobody had stopped them then. Getting out was an entirely different matter. As the flames engulfed the entire ground floor and even the billiard table began to burn, they found the stairs to the second floor and went up them. It was an unwise move. Only Frank Midden, a retired and rather lame ostrich farmer from the Cape, had the good sense to hurl himself onto the roof of the verandah and roll down it. He didn't care if he was shot. It was better than being burnt alive in that awful house.

Above him in one of the roof turrets even Buffalo was coming to a similar conclusion. A ball of flame, a positive fireball, issuing with a terrible whoosh, alerted him, in so far as anything was capable of alerting the idiotic old man, that his enemies were employing a new and dreadful method to flush him out. It was hardly the method he had anticipated but it showed how ruthless terrorists were. They were deliberately burning the Middenhall to the ground, presumably as some sort of propaganda victory like blowing up that Pan-Am Jumbo. Since Buffalo had blown up any number of jumbos – he had once driven a herd of elephants across a minefield he had constructed from mines collected in Mozambique to see what would happen – he knew what blowing up jumbos meant. Or thought he did. Well, two could play that game and he intended to go, if go he must – and it was beginning to look like it – with a bang. Bugger the whimpers. And he had just seen two men in those sinister black overalls make a dash under cover of smoke from the kitchen window to take up positions behind the huge propane tank that supplied the heating and cooking gas to the Middenhall. Snatching a Very pistol from the satchel that held his ammunition, he aimed it at the propane tank.

Then he hesitated. He wasn't sure about a Very pistol's penetrating power. He'd seen what it did to a warthog, and he'd once brought down a circling vulture with the thing by pretending to be dead and waiting for it to come down and have a snack, but even to Buffalo's simple and murderous mind there was a very great difference between warthogs (ugly bastards, they were) and vultures and propane gas tanks. It might be wiser to hole the tank with the rifle first, and then fire the Very pistol's flare at the escaping gas. Much better. Bigger bang and damn-all whimper.

The resulting bang, which was heard as far away as Tween, had all the characteristics of a blended thunderclap and an exploding oil refinery. Something like the Oklahoma City bomb went off at the back of the Middenall. Even Phoebe Turnbird, dragging the unresisting Detective Markin with an arm-lock that occasionally lifted him off the ground, was struck by the explosion. Other people were less fortunate. They were struck by pieces of the Middenhall itself. Two vast ornamental Corinthian columns on the façade broke loose and crashed onto some of the trucks and police cars on the drive (it was at this point that Inspector Rascombe realized that his top priorities had fuck-all to do with rescuing kiddies from having their throats cut on altars, and made a dash for the lake); a mock Tudor chimney of unnatural proportions toppled onto and through the leaded roof (which hadn't been strengthened by the fireball from the kitchen); several Child Abuse Trauma Specialists had reason for genuine concern, but weren't cared for by their comrades-in-arms who went screaming hysterically up the drive pursued by maddened German Shepherd police dogs sensibly released by their handlers from the overheated van; only the prostitutes stood their ground and did anything useful. They had seen police dogs in action and, being uneducated and high on heroin, they were also unconcerned. But they did care. They helped those earnest caring women who despised them, those who could stand up on their feet, and led them away and bandaged their wounds as best they could, as a result of which some of the wounded CATS contracted AIDS.

The police marksmen previously behind the propane tank neither cared nor were concerned. Ashes to ashes and dust to dust just about summed up their condition. They were part of the mushroom cloud that rose over the remains of Black Midden's architectural gravestone. Buffalo Midden rose with them but, remarkably, in one piece. He landed in a huge pile of manure that had been fermenting nicely on the far side of the kitchen garden and emerged half an hour later uncertain what had happened and wondering why it was he seemed to smell so strongly of pig and singed hair.

He wandered away from the inferno unsteadily and stopped to ask one of the Armed Quick Response Team, one he had shot and killed, the way to Piccadilly Circus. 'Rude bastard. Can't get a civil word out of anyone in this accursed country,' he muttered as he stumbled away.

Behind him the Middenhall blazed and slowly folded in on itself. And on the other unfortunate Middens who had seen it as their home from home with free board and lodging and all the trimmings, like being as rude to domestic servants as they had been accustomed to be in the tropics. There were few servants left for them to be rude to if they had lived. The cook and her daughter and the other helpers in the kitchen were saved by the water tank above them, which burst and flooded the cellar. Even so they were almost boiled alive. The arrival of a fleet of fire engines did nothing to assist. They couldn't get past the cars blocking the drive and the

230

lodge gates. In any case there was nothing they could have done. The Middenhall, that brick, stone, and mortar construction of abysmal taste, that monument to Imperial vanity and stupidity and greed, had become the mausoleum Black Midden had intended, though not in the way he had hoped. It would go down in the history of Twixt and Tween. It had already gone down in just about every other respect. The great billiard table – a massive piece of slate was all that remained – had crashed into the wine cellar destroying the last vestiges of a fine collection of port, claret and sweet dessert wines he and his successors had laid down there and the colonial Middens had not been able to find and drink.

And through it all, through the mayhem and the maelstrom of disaster that had engulfed the Middenhall and its inhabitants, Miss Midden sat impassively by the phone in the hall of the old Midden farmhouse and talked insistently and incessantly to an old school friend in Devon about things that were not happening around her, about happy memories of other days when she and Hilda had hitch-hiked to Land's End. She was establishing an unbreakable alibi. No one would ever be able to say she had been responsible for the destruction of the loathsome house that had broken her father.

Chapter 28

The scene that greeted Lennox Midden – though greeted was hardly the most appropriate word – on his arrival at the Middenhall (there was so much traffic he'd had to walk over half a mile) was not one to reassure a decent suburban solicitor who had woken only a few hours earlier expecting to play in the Urnmouth Golf Club's Annual Competition. There was nothing of the smooth greens, the broad fairways, and the bantering camaraderie in the clubhouse afterwards of men who believe that hitting a small white ball into the distance gives life meaning. A great gulf was fixed, an abyss, between that comfortable world and what was happening at the Middenhall. There were snatches of green through the smoke where the lawns ran down to the lake, but they were not smooth. Lumps of concrete blown from the crenellations and the ornate turrets of the roof lay embedded in the turf, with the occasional dead or wounded police marksman lying poignantly among them. Smashed trucks and police cars burnt vigorously on the drive. The vast verandah burnt too, while the shell of the great building steamed and smoked hideously, flames suddenly erupting from its depths like some volcano on heat. A German survivor of the final Russian assault at Stalingrad, or an American soldier surveying the devastation unnecessarily and barbarously inflicted on the Iraqi convoy north of Kuwait City, would have found the sights and smells familiar.

Lennox Midden in his plus-fours didn't. He had never been in the presence of death and destruction on this scale before, and with each dread step he took along the road and down the drive, past stragglers of the Child Abuse Trauma Specialists, past wounded policemen, past hideous but stalwart prostitutes with smoke-

blackened faces, past maddened German Shepherds with smouldering tails and burnt whiskers, even past Buffalo Midden,
unrecognizable beneath his coating of pig manure but still wanting
to know the way to Piccadilly Circus, Lennox Midden's faith in the
suburban values faltered. By the time he reached the bottom of the
drive, where firemen had gathered to watch in awe what they had
come to extinguish, the solicitor's hopes had vanished. There was
nothing to be saved from the Middenhall. Chunks of the upper
storeys were still crashing at intervals into the inferno below,
sending up clouds of dust and smoke. The smell was appalling.
Even to Lennox it was obvious that more than his great
grandfather's fantastic mansion had been burnt. The stench of
barbecued relatives, those Middens from Africa and India and
faraway turbulent places who had sought safety and comfort for
their retirement in the house, hung nauseatingly on the summer air.

Lennox Midden couldn't understand it at all, but being a lawyer
he looked round for someone to blame. And to sue. He learnt what
he needed from Frank Midden, the ostrich farmer who had sensibly
leapt from his bedroom window and rolled down the verandah roof
to land on the top of a police van.

'Those bastards started it,' Frank moaned (he was lame in his
other leg now and didn't care) and pointed at the body of a police
marksman in his black overalls. 'They drove down the drive in
those vans like madmen and started shooting at anyone they could
see. I saw them kill Mrs Devizes at the window of her room and all
she was asking was what they were doing. Don't suppose she'll
ever know now.'

'But they're policemen,' said Lennox, who had seen the
markings on the vans, 'they must have had some reason for starting
to shoot.'

Frank Midden wasn't having it. 'Reason? Policemen? If they're
British policemen, I'm going back to South Africa. Our lot are bad
enough but these bastards are . . .' He couldn't find words to
describe what he thought of them. Lennox Midden didn't need to
hear any more. If the Twixt and Tween Constabulary had been

responsible for this murderous attack on people and property, they were going to pay for it. He was more concerned about the property which, while it could never have found a buyer, had cost a fortune to build. Now, in its smouldering state, it was of incalculable value. The dead Middens had their uses too. His legal mind, honed to perfection by years of litigation in matters of compensation and damages, couldn't begin to imagine what this little lot was going to bring in. Or, as he put it, with more accurate irony than he dreamt, to Miss Midden when he found her still on the phone at the farmhouse, 'Talk about bringing home the bacon.'

Miss Midden kept her thoughts to herself. She had no real idea what had started the catastrophic events of the morning or why Buffalo had begun firing his rifle but, whatever it was, she was macabrely grateful. The curse of the Middenhall had been broken.

So had Inspector Rascombe's spectacles. Not that he needed them to see in a blurred way, his mind was pretty blurred too, that he had been partly responsible for the destruction of a huge house, the deaths of at least half a dozen police marksmen from the Armed Quick Response Team, and, to judge by the dreadful smell, some of the previous occupants of the fucking place. As he dragged himself though the mud out of the artificial lake where he had taken refuge, he had the sense to know his career as a police officer was at an end. God alone knew what the Chief Constable would say when he heard about this debacle and, from the sound of several helicopters now flying overhead, he'd probably heard already and was rabidly seeking whom he might – fuck the 'might', whom he would devour. The Inspector's only hope, and it was a very, very slight though sincere one, was that Sir Arnold Gonders had had an apoplectic fit or a fatal heart attack.

In fact the Chief Constable hadn't heard what malignant fate had in store for him that Sunday. He had been spared that knowledge by giving the congregation of the Church of the Holy Monument in Boggington, some thirty miles to the north of Tween, the benefit of his colloquies with God. They consisted very largely of a series of admonitions which made God sound like the Great Lady herself at her most mercenary.

'I say unto you that unless we maintain the bonds of free enterprise and free endeavour we shall be bounden to do the Devil's work,' he announced from the pulpit. 'Our business in the world is to augment the goodness that is God's love with the fruition of free enterprise and to put aside those things which the Welfare State handed us on a plate and thus deprived us of the need to which we must pay homage. That need, dear brothers and sisters in God, is to take care of ourselves as individuals and so save the rest of the community doing it out of the taxpayer's pocket. Only this week I have been encouraged to see how many Watch Committees and Neighbourhood Watches have been set up to augment the splendid work being done by the Police everywhere and in particular by the men under my command. It is not often that I have a chance or, I might say, the opportunity to do the Lord's work in the way he would have me do, namely, like your goodselves, to encourage others to free themselves from the shackles of passivity and acceptance and to go forth into the world to bring the positive and active blessings of health, wealth and happiness to those less fortunate than ourselves. This is not to say that we must bow the knee to social need or so-called deprivation. Instead we must make of ourselves and our gifts in business and in wealth whatsoever we can. As the Lord has told me, there are as many numerous spin-offs on the way to Heaven as there are hand-outs on the slippery road to Hell. It is one thing to give a penny to a beggar: it is another to beg oneself. And so I say to you, dear friends, assist the police wherever you can in the prevention of crime and in the pursuit of justice but never forget that the way of righteousness is the way of self-service and not the other way round. And so let us pray.'

In front of him the congregation solemnly bowed their heads as the Chief Constable, calling on all his powers of rhetoric, launched into a prayer for the anti-vehicle-theft campaign and ancillary individual schemes. It was a great performance.

'I think you missed your vocation, Sir Arnold,' said the Minister afterwards as the Chief Constable left. 'Still, when you finally give up the wonderful work you are doing as Chief Constable you may feel the call to the ministry. There are many opportunities for a man of vision.'

'Indeed,' said Sir Arnold, who didn't enjoy references to his retirement, 'but I see myself in an altogether more humble role, Reverend, as a poor sinner who finds joy in his heart bringing the message of the good book to –'

'Quite so, Sir Arnold, quite so,' said the Minister, anxious to stem the flow of the Chief Constable's oratory before it got going. 'Splendid sermon. Splendid.'

He turned away to attend to one of the congregation and Sir Arnold went down the steps to his car. As he drove back to Sweep's Place he considered how best to use the moral virtue that talking about God always stimulated in him. 'That ought to put paid to anything like Job got,' he thought to himself. 'Even God wouldn't want to interfere with the maintenance of Law and Order on my patch.'

His hope didn't last long. Turning the car radio on he caught a news flash and very nearly smashed into a bus shelter as a result.

'The battle at Middenhall, which was the subject of police action this morning, is over. The building is in flames and there has been an enormous explosion. Police casualties are said to number nine dead. There are no figures for the occupants of the mansion itself. We shall be bringing you fresh updates as soon as we can.'

The Chief Constable pulled into the side of the road and stared at the radio. Nine coppers dead? Nine of his lads? It wasn't possible. Not his lads. They weren't lads any more. They were corpses. Dear shit, and Job thought he'd been given a hard time, the whingeing swine. But Sir Arnold knew why he'd cursed the day. He did too. The day he'd ever made that fucking moron Rascombe Head of the Serious Crime Squad. That was the day Sir Arnold cursed. And

236

God, of course, for having created Rascombe in the first place. The old swine should have had more sense. Even as a sperm it must have been possible to spot that he hadn't got the brains of a . . . well, a sperm at any rate. And what sort of gormless ovum had invited him in? Must have been off its tod, that fucking ovum. If Sir Arnold Gonders had had his way he'd have wrung that evil little sperm's neck and kicked that moronic ovum into the street. And if that had failed, and he rather thought it might have been too difficult, he wouldn't have hesitated to use a knitting-needle to get at that vile sperm and ovum. Or, better still, give Mrs Rascombe a uterine washout with some Harpic or Domestos, something that would make her think twice about having it off with Rascombe's bloody dad ever again.

Sitting in his Jag outside one of the mining villages of Twixt and Tween he had helped so ruthlessly to turn into a workless place, the Chief Constable saw the bright summer day differently from other people. It was a dark overcast day with great thunderclouds spread out across it, black and menacing, as black and menacing as the row of miners' cottages, meagre and pitiless places with empty cans of lager in the gutters of the street. Some had boarded windows and some were occupied by miserable men who would never work again, who if they were old had miner's lung, and by their brutish offspring. But even they, in their miserable hovels, would find joy in the downfall of the man who had ordered his men to break their picket lines and any heads that got in the way, and to hell with the consequences. The bastards in those houses would probably hold street parties to celebrate his disgrace and drink themselves sick to his unhealth. The Chief Constable drove on hurriedly to escape this terrifying vision of his future. He had many illusions about many things but he knew his friends and political allies. They would drop him like a hot cake, hot dogshit more like, the Bloads and the Sents and the high-and-fucking-mighty he had helped like Pulborough, the Waterworks magnate. Fair-weather bastards all of them, and the Gonders weather had turned very foul indeed. In his imagination it had begun to rain and the wind was blowing it into his face.

Another news flash. The police casualty rate had gone up to thirteen and the estimated number of dead in the Middenhall was now put at ten. The Chief Constable was disgusted. The Armed Quick Response Team clearly couldn't even shoot to kill straight. Attempts to reach the Chief Constable had failed but his Deputy, Henry Hodge, speaking from his home, had admitted that he knew of no authorization for an armed raid on the Middenhall. It was news to him.

'Stupid little fucker,' the Chief Constable shouted at the radio, 'couldn't he have kept himself to "No bloody comment"?'

It was a stupid question to ask. Even Sir Arnold could see that. The bastard wanted Sir Arnold's job, that's why he was passing the buck and landing him in the shit. And there was no way he was going to get into his house in Sweep's Place. It would be blocked by reporters and people from the BBC with cameras and mikes who'd always been out for his blood. Well, they'd got it now. With all the keen cunning of a cornered plague rat, Sir Arnold sought for a way out of the trap he was in. And found it. In violent illness.

Somewhere along the line of his sordid and brutal life he had heard that eating a tube of toothpaste gave one some pretty ghastly and seemingly authentic symptoms. He stopped at an open supermarket and bought two large tubes of differing kinds – one brand might not do the trick – and a bottle of tonic water. He'd be found slumped in his car somewhere very near the Tween General Infirmary – he didn't want to die – and be rushed in and treated. With fresh determination and fortitude the Chief Constable drove into Tween and, having parked just outside the gates of the hospital, managed with the utmost difficulty to get those tubes of toothpaste down with the help of the tonic. It was a move he was going to regret. The effect was almost instantaneous. And horrible. He stumbled from the Jag and collapsed on the road. He wasn't shamming. He hadn't known he had an ulcer. He knew it now with a vengeance. Hiatus hernia it wasn't. Could be fluoride poisoning though. Christ, he hadn't thought of that. As he crawled towards the hospital gates he knew he was going to die. He had to be dying. That damned malingering skunk had been bullshitting about toothpaste, lying through his fucking teeth. It had been a terrible mistake.

An hour later he knew just what a mistake it had been, in more senses than one.

'First time I've ever known a case of attempted suicide with toothpaste,' said the doctor who had pumped his stomach out. 'He must have been out of his mind.'

This opinion was shared in Whitehall. Even the Prime Minister, who had seen the inferno at the Middenhall on television (those helicopters had done sterling service for the media) and who would cheerfully have strangled Sir Arnold with his own bare little hands, found the news that the Chief Constable, having attempted suicide by eating at least two tubes of toothpaste, was still alive quite astonishing. He was also horrified to learn from the Head of Internal Intelligence that the Special Branch men flown up from London to check the contents of the house in Sweep's Place had unearthed scores of videotapes taken in a brothel in which important members of the local party, prominent businessmen, and important contributors to central party funds figured largely. There had also been a great deal of damaging information on Sir Arnold's hard disk and database.

'He'll have to go,' he told the Home Secretary. 'I don't care what arguments you put to me, I will not have such a corrupt person in a position of high public responsibility. I won't.' It was a strong statement from such a weak man. But the Home Secretary had no intention of opposing the Prime Minister. He too would willingly have strangled the Chief Constable, not only for what he had done to the Middenhall, but more personally for what he had done to the Home Secretary. Someone ought to have warned him about that establishment at Urnmouth and the fact that he might be filmed in his role of Marlene Dietrich. To put it mildly, Sir Arnold Gonders' future was not going to be a pleasant one.

'On the other hand, we mustn't rock the local party boat too much,' the Prime Minister went on. He really was a very weak man.

The Home Secretary couldn't bring himself to agree. He was in a very ugly mood. He'd have torpedoed the bloody boat and machine-gunned any survivors.

Chapter 29

As the last marksman was carried from the front lawn and the forensic experts flown in from Scotland Yard ('The hell with what that moron Gonders says, I'm putting you in command,' the Home Secretary told the Commissioner of Police) began the almost impossible task of distinguishing the remains of Mrs Devizes from those of Mrs Laura Midden Rayter and the other burnt corpses (only DNA tests might do that); while the lobster-coloured cook explained to a TV audience of at least fifteen million how she and the other kitchen staff had escaped the holocaust by hiding in the cellar and being boiled; as the persons who cared and were concerned went back to their extremely expensive conference hotel to discuss the sphincter in an entirely different context, namely as it applied to those arseholes of the anti-feminist State, the police; in short as things got back to normal, the Dean led the Porterhouse Mission to the Isle of Dogs away from the smouldering squalor that had been the Middenhall. In the thicket Consuelo McKoy fumbled with her silver cat suit and wondered if she would ever feel the same way about small boys.

Inspector Roscombe knew he wouldn't. In the back of a police van he had no interest whatsoever in the fate of little kiddies. As far as he was concerned they could hold Black Masses and slaughter the little buggers on an hourly basis and he would rejoice. He had nothing else to rejoice about. They were waiting for him at Police Headquarters and the two detectives who had collected him said some Special Interrogators had been flown up from London to have a little chat with him. Roscombe knew what that meant. He had had 'little chats' with people before, and they hadn't enjoyed the process.

Behind him in the wood Phoebe Turnbird left Detective

Constable Markin with his thumbs tied together round the back of a tree, a trick she had been taught by old Brigadier General Turnbird, who had done the same thing to a great many captured PoWs before interrogating them. Then she headed triumphantly up to the Midden farmhouse in her stained and torn white frock and battered hat. She wanted to console poor Marjorie Midden and let her know how desperately, but desperately sorry she was and how she felt for her in her moment of loss. To her amazement she found Miss Midden sitting outside the front door looking remarkably cheerful for a woman who had lost everything.

'Oh, my poor dear . . .' Phoebe began, disregarding the glow of satisfaction on Miss Midden's face. Miss Turnbird, in spite of her love of poetry, was not a deeply sensitive or perceptive woman, or perhaps poetry was a substitute for sensitivity and perception. She had come up to sympathize with poor dear Marjorie (and to patronize her) and she was going to do it, come hell or high water. Hell there had already been, and as far as the cook was concerned high water had been exceedingly helpful. But Miss Midden had had too good a day to put up with sentimental slush from Phoebe Turnbird, slush and odious sympathy. Besides, it was plain to see that wherever Phoebe had been she hadn't been in church all day. The leaf mould on her face and hands and the state of her dress indicated that. She had obviously been rolling on the ground, having a whale of time.

Looking at her, Miss Midden was struck by a sudden inspiration. She raised her hand and her voice. 'Stop that at once, Phoebe. I won't have it. Now get yourself a chair . . . no, go upstairs and wash your face first. You look like Barbara Cart – You don't look your usual self. Lipstick doesn't suit you. I suppose you put it on for that dreadful old Dean because he once said . . . Never mind. I shall make a nice pot of tea and then tell you all about it.'

Phoebe lumbered upstairs, and when she came down she looked a good deal better. At least the lipstick had gone, though her attempt the previous evening to pluck her eyebrows was now revealed with mottled clarity to have been a mistake. She fetched a chair and joined Miss Midden in the garden.

'Now then, Phoebe, I have something to tell you. So I want you to listen carefully. I am afraid I have presumed on your hospitality,' she said as she handed Miss Turnbird a very large cup and saucer. 'I've had a very nice boy staying here. He's had a nervous breakdown and he's a bit jumpy. So this morning when the shindig down at the Middenhall . . . No, dear, do not say anything. I won't discuss it. This is far more important. As I say, when the police began to kill all those people down there, I immediately thought of you and Carryclogs as the perfect place to send the poor boy. Well, to be truthful, he isn't exactly a boy, more a hulking great brute of twenty-eight and not frightfully bright. He likes to call himself Bright, Timothy Bright, but he isn't. That's part of his nervous problem. He's been something in the City and the stress has affected him. He suffers terrible nightmares, and I'm not at all surprised. No one should put a healthy young man in front of a computer screen all day and ask him to make instant decisions about money. It isn't natural. Now, given the healing hand of time and fond affection and plenty of food and fresh air – I'm sure he shoots well and rides, he's that sort – he'll soon be as right as rain. So I sent him over to your place because I know how good you are and kind and affectionate. He's your class, too. I've met his uncle and the family is a very good one indeed. And his manners aren't bad. I'm sure you'll be able to help the poor boy. Now, I hope you don't mind my taking advantage of you like this but I thought . . .'

What Miss Midden really thought she kept firmly to herself. If Phoebe Turnbird didn't take that ghastly lout to her ample bosom and to the altar, her own name wasn't Marjorie Midden, the daughter of Bernard Foss Midden and Cloacina von Misthaufen, daughter of General von Misthaufen, whom her father had met and married when she was allowed over to visit the dying General at the Middenhall in 1949. Miss Midden had never known her mother, who had died in childbirth, but her father had always spoken of her as an immensely strong-minded woman whose plain

German cooking had suited his ailing stomach to perfection. 'Dear Clo,' he would say, 'I miss her Blutwurst and Nachspeise sometimes. She had a wonderful appetite, your mother. It was a pleasure to watch her eat. She used to say to me, "We're not really 'vons'. Or Misthaufens. Affectation. We were just plain Scheisse, like you Middens, until the Kaiser came along and somehow we became von Misthaufens. Scheisse is better. Down to earth and no pretendings." And there was a lot of truth in what she said. Your mother was a remarkable woman. She saw things clearly.'

Presently, with the smoke drifting across the sky behind her, Miss Midden drove Phoebe over to Carryclogs and picked up Major MacPhee. She was rid of the Middenhall with all its pretendings and she needn't think about it any more.

She wouldn't have to think about money either. On top of her wardrobe in a cardboard box there was a brown paper parcel containing thousands and thousands of pounds from the man with the razor who had so terrified Timothy Bright. It was never going anywhere now. The Brights had their money back and Phoebe had a fiancé in waiting. Miss Midden herself would go on living at the Midden while Lennox exacted every penny from the authorities for the destruction of the Middenhall. But she would never go to Phoebe's wedding, though Phoebe would undoubtedly want her to. As a bridesmaid.

Miss Midden shuddered at the thought. It would be a hideously noisy wedding and in any case she was not a maid and never intended to be a bride. She would stay the way she was and always would be, an independent woman. She had no intention of marrying for the sheer hell of it. There were enough Middens in the world already without creating any more. And the Major could stay if he wanted to. She didn't much care one way or another. He was a pathetic little creature and she could do with help in the house. But she doubted if he would. The Major's taste for the life of the gutter, she had once heard it called nostalgie de la boue, though in his case it was less boue than ordure, would call to him. As the old Humber drove past Six Lanes End she saw, limping towards them, a tattered and besmirched figure. Miss Midden stopped and asked if she could be of any assistance.

'Very kind of you, I'm sure. I'm trying to find the way to Piccadilly Circus, but no one round here seems to know.' It was Buffalo Midden and the boue in his case was entirely genuine.

'Get in,' said Miss Midden, 'I'm going that way myself.'

Beside her Major MacPhee began to gibber a protest. 'Shut up,' said Miss Midden. 'Shut up or get out and walk.' The Major shut up. He had walked far enough that day.

As they drove into the farmyard Miss Midden knew she would never be rid of stupid old men and their mad fantasies. Being a kindly, sensible woman, she didn't mind. In a way, it was her calling.